Ibrahim Bangura

THE GRIP OF DEATH

Stories of Children and the Conflict in Sierra Leone

Miraclaire Publishing
Kansas City / Yaounde

MIRACLAIRE PUBLISHING LLC
Kansas City, (MO) USA

Kansas City, MO 64133, USA
Email: info@miraclairepublishing.com
Website: www.miraclairepublishing.com

P.O. Box 8616 Yaounde 14,
Yaounde, Cameroon

ISBN-13: 978-0615823621

ISBN-10: 0615823629

Miraclaire Publishing makes every effort to ensure the accuracy of all the information ("Content") in its publications. However, Miraclaire and its agents and licensors make no representations or warranties whatsoever as to the accuracy, completeness, or suitability for any purpose of the Content and disclaim all such representations and warranties, whether expressed or implied to the maximum extent permitted by law. Any views expressed in this publication are the views of the author and are not necessarily the views of Miraclaire.

For all the children across the world caught in violent conflicts, which they played no part in designing.

I wish to thank all those who in various ways assisted me in the development of this book. My dear friends Prof. Dr. Arnis Vilks, Abdul Karim Koroma (AKK), Irma Specht, Sarah Danso, Nagayo Sawa, Emily Marr, Dr. Henry Mbawa Jnr, Janice Wang, Peter Seary, Ojoma Ali, Arthur Smith, Zhengzheng Qu, Eldridge Adolfo, Fatuma Hamidali Ibrahim and Albert Samah. My greatest thanks go to those who shared their stories with me. You know who you are and I will leave it at that.

Preface

Sierra Leone, a small and beautiful country in West Africa, went through the harrowing experience of a particularly brutal conflict from 1991 to 2002. The conflict had a heavy toll on the country, with approximately 55,000 people killed, thousands raped and sexually assaulted, hundreds amputated, and over a million becoming internally displaced or refugees in neighbouring countries.

Saturated in this decade-long mayhem, children, boys and girls alike were conscripted as combatants, spies, cooks, porters and sex slaves. In the aftermath of the conflict, the debate over the loyalty of conscripted children grew into a storm. Were they merely victims of circumstance, or partners in crime? The exploration and examination of this question is the primary inspiration and purpose of this book. It, however, does not make pretense at providing a cut-and-dried answer to the question. The activities of children in and during the unfurling violence are presented as narrated to the author.

The Grip of Death consists of eleven stories, each narrating the experience of children who were associated with different fighting factions and played different roles. These are true accounts fictionalised to conceal the identities of the children in the stories but more importantly to respect their gruesome experiences. The eleven stories herein are arranged under individual themes ranging from voluntary to forced conscription, disarmament and reintegration of child combatants, and one of the key topics under debate: whether or not Children Associated with Armed Forces and Groups (CAAFAG) should be part of transitional justice mechanisms such as Truth and Reconciliation Commissions. While these themes cover several strands of Sierra Leone's tragic experience, it should be naturally be underscored that the eleven stories do not provide an all-encompassing account of the conflict and its aftermath. In itself, it is this author's attempt to portray the activities and plight of children during the conflict: how they were recruited, reasons that compelled some to volunteer into the different fighting groups, and the roles played among others. Most of the accounts are gruesome and vivid. This is intentional, both to respect the experiences of the individuals, and also to let the reader appreciate that conflict is real and that behind the media and motion pictures on their screens are most often untold stories of 'less important' survivors of conflict.

My intention of writing a book about the experiences of children in the Sierra Leone conflict-which I, myself experienced with vivid memories—is twofold: First, despite attempts by various institutions such as the Truth and Reconciliation Commission (TRC) and the Special Court for Sierra Leone (SCSL) to document accounts of the conflict, most victims and perpetrators of the violence feel that more work has to be done in documenting their experiences. They believe it will be beneficial to the future generation and also to those who find official accounts as watered-down versions of actual experiences. Second, and perhaps most importantly, that it will serve as a source of inspiration and a call to action to the reader, to work toward the betterment of the lives of children, and their protection from danger.

Ibrahim Bangura
September 2013

CONTENTS

The Burning Heart

It was the last week of July, the height of the rainy season, deep in the tropical rainforest of Sierra Leone in West Africa, 10 degrees north of the equator, bathed by the Atlantic Ocean breeze. The south-westerly wind, which flows through the country between May and September, is laden with moisture which forms dark clouds that spread out and pour rain on the heads of the people with fierce and unrelenting intensity. As the clouds block out the sun for hours, sometimes days, temperatures uncharacteristically drop. Those used to moving about bare-chested, or in thin cotton, are met by rain pounding onto patchwork tin roofs.

There was unceasing firing from the village. It was not sporadic, which could have indicated that they were merely warning shots or people being summarily executed. The contrasting continual ratatat of machine gun fire made it clear to us that there was a full battle raging on. The Government soldiers were likely engaging the rebels. There was the punctuating sound of rocket-propelled grenades (RPGs), and heavy machine guns that would reverberate the rafters of any hut in sight. We were convulsing, and our eyes felt as if they would pop out of our heads.

I was very scared. I had been in this forest for two days with other children from my village. By chance, we were out playing football when the village was attacked.

My brain was racing unstoppably, like a canoe in fast water with no oar. I needed a solution and I needed it quickly. Running back to the village was dangerous, staying in the forest equally so, since we never knew who would emerge from the undergrowth.

"I'm hungry, I want something to eat," Foray, my little cousin of eleven started crying. I pleaded with him to hold on, that very soon the fighting would die down and we would return to the village where he could find some food. I was dying inside, as I was myself just a child lost in the midst of chaos. Hunger was getting the better of me also and I felt like very soon I would be crying like Foray. Yet I was summoning every willpower in me to maintain a brave front and not let go of what little shred of hope I was clinging to, for little Foray's sake. The forest we were in was vast and very close to our village. Our parents always warned us never to go into it and told us very horrible stories when we asked why.

My grandmother once told me that when she was young, people used to throw baby twins into that forest because they were regarded as evil, and were left to die there. She said the restless souls of those twins were still roaming the dark forest, seeking to exact vengeance on the descendants of those who threw them there. Yet, to me, the forest looked peaceful and I frequented it in search of wild birds and to be closer to nature. A one-time encounter with a large python almost made me jump out of my skin and I ran like a gazelle all the way back to the village. However, this did not stop me from frequenting the forest. Now, having been hiding out in the forest for two days from the attack without 'meeting' the devil or seeing any sign of restless evil souls lurking around, I concluded that the stories were all made-up and were meant to keep us from straying too far into the forest. This time around, the real devils, from whom we were hiding, were actually in the village and not the forest and we had been told that they would kill us as soon as they set eyes on us; and this story I did believe. I was shuddering with fear and could clearly hear the palpitation of my heart and my cousin's, to whom I pretended to be strong as I was his last hope.

•••••

It was on Monday when I was in school taking a test that the headmaster entered and ordered that everyone go home. We were surprised, but since we were all very afraid of him, no one questioned it. In our village, it was uncommon for one to question a knowledge-giver. We all believed that one needed the blessings of your teacher to succeed in life. As such, questioning the authority of a teacher was an anathema. On my way home, I met my dad sprinting like a Kenyan athlete towards my school. He grabbed me by the wrist and made a U-Turn in the direction home. On the way, he told me that a strange letter addressed to the chief had been found in the village centre. The contents of the letter carried the spectre of death, destruction and decay. It was not a threat but a clear message of an imminent attack on the village. For months we had been hearing of the fighting going on in the country and the atrocious means in which rebels were killing and maiming people. Our village had hosted several people running from this fighting and now we were about to witness this, until now distant war. I could not believe my ears.

The letter must have been a mistake. I prayed that someone could come out and laugh at the villagers, saying it was only meant to scare people. My suspicion fell on Jusu, the local rastafarian. My mom was sobbing as she dressed my baby sister Isatu, who was suffering from malaria; a disease that had a permanent home in my village. It disregarded life, and made no distinction between young and old. It swept away most of those that it came across. Unfortunately for us, there was no medical centre or clinic in our village. The nearest was about 36 miles away. My father looked hopeless as he stood there

3

in oblivion as if he was asking himself, "What should I do?" While we stood in looking lost, we heard the village crier summoning everyone to the village centre for a meeting with the chief. My father asked my mother to stay at home with Isatu while he went to the meeting with me. I liked attending meetings with my dad even though I had little interest in what was discussed, but this day was different. I was eager to attend and know what the men in the village planned to do.

•••••

Our village is a very small one with less than one hundred houses. There was unity in the village and everyone referred to the other as brother, sister, uncle or aunt. We were one big happy family. When we entered the village centre we found it crowded, with the chief standing aside brainstorming with the council of elders. There was tension in the air with pockets of meetings taking place with people shaking their heads, resolute. I had the feeling that things were no longer going to be the same. I sensed that something ominous would happen, out of our control, and that we were all doomed. I was overwhelmed with fear and doubt, and silently cried for the first time in a long time. But then I told myself that I was a man and men should never cry. I wiped my tears and sat by my dad, who was talking with his friends, trying to find comfort in the conviction that he would protect me. The child in me could however not be shut out for long and despite the gravity of the gathering, I started looking around for my friends to play.

After a minute or two, the crowd was called to attention by the chief, "My people, I called you here today because a letter was discovered right where you are standing. The letter states that the rebels, those evil ones fighting the Government, will attack our village tomorrow. When I read the letter given to me by Pa Sorie, I thought my eyes were deceiving me. So I sent for my glasses, but after reading it for a second and then a third time, I

4

realised that what I was looking at was real and not a bad joke. This is a bad message for all of us, so I have called you here because I want us to decide on what we should do."

Thaimu, the village carpenter, who had the body shape of a barrel and head as flat as the seat of a bicycle put his hand up and said, "Chief, we must fight them. Let us never give up. They will rape our wives. They will kill us and kill our children. They will take our cattle, and they will burn our houses. We will lose all we have ever lived for and we will be left useless after they have left. I want us to fight. We all have our machetes and hunting guns. Let us stand up to them." There was a round of applause and it seemed that everyone supported Thaimu's suggestion. All others who spoke including my father supported fighting. Looking at Thaimu and his physique I doubted if he could possibly be among those who would actually fight. The thought of him fighting made me forget about the seriousness of the moment and a smile formed on my face. It seemed they were buoyed by the stance of another village, which had repelled a rebel attack by setting up vigilante groups that kept an eagle eye out for strange activities and individuals.

The chief cried for silence and spoke, "I have heard all of your thoughts and I want to tell you this: I have seen war, I have fought in them. I fought in the Great War, and I fought like a man. My question here is: can we fight the rebels? They have big guns and they are trained killers. We are ordinary village people. Do you truly believe you can put up a fight if they come?" Everyone shouted, "Yes! Yes!", "Okay," the chief agreed, "Mobilize yourselves and we will give them a hard time when they come. We should be as brave as possible." Everyone went home and had lunch. My mother had prepared cassava leaves with rice. I loved cassava leaves especially the way she prepared them. I momentarily stopped thinking about the letter and the threat of attack when I started eating.

5

•••••

That afternoon my dad left for the mobilisation meeting with the other men of the village. He asked us not to leave the house and to lie on the floor should we hear any gun shot. The directive helped to intensify our heartbeats. I was the man of the house and had to protect my mom and younger sister in the absence of my dad. Not a word was spoken amongst us as we sat helplessly looking at each other. I decided to read my literature book for comfort. I loved the story of Robinson Crusoe. I was very much interested in adventure stories. After thirty minutes or so I fell asleep and I dreamt of fighting and of people chasing me. I must have screamed in my sleep, for my mother woke me up and asked me what was wrong. I said nothing, got up, washed my face and checked the pots for more rice and cassava leaves. Dad arrived late at night and told us that he would not be sleeping in the house but would keep watch with the other men of the village. He assured us that all would be well, but that we should not leave the house at any cost.

•••••

Early in the morning dad came home, rested for a while, ate and then went again to join his colleagues. By this time, the health of my sister was improving, as my mother was loading her with Chloroquine and Panadol. My mother always told me that Chloroquine is good for malaria. If even it was not as good as they claimed, there was no other option, as it was one of the few drugs that we could get in the village. My grandmother always insisted when we visited her that we stop taking the Whiteman's medicines and instead take gbangba, the locally produced herb in the village. This she claimed made one grow strong and healthy. The elder brother of my mom, uncle Morlai, who lived in the city, was completely opposed to my grandmother. To him, taking native herbs was to some extent suicidal as they were not approved by medical professionals and were not measured to avoid overdose.

6

He sometimes exaggerated and pushed his facts too far by occasionally stating that some of the herbs have been scientifically tested and were said to be harmful. My grandmother would always dismiss him, telling him that he had lost his heritage and that he had been spoiled by the city. I was happy that my sister's health was improving. She was eight, and was very cute. There was a natural bond between us and she looked up to me when faced with any challenge especially in school where I protected her from bullying class-mates.

•••••

Tuesday came and went and there was no attack. We were all happy and as the tension eased and days went by, complacency set in and with a natural air of calm, business as usual started to re-establish itself. Some of the men in the village boasted that the rebels must have learnt of their plan and decided to avoid the imminent wrath that was in store for them. Some were even saying that if the rebels had dared come close, every one of them would have been killed. The chief sensing the change, laxity as well as excitement, among the men cautioned them to remain alert and report any suspicious activity. He garnished the advice with stories of how his battalion was caught in surprise attacks during the Great War. Such stories increased the respect people had for him. As a gifted orator with a dramatic character, he earned the respect of both the young and old. Even though I was very young, I suspected that the seed of ignorance had taken root in the minds of the villagers so that they believed anything the chief said. It reminded me of the saying, "In the land of the blind, the one-eyed man is king." My father had told me that the chief had been educated in the capital, and later became a soldier who was taken to fight in Asia during the Great War. Nonetheless, he was a good man who took interest in issues affecting his people and was always there when needed. His selflessness earned him the trust and respect of his people.

Few days later, things returned to a complete state of normalcy. My father allowed me to visit my friends but asked me not to stay out for long. I was happy that the rebels had not come and that once again life was as it used to be. That evening, a bull was slaughtered and barbequed in the chief's compound and the entire village was invited to feast with the chief. My father brought me along. I met my cousins, Foray and Abdul, who were there with Uncle John, my dad's younger brother. They lived at the other end of the village, five minutes from our house. They were my usual playmates but I had a difficult relationship with Abdul and our inability to peacefully settle our differences always culminated into us throwing fists at each other. Unfortunately for me, he was older and stronger and could relentlessly rain blows on me with the ferocity of Muhammad Ali. On one occasion, I had no option but to take to my heels in the full view of my friends. I preferred to be laughed at than to suffer the consequences of reckless bravery.

The aroma of frying and stewing was permeating every corner of the village as people decided to make the feast an occasion to celebrate life. Even the dogs and vultures could not wait to have their own share. I ate till I could eat no more. Having my sister in mind, I carefully wrapped two huge chunks of meat in a banana leaf. Even though I doubted if she could eat as she was still quite weak, I wanted her to know that I was thinking of her. Traditional dances were performed, while the chief and some of the elders told stories of their past, the village, the forest and the river that ran through the village. They told stories of the heroes and heroines, who once lived in our village. The chief said he had decided to make a feast because he wanted people to calm down after the stress of the last few days and move on with life. He said that the letter was probably just the work of a miscreant who had wanted to disturb the peace of the village, but wanted the person to know that it was a bad joke that should never be repeated. People laughed and the men passed palm wine around and smoked cigarettes.

Thaimu, the carpenter, told the chief that the security measures put in place would continue and the men would do all they could to keep the village safe. He reassured us that they would prefer to die than let rebels destroy our beautiful village. I was touched by the words of Thaimu, but I did not take him seriously as I knew he was only good at talking and did not have the capacity to defend the village. While the others were drinking, he was moving around like a local unit commander, checking to see if everything was okay. I looked up at the sky, and it looked very peaceful with the stars providing a kaleidoscopic canopy that capped our village. I prayed in my heart for my people as the effect of a full stomach sent me to sleep, while my dad continued with the celebration and sharing of palm wine. He and the other men drank generously from no shortage of bottles. He hadn't noticed that I was sleeping until his friends asked him to take me home. He was drunk and I was sleepy but nonetheless, we made our way home.

•••••

The following Monday, school resumed and I was happy to see my friends again. The day was consumed with the events of the previous days vigil. Our teachers abandoned their classes to engage each other on lengthy discussions. It appeared that some of my classmates did not grasp even the faintest picture of what could have happened if the village had been attacked. Their sense of excitement and wishes that the rebels should have attacked and beat the hell out of our wicked teachers for giving them difficult assignments drew me back to the reality that we were just kids. We were too young to fully comprehend what was going on in the country and what the fighting was all about. The chief and the others called the rebels the 'evil ones', who were bent on destroying everything good. I kept pondering over that. Once I asked my father if rebels were humans like us, or if they had tails or wings, and if they were more powerful than ordinary people like us. He faked a smile and sadly said that they were ordinary people who chose to conduct themselves in such a manner that made even Satan appear to be peaceful. I sensed a tinge of fear in my dad's voice as he spoke and the passing moments of silence triggered, for the first time, the feeling that my powerful dad was not the superhuman I had thought him to be. He was scared of the rebels and felt uncomfortable talking about them. My class was soon caught up in talking about war and the bravery of movie stars like Arnold Schwarzenegger and Sylvester Stallone who could take on several enemies and kill them all. I stood by an open window overlooking the staff room and looked on as the teachers engaged in a heated discussion.

I saw my favorite teacher Mr. Fofanah sending a kick, demonstrating to those around him how he would have attacked any rebel who had dared enter his house. Unfortunately, he raised his foot too high, lost balance and fell. This started a chain of laughter that heavily resonated across the school. He got up, dusted himself and joined in the laughing to make light what had happened. I felt sorry for him as he was a nice man and I usually helped him at his farm. He however, had the reputation of having the largest appetite in the village. Families think twice before inviting him to their house. His wife was given the nickname 'Kitchener' as she spent more time in the kitchen than any other place in their house.

•••••

The usual household chores occupied my time when I returned home from school. Even though I had made up my mind to stay at home and take a nap I had the sudden urge to go look for wild birds. I love watching birds and their rhythmic chirping has an effect on me. I envy their freedom and peace; flying above all humanity, going wherever they please with such ease and comfort, and returning when they feel; if they ever want to return. My mother, who could not understand my love for them, sometimes hinted that maybe I was a bird in my past life. Mr. Fofanah once told me that it was from the manner in which birds fly that airplanes were designed. Unfortunately, my cousin Abdul took pleasure in killing them and to hurt me he made sure I saw their remains. My fellow explorer friends were Gibril and Kakay, and although their primary interest were rodents they occasionally also spent time looking for pigeons and hawks. They were great hunters and fun to be with. Gibril had a good sense of humour and could cause one to laugh uncontrollably. His stories flowed endlessly and he had a good joke about every person in the village.

The urge to go bird-searching was interrupted by the aroma of cassava and stew that started floating its way through my nostrils. My mother was an exceptional cook and she succeeded in earning the reputation of our neighbours who made it their business to be visiting her kitchen even when they were uninvited. Other women in the village were not particularly enthused with the regular mentioning of my mother by their husbands whenever the topic of how a good meal should taste was discussed. I devoured my food with the speed and uncouthness of the hyena, and comfortably finished Isatu's leftovers. She had fully recovered from the malaria and had started playing with her friends.

•••••

"Pass me the ball, Foray, pass it to me!" I yelled. We were locked in the battle for supremacy. Football was the sport of the village and sometimes it appeared to be more of a wrestling match. Foray was a better player than I was, but I had more stamina and could play longer. The school compound served as our football field and we usually waited for all the teachers to leave before we took out what was our football. The frequent use, if not constant and relentless abuse, had battered the only football that graced our childhood. Our plea for a new football fell on deaf ears and I soon realised that my father's ceaseless promises to get us one were simply uttered to bring him immediate peace as my pleading took a monotonous rhythm. Like my friends, I finally gave up and we settled on what we had, a socks-ball.

"Saidu, you are hogging the ball, pass it so we can play," Foray called. I passed the ball on to Musa who was also in our team. Suddenly there was an explosion "Pan pan pan, thudom, thudom, pow pow pow"… sporadic gunshots engulfed our village and our football came to an abrupt end with everyone running for his dear life. I was gripped by fear with the dawning realization that the rebels had finally attacked the village. Despite the loss of rationality to the emerging chaos, I was able to pull Foray alongside me as I took off like a cheetah. The destination was my house but on nearing the chief's compound, we saw men dressed in black with red bandanas tied on their heads, screaming, "Where is he? Where is the chief? Let the bastard come out now or we will kill him when we find him!" I never knew I had a reverse gear and immediately made a 360 degrees turn around and run in a different direction. At this stage, the boys were religiously following me as if I knew what I was doing or where I was going. We made a clean dash for the forest, which was our safe haven.

All main paths were avoided as we took the less frequented routes. We had no final destination in mind. The key objective was to get as far away as possible from the village and the rebels. My knees almost gave way and I was consumed by nausea. I was facing the worst moment of my life, which was further worsened by the mixed feeling of wanting to return to the comfort of my family in the village, but at the same time fearful of what may befall us. The weight of the dilemma was tearing me apart. The push and pull was breaking my heart. I went close to

Foray, hugged him and we broke into an endless flow of tears. As a child I was very unprepared for what I was facing.

The momentary silence in the forest was shattered by a fresh wave of gunshots from the village with people screaming, either from being shot or out of panic. It suddenly dawned on me that we were eight vulnerable children who could easily fall into the hands of the rebels. I asked myself 'What should we do?' 'Where should we go?' The constant flow of questions yielded no answers to curb the effects of the trauma. Our young minds were pre-occupied but all eyes were glued on me. Alusine and I were older than the rest. The youngest was Deen who was 10. We found a thick bush covered with trees and savanna like grasses that made good for hiding. I asked everyone to stay calm and not to make any noise that might attract the rebels. We clung together like animals in hibernation. We felt that letting go of each other would lead to some of us mystically disappearing. We sat like that for over six hours until some of the boys fell asleep. The burden of the six younger ones laid squarely on Alusine and I. We had to do all we could to make sure that they were safe.

•••••

"Alusine! Alusine! Wake up; we must keep watch while they sleep. We can't afford to fall asleep." I called on Alusine who was also dosing off. He sat up and tried futilely to stay awake, but the need to sleep could not be denied, the rhythmic nodding of his head and its frequent contact with the tree made me feel sorry for him. I decided to let him sleep while I kept watch. By now the guns had fallen silent and darkness was fast falling. After a few hours, I heard people moving in our direction. I woke everybody and instructed all to keep very quiet and still while I climbed a tree to take a good look at those passing. They passed very close to us, heading towards the village. They were about forty in number and they were carrying loads, guns and ammunition. I realised immediately that

13

they were rebels going to join their colleagues. After they had passed, Alusine, now wide awake, joined me in keeping watch. This time I chose to stay on a tree looking west while Alusine took a tree facing east.

The rumbling in my stomach alerted me to the hunger that was about to harass me. I started looking for trees that had fruits; I spotted one with mangoes, and made a sign to Alusine to let him know where I was going. I got on the tree, removed my cloth and used it as a sack for the mangoes. When I returned, I gave three to each of us. We devoured the fruits like wolves on a fresh kill. The next concern was water but going in search of it was quite challenging. However, as the shooting in the village had died down, I decided to go to a stream in the forest I had been to before. The heavy protests of Alusine almost made me change my mind. He drummed the possibility of me meeting rebels on the way. I sensed he was cloaked in fear and did not want to be left alone with the kids or was probably nervous that something would happen to me. I carefully scouted the areas closer to us but could not find any water source so I returned to our hideout. We passed the night without anything to drink. I was restless and could hardly close my eyes so I started a conversation with Alusine and we talked for the remainder of the night while the boys slept.

Mosquitoes descended on us like locusts, and every exposed part of our body was lost to them in spite of the quiet slaps we landed on our bodies to kill or ward them off. I thought of Robinson Crusoe, his stay on an island and the bravery and courage that enabled him come out alive. The real and present fear of rebels was coupled with the fear of snakes and beasts entering our hideout. The thought of those slithering creatures, goose-bumped my skin. Alusine assured me that snakes avoid human beings and reminded me that the anti-snake marks on our bodies will protect us from any snake. I took solace from this, but couldn't help the intermittent scanning of our surrounding to ensure that we were safe.

•••••

Gunshots from the village jolted me out of my semi-conscious, as I realised I had been completely lost in my thoughts for a while. Were the rebels now settled in our village? I wondered. Having gotten used to the sound of the gunshots, I set about thinking of food. I woke everybody up and ascended the tree to see how it could help in our fight against hunger. Alusine discovered a guava tree close to the mango tree earlier visited and our store was filled with it. By then, the desire to go and see what was happening in the village and find my family had overwhelmed me and throwing caution to the wind, I decided to give it a try. Alusine as usual protested but gave up when he realised that my mind was made up and nothing could change it. We did not tell the other kids what I was going to do because I thought they would be against my leaving.

"Foray, Hamid, I am going to look for more food, I know there are more fruits around, I will be back soon," I said. I saw the look of despair in Foray's eyes as he asked, "Saidu, can I come with you?", "No Foray, it will be better if you stay with the group. The closer we stay the better. I will be back very soon and Alusine is here to take care of you while I am away. I promise you, I won't be long." Alusine wished me well and off I went. I was as careful as I could be to avoid stepping on twigs that would snap and betray my position. I took the route where the forest was particularly thick and canopies hung. On reaching the outskirt of the village, I climbed a tree to observe the village from a safe distance. I chose a very big one with lots of branches and leaves that would make for an easy cover. From the tree I could see smoke coming from several parts of the village, and there were burnt huts with people lying dead on the ground. I could not see my house because it was on the other side of the forest. I could hear people shouting and crying but I could not see their faces. However, from their screams I was convinced that they were been tortured. I climbed down and took the direction of my house through the forest. An adrenalin rush was swelling in me. Several questions were rushing through my mind: What if my parents were dead? What if the soldiers had taken them away? I felt so disturbed that I vomited.

Before the letter found its way to the village, I never for one moment thought that life could be so horrible. I was always reading stories with the ending "They lived happily ever after"; it never crossed my mind that humans were capable of hunting each other down like wild beasts. It was too much for me. As I tried to make sense out of what was happening, my confusion only intensified.

Getting closer to my house, I saw rebels sitting in an open space between our house and Lamin's, our neighbour. There was no movement in our house. The door was broken down and our stuffs were scattered on the verandah. I could not see my parents or my sister. I had to hide myself behind trees waiting to see if they would leave so that I could enter the house. The rebels seemed happy. They were playing Ludo, smoking marijuana (which I had seen some young men in our village smoking), and drinking palm wine. The regular cacophonous outbursts from someone winning or losing showed how indiscreet the rebels were. They appeared to be very relaxed and not thinking of a counter-attack by Government forces. There were two women sweating from the strain of cooking in the heat. I recognised the pot being used as ours; my mother had told me it was given to her as a wedding gift by my grandmother.

•••••

Hours of immobility waiting for the rebels to leave caused my muscles to cramp so I changed plan and retraced my steps back into the forest and re-routed to the chief's compound. Caution was my mantra. However, considering the way the rebels were running towards that compound when they attacked, I doubted if there would be much left of it. Trying to make as little noise as possible, I reached the back of the compound. I saw that half of it had been burnt down. While watching from what appeared to be a secure location, someone in a close hiding spot whispered my name. "Saidu, come here. It's me, Mabinty." I almost had a heart attack when I heard someone calling my name. The shock was compounded by the fact that I assumed I was alone in my hiding place. Mabinty, the chief's daughter was lying on the ground looking exhausted and petrified. I decided to take her to a safe location in the forest before bombarding her with questions. "Where is the chief and everyone else?" I asked her.

She broke down crying, "They have killed Papa, they have killed him. They cut off his head when they got hold of him. My sisters are with them. They raped Jariatu and Femusu. They also killed Thaimu in our house. He was with Papa when the attack took place. He wanted to fight back but was shot in the head. They have taken everyone to the field and I believe they are going to kill them." I tried to calm her down but it proved to be a daunting task. She was overwhelmed with grief, fear, panic and confusion. Her eyes were as red and alert as someone who had taken a cocktail of drugs. My mother once told me that crying is good for women especially after they have faced a traumatic situation, so I let her exhaust her pain and sorrow before asking more questions, "Where were you when all this was happening?" I asked. "I was in my room. After they killed Papa and Thaimu, I heard one of them telling the others to take the rest to the school where they would be killed. At that point I jumped through the window and ran into the forest," she explained through her tears. I asked her to calm down and wait while I went back to their compound to get some food and water. She directed me to where I could get them and I left her.

When I reached the compound, it had the deafening silence of a graveyard. Indeed, it was a graveyard. Death hung in the air and I knew that murder and chaos had pitched tent not too far away. I climbed through an open window, which I believed was the one used by Mabinty, and entered the main house, or at least what was left of it. I navigated my way into the store and threw bread, butter, cassava and tins of sardines into a bag. Luckily, there was a small container filled with water, which made things easy for me. So I grabbed it, satisfied my thirst, then climbed out and ran off to the forest to meet Mabinty. When I found her, we set off to where Alusine and the other boys were. We walked in silence, each heavy-hearted with grief. Alusine and the others were happy to see us but they could see the sadness on our faces. The food and water however caught their attention, and they focused on them instead. After eating, they started asking questions. I recounted what I saw and Mabinty explained everything that happened at their compound. Tears were streaming down all of our faces as she spoke. There was no way to comfort anyone.

•••••

That night it rained heavily and we were all wet for there was no place to hide from the rain. I went in search of banana leaves to shelter the younger ones and Mabinty, but I could not find any so I brought back palm leaves which did not do much good. We huddled together, weathering the storm. At that moment I thought of my sister and I prayed that no harm would befall her. As the rain became unbearable and I started feeling cold, I stood up and walked around to kill time. I could see that the cold was also affecting my friends but there was nothing I could do but ask them to be patient, whilst reassuring them that all this madness would end very soon. Then we could go back to the village.

Unfortunately for us, the rain continued throughout the night and the next day. August is a rainy month and sometimes it could rain for days. I always hated going to the farm with my father in August, as the roads were muddy and very slippery. I never knew that there would come a time when the rain would be beating me as crazily as it was doing now. Foray called me aside and said, "I am really tired. I think it would be better to die than go through this. You did not tell me anything about my family, something bad must have happened to them. Please talk to me." I did not know what to say to him but I decided to say something to calm him down, "Foray, we are in this together like everyone here. We do not like being here but we have to be. The rebels will kill us if we return to the village, but I know this will not last forever. The God that created us will definitely get us out of here and He will see us through this. Please hang on. I will do all I can to make you safe. I believe that our families are safe. They must have gone somewhere safe. We will find them after the rebels have left the village. Please do me this favour, hang on and try to be strong. Our parents would want us to be strong at this moment, please Foray."

He just stood there staring at me. I really hoped that I was telling him the truth, that all would be well. I was trying to give him hope and courage. Keep hope alive as they say because hope is the last thing that should die in a person, if it dies then you are doomed. I never understood where my strength was coming from, but the boys and Mabinty saw me as the leader. They were all listening to me, even Alusine. Probably it was that which gave me strength. I did not want to fail them, so I swore to myself that I would not. The following morning the rain stopped and by then we had had the last of the food and water I brought from the chief's compound. I decided that it was time for me to go back to the village, the only place I knew there could be food, water and blankets, if I could find any. Alusine volunteered to go with me but I encouraged him to stay with the others. This time I took the route that led to the school. I wanted to see what was going on there. The living quarter of the head teacher was very close to the forest and if I took the path that led to the back of his house it would be very difficult for anyone to see me unless there was someone lying there waiting to attack. I decided to take the risk. As I approached, I heard noises coming from the schoolyard and then two shots being fired. I braved it to the head teacher's quarter and entered the pit latrine that was built by the side of the house. From there I could see the schoolyard since there were holes in the wall. I prayed that no one enters there as I would be caught or killed.

From the peephole, I saw about fifteen rebels, most of them around my age standing with guns almost the height of some of them and smoking marijuana. Two of the young rebels were kicking a man lying on the ground. I could only see the back of the person, but not his face. Around twenty to twenty-five people were sitting on the grass and I saw one of the rebels urinating on a man I recognised to be Pa Turay, the chief's messenger. I also saw the father of Alusine, and Mammy Kamara, the old woman who sold rice at the village center. The other faces I could not make out. They were very far away. At least I had some news to take to Alusine that his father was alive, but what would happen next I did not know. From the school hall I could hear someone crying between the loud cracks of a whip.

As I watched, concentrating, I heard someone coming close to the toilet. I almost urinated where I stood. I leaned on the wall adjacent to the door and for a second thought of jumping into the latrine. I also contemplated taking whoever it was by surprise by hitting them with the stick that was on the ground, and then run away into the forest. While all these thoughts were parading through my mind, the person continued past the toilet. I gasped for breath. I knew it was time to go in search of food and try to avoid human contact. I opened the door and slowly walked my way into the forest and then to the chief's compound. Only a few tins of sardines and some cassava could be found in the chief's compound. I guessed that someone else had visited the store and probably the person was still close by. I immediately took what I could and jumped out through the window. However, what I got was too small to take back to my friends so I decided to look around the town a bit to see what I might come across. Curiosity led me to our house and this time there was no one sitting there. I could see my mother's pots lying strewn across the floor. I tried the window to see if I could enter the house from the back but the wire-mesh we used to prevent mosquitoes from entering the room was quite strong and I did not want to cause any noise that would draw attention to me. I crawled through the door and entered the house. Everything was scattered around but I was happy not to see any dead bodies. I became hopeful that my family was still alive. I collected all the food and water that I could carry and headed towards my new camp in the forest.

•••••

Alusine was wearing a troubled look when I returned. I saw Bakarr, one of the younger boys, lying on his lap. He told me that Bakarr had been throwing up since I left, and his temperature was high. I touched him and could feel that he had a high fever. We sat him up and gave him something to eat. However, he was eating with serious difficulties. He threw up immediately after he finished eating. I had taken two towels from my house, I soaked and placed one over him to cool his temperature, found a dry spot to lay him down and covered him with the other. He was very weak but there was nothing more we could do, and we had no experience on how to handle a sick person. Foray told us that Bakarr had sickle cell. I checked everybody, putting my hands on their foreheads and necks to see if they too had a fever. The rest of my friends seemed fine except Bakarr. I told Alusine that I saw his father at the schoolyard. I also told him that we should stop telling the children what I saw each time I went to the village because it was only increasing their fears and that was not good for their health.

After eating, we took turns drinking from the rubber container of water I had brought. I intermittently checked on Bakarr who was sleeping: a poor, sick child, sleeping on the floor of the forest. Luckily for us, it did not rain that night. So we sat together telling stories we heard from our parents - like the story of the spider who had invitations to several feasts. Wanting to attend all of them, he asked his friends to tie eight ropes round him and draw him to the first one to get started, and after some time the next person should draw him to another feast. Unfortunately for the spider, all the feasts began at the same time, and he was drawn from all the sections and that is why he has eight legs and a small middle. That was the most popular children's story in our village. The minute Foray raised his hand, I knew he wanted to tell that story, and I could see him smiling as he did. He was in love with the story and could tell it a thousand times. Seeing him smile made me happy, it was the first time he had smiled in days.

•••••

"Bakarr, Bakarr," I called, but he didn't answer. He lay there exactly as he had when I checked on him the night before. I moved over to check his temperature. I turned him slightly, not wanting to wake him if he was sleeping. Then I saw froth from his mouth thickly glued to the ground and ants all over his face. I panicked and cried out, "Bakarr, wake up, do not do this to us, please don't! Wake up, wake up!" Alusine and the others rushed to us, and they saw the froth and the ants. It was a very terrible and pitiful sight. We started tugging and calling on him as we cried. We could not believe that he was gone. We surrounded him and wept for hours. We intermittently shook him to see if he would respond, but he did not; we had lost him and that was not going to change.

I felt the urge to leave our hide out and seek refuge where there were people older than us. The death of Bakarr was too much to handle. The pressure was augmenting and my head was at a point of explosion. I was losing it, and my being a child was manifesting my limitations. My head was spinning and I felt like screaming. After trying to gain control of myself I asked my friends if we should leave the forest and try to reach the other villages. Six sets of lips instantly screamed a resounding 'No!' which killed all intentions to debate the issue. I saw that everyone had surrendered to fate and were not prepared to move an inch. The fear of the unknown was preventing us from moving. My silence seemed to bother Alusine and he came close to me and stated that the rebels had probably captured all the other villages as well, and we could not cross the river to the village on the other side of the forest without a boat.

In the early hours of the afternoon, we buried Bakarr. We used sticks to dig the grave by a massive cotton tree so we could not forget the spot. This was never something I thought I would do as a child. I wished I was not doing what I was doing, but I was left with no choice. It was a sobering moment for all of us, and everyone was crying as we dug. Alusine prayed for him, reciting verses from the Koran as we laid him gently in the ground and covered him with earth.

Bakarr's death imposed a cathedral silence on the entire group. Hardly anyone spoke. We could not sleep so we just sat looking at each other. In the morning we shared the remaining water. I was physically and emotionally paralyzed, I could not move an inch, even to go in search of food. The burden of the past days was weighing heavily on me now. My faith was heavily tested, for the first time I was seriously thinking of God, life, and the evils in the world. The image of Bakarr was etched indelibly in my head and appeared vividly regardless of my eyes being closed or not. I was no longer scared of dying. I had had my first encounter with death and it was someone very close to me. If Bakarr could die, then any one of us could die at any point in time. I cried endlessly, not caring who was watching me or what effect my crying might have on the others. Alusine went in search of fruits and came back with a big full of assorted fruits and nuts. All efforts by Mabinty and the boys to cheer me up had no effect. Sensing that Bakarr's death had left me deranged and flustered, Foray came to me and lay down with his head across my chest. I was touched by this act and hugged him as I cried.

•••••

Emotionally and physically drained from the trials of the day, we surrendered to nature. We drifted off to sleep but not for long. "Who are you? Raise your hands or we will shoot!" We awoke to see soldiers standing over us, their guns pointed at us. My hands shot up high, raised to avoid any misunderstanding. Despite being used to such form of punishment in school, some of my friends hardly knew how to respond. We could see that they were surprised to see that we were children. The commander asked, "What are you doing here? We could have shot you." Alusine explained to them that the rebels had captured our village, and that we had escaped into the forest. He also told the leader that one of us had died, and showed him where we had buried Bakarr. The soldiers were many and they were well armed. The leader explained that they were Government forces liberating the villages in the area from the rebels. We were so happy to see them that we shed tears of joy. They gave us food and water. The leader asked us to remain calm and left us in the care of two officers with the promise that we would soon be returned to the village once it had been liberated.

•••••

We heard heavy firing in the village few hours after they left us. There was a heavy downpour but this time we cared less about it. We were only waiting for the end of the fighting and our return to the village. From the gunshots we heard, we could tell that the battle was fierce. We waited until mid-afternoon before we saw one of the soldiers returning to us. He told us that the village had been liberated! Some rebels were killed and others had fled. We began to celebrate, but when I thought of Bakarr, I stopped. We were returning to the village without him.

We were taken to the school compound, where we met the commander of the soldiers who told us of how they took the rebels by surprise and killed most of them. He went with us to the chief's compound where the remaining villagers had assembled. Foray's dad hugged us and started crying. I asked him why he was crying but he could not tell me. He held me and continued sobbing. I asked if he knew where my family was. This drew more tears and I immediately suspected that something bad had happened to them. He told me that they had been killed and thrown down a well. My legs gave way beneath me as I passed out. On regaining consciousness, I saw people fanning me but the horrific image of the way my family had been killed flooded back and I passed out for the second time. When I came to for the second time and was able to stand on my feet, the commander took me aside and gave me some medicine while asking me to be courageous, to take the news like a man and have faith in God. Why was I being asked to take it like a man, when I was just a small boy presented with challenges even adults could hardly overcome? How was I supposed to act like a man, when I was just a boy whose world has been crushed, his entire family brutally murdered? I cried, asking God: how can anyone deserve this?

The Draw of the Unknown

The streets of Freetown are dark and quiet. The people lay securely within the comfort of their homes for the duration of the evening. The cool harmattan breeze, which usually tempts people to escape the thick hot air trapped in their homes, could not even draw a single person out. Windows were tightly shut and the kerosene lamps that usually lit the houses were either put out or dimmed to provide a shadowy intimate light. We are waiting, waiting for the inevitable. We know the city will fall into the hands of the combined forces of rebels and renegade soldiers. The Nigerian head of the Sierra Leone Army (SLA) came on the radio, making bellicose speeches, fanning the flames of war, while claiming to have the situation under control. This time around, the people are not with him, they know his words are empty; it is just a matter of time before the rebels attack our precious city.

In the preceding days, Freetown had been inundated with displaced persons who were running from communities taken over by the rebels. The evidence of what the rebels could do was clear for all to see: the amputees, the mutilated bodies and the blood that painted the streets. People who were more dead than alive flooded the hospitals, clinics and pharmacies; every edifice that had a medical sign was gradually filled up. A thick pungent smell of blood from the street gutters filled the air. Those who could talk narrated their experiences, depicting how the rebels cut off hands or arms from either the elbow or wrist, after giving the victims the choice of 'short or long sleeve'.

Rumours had ruled our lives with fear and anguish for the last eight years. They began to spread, this time though, they came eerily close to home. Word spread that the President had left the city and had set up camp at the base of the Economic Community of West African States Monitoring Group (ECOMOG), the military wing of the Economic Community of West African States (ECOWAS). ECOMOG had helped to restore President Ahmad Tejan Kabba in 1998 after he was overthrown by the military in 1997. Another school of rumor firmly believed that the President was still in his residence at Hill Station, and that he was confident that the rebels would not be able to break the defensive perimeter set up by the ECOMOG and SLA.

Food was left untouched as we glued our ears to radios, continuously waiting for updates. We were all lost in our thoughts. Bags packed, jeans and t-shirts worn, shoes laced, we were ready to run whenever we heard a shot. But the question was "where could one run to, and which area was safe?" There was no clear answer. The rebels were expected to come from the eastern part of the city, but it was equally possible to use the peninsula and attack from the West.

•••••

As night fell, the call to prayer from the mosque near our house began to echo throughout the house. It was the month of Ramadan, but few dared to walk the streets in these times. We quietly prayed and then decided not to fast the next day. There were three of us in a small room that had been rented by our now deceased aunt, in order to care for us. There was Momodu, who was the oldest of us, a thick-framed guy with an egg-shaped head. Momodu had a beautiful and peaceful heart, his calming presence kept me somewhat assured. Kolorie, my elder brother worked as a football coach for one of the local teams in the centre of Freetown. Since becoming a member of the Commonwealth, football developed a strong following in Sierra Leone which remains till this day. Kolorie had been lying on the bed the entire day without talking, his face turned to the wall. Usually talkative, with an opinion on every issue, he had lost his strength that day. His somber mood worried me.

The house was big and unkempt. It was divided into several apartments. As small as they were, some of the rooms housed more than eight people at various points in time. The toilet was by far the worst part of the house, hosting more than 40 people per day, each visiting more than once. The stench spread across the surrounding rooms, and it was always wretchedly filthy, making me gag every time I walked into the vicinity. Having little choice, we had to make do with what was available and being the youngest of the three did not help. I was responsible for cleaning the toilets when it was our turn to do so. No matter how long I spent scrubbing my body afterwards, I would still feel contaminated and dirty.

Momodu said "If anyone had told me that these boys could come so close to the city I would have denied it. Yet this idiot keeps talking nonsense on the radio. The President is probably not even in this city. These guys always disappear when things are hot, leaving us to suffer, chai, man pikin dae suffer." He had a funny way of talking that always made me laugh and even when he was serious he spoke with a funny tone. My brother got up, took his ablutions, prayed, and lay down again. Momodu and I exchanged glances and I had the impulse to engage my brother in a discussion to change his mood but decided to let him be. It was as if his self-assured and calming nature had been sucked out of him, leaving an empty hell with nothing behind his eyes but a growing fear, which seemed to be quickly turning into apathy and withdrawal.

•••••

"Knock, knock, knock!" We all jumped. "Who is it?" I shouted after a brief moment of hesitation. "God damn them" I swore under my breath. "It's me, Tamia." I opened the door for him. Tamia was a friend of Kolorie who lived in one of the rooms in our house. He was a midfielder at the club that Kolorie was coaching. "Man, I just received a phone call from my aunt at Calaba Town. She says the rebels are advancing towards the city and the Nigerian soldiers are running away. She said she saw a big crowd with people coming towards their area and that there is a lot of shooting going on at the moment."

This caught the full attention of Kolorie who sat upright on the bed with his head in his hands. At that moment Tamia's mobile phone rang (then there were very few mobile phones and operators in Sierra Leone, Tamia and his aunt had Mobitel phones provided by a relative of theirs who was working for Mobitel), "It's my aunt," he said. "Put it on speaker so we can hear her," demanded Momodu. "Tamia! The rebels are here! They are here and I do not know where to go or what to do," she cried. In the background, we could hear the sound of heavy shooting. It was so loud! "God save us, we are finished!" The phone went off. Tamia tried calling again but it was not answered. We exchanged fearful glances, waiting for someone to come up with a plan or even a direction, but none of us could believe that this was actually happening.

"Where can we go now, where?" Tamia asked. Even though I was wearing a sweater, I was very cold and could feel my blood running through me like ice. I was coming face to face with the reality as I sat there hopelessly anticipating the ideas that the older two would surely offer. The radio announced that at 8:45 p.m. the Minister of Internal Affairs would make a statement. I checked my watch; it was 8:40 p.m.

"Tune this radio properly and increase the volume," Tamia instructed. I increased the volume and looked for the wire I normally fixed onto the tip of the antenna to give it better coverage. At 8:45 p.m. the Minister started speaking: "Fellow citizens, the Government would like you to know that there is heavy fighting going on in the eastern part of Freetown, between Waterloo and Calaba Town. Joint forces of ECOMOG, SLA, and Kamajors are protecting us from the rebels. Reinforcements have been sent to the front and we are asking everybody to stay calm and remain indoors. A dusk to dawn curfew is now in place and violators will be punished. On behalf of the President, and his entire cabinet, I want to assure you that we will do all we can to protect the citizens of this our great land. We will never allow evil to triumph over good. At this moment of difficulty, we count on the support of all patriotic Sierra Leoneans. We ask you to stand shoulder to shoulder with us as we march to victory. We shall overcome, God bless us all and God bless Sierra Leone."

Immediately the speech ended, Tamia jumped into frenzy, "Listen to him, big mouth and empty words, empty words. While we would be slaughtered like chickens, he will be in a foreign land. They have money to run, we have nothing. Empty talk! Liars!" Momodu, in an attempt to calm Tamia down, added, "Hey, come on, let's hope they stop them. Let's not get angry, it won't solve the problem." Tamia's expression did not change. "I can't believe the rebels would overcome the Nigerians, the Ghanaians and the Guineans. They are surely not that equipped, and ECOMOG forces should be better trained" I said. Looking back at the easy way ECOMOG kicked out the army and the rebels from power in 1998, I doubted if the rebels would be any match for them. Yet, considering the distance the rebels and the renegade soldiers had covered, from the Liberian border right to the outskirts of Freetown, a part of me was not sure they could be stopped. It was a moment of internal chaos. I decided to lie down on the cold floor and ease the bubbling anxiety that was rushing through my veins.

Rumours of the rebels wanting to attack Freetown had started coming in by early December 1998. Rich middle class families immediately started sending their children out of the country. The normally loud and rumbustious Christmas season was dull and unobtrusive. There was tension building in the air and one could sense it growing daily. The pattern in the city changed and the early evenings were clouded with pockets of people standing at junctions or in front of their houses talking. Schools were closed as parents were afraid of their children going far from their homes. After 6:00 p.m. very few people could be seen outside. Periodically there were rumours of spies captured in the city who stated that some rebels were already in the city, waiting for the order to attack.

No one knew who to trust so people only talked to those they knew, and when they saw a stranger heading their way, they would immediately stop talking. This had gone on for weeks until we heard the rebels had attacked Waterloo, about 30 miles from the centre of Freetown. The Government initially dismissed these reports as untrue, and it was only when the city became deluged with those fleeing the violence that it confirmed the rumours. Calaba Town, which served as the gate of Freetown, was captured in quick succession. I thought of my friends staying there and what their situation would be. Tamia joined me on the floor as I slowly drifted into a deep sleep.

•••••

At 5:00 a.m. on the 6th of January 1999, Aunty Kadie, one of our neighbours, woke us up. She thought we would be fasting. Still drowsy I made my way outside to empty my bowels when I heard a massive explosion. I dashed inside and like the others spread myself on the floor. After about an hour, we went outside as we had heard our neighbours opening their doors. Brima, a police officer who lived in the room just above ours, said, "No

31

need to worry. The Navy is testing the gun boats bought from China. You can go back to sleep, everything is under control."

"Who would want to go to sleep at this moment?" Tamia asked him. Bang! Gbooooon! That sound was horrifying, I had never heard something like that before and I hoped to never hear it again. The sound of military helicopters was heard and Brima continued, "The Nigerians are truly trained soldiers. Now they're stepping up their attack." Brima was known to be a talkative who took pleasure in talking about things he had little knowledge of, so we always dismissed his statements as untrue.

'Bang!' The sound came again, this time closer. We all dashed for our rooms, with my intuition telling me that doomsday had arrived. Subsequent gunshots were heard from all angles in the city, with regular explosions going off. Tamia cried, "Kolorie! They are here! I swear to God, they're here!" Kolorie told him, "Please, let's be quiet. Our destiny is in the hands of God." With eyes bulging and rivulets of sweat engulfing my whole being, I dived for cover on the floor with many thoughts rushing through my mind. The shootings were even more intense now and coming from every direction. A few minutes later, we heard vehicles moving with people cursing as they passed, "You bastards thought we would not come. Now here we are. Get the fuck out of your hiding places! We will find you, no matter where you are!" "Let's open one of the windows and see what's going on outside," Momodu said. "You must be crazy, you can go outside if you want, we're not opening any window" my brother replied. We heard someone banging the door of Aunty Joe, a very fat woman whose room was adjacent Brima's. She was commonly known to be a coward and I wondered what she would do at a moment like this.

"Open the window, Samuel, we will jump out if someone tries breaking the door," Kolorie said in a whisper. I opened it quietly not wanting to draw any attention. We heard Aunty Joe crying. A shot went off followed by the sound of someone running. After a while, we heard doors opening. So we decided to open ours. Aunty Joe was sitting by her door crying. I was happy to know that she was not the one shot, but then she said, "They've taken all my money and almost killed me. When I resisted, they shot the ground and I let go." Kadie said, "Aunty Joe, be happy you're alive. These rebels could have done worse. Money will come and go, pray for good health and security."

We decided to go and look for Brima. When we entered his room, he was lying flat under his bed. He looked visibly shaken. He came out saying, "I have to throw away my uniform, if those guys see them, they will kill me. They will do me evil before killing me." "I think so too, and all of us will be in trouble along with you. Just put them in a plastic bag and dump them in the toilet," Kolorie said. We helped him pack his police regalia and he threw them into the toilet. We had heard stories of how rebels treated police officers and police stations, as they were moving towards Freetown.

All seemed quiet for a while. We barricaded the main gate and sat in the compound. Everybody came out of their apartments and the women set about preparing food for their children. "Sammy," Tamia called, "I think we should boil the cassava we have, let's eat while we can." "Be quiet!" Kolorie hushed him and said, "There is someone talking on the radio." So I ran closer to get the latest development.

The speaker on the radio said, "As I speak to you, our boys have captured the State House and Parliament Building, and they are moving towards the western part of the city. ECOMOG escaped from our boys with their tails between their legs! They could not match us with all their fire-power. We have better, stronger fighters." The journalist broadcasting posed a question to the speaker,

"There are reports of heavy civilian casualties. What is your estimation?" "I am sure there are civilian casualties but I cannot give you a specific figure. Some of those killed were caught in cross-fire, but I want to assure you that we do not target civilians," the speaker replied.

The journalist continued, "But in the past months there have been amputations and horrible acts of violence perpetrated by your boys. There have also been lootings and targeting of innocent people. You use them as human shields, which is clearly a horrendous act, not to mention a violation of the Geneva Convention. Why would you do this to people you claim you are fighting to liberate?" "Our movement is a highly disciplined one, and our commanders are warned regularly that innocent people should be protected and not targeted. If anyone is caught committing atrocities that person will be punished." "What are your plans now that you have taken the capital city?" "Once we succeed in weeding out the pockets of resistance we are facing, directives will come from the high command of the movement. For now, I cannot say what those directives will be." "That was General Kamzo in Freetown, Sierra Leone. We will give you updates of the situation on the ground later." The British Broadcasting Corporation (BBC) journalist concluded the interview.

As the broadcast ended Kolorie put off the radio and said, "The time has come for monkey to chew pepper. Now we are in the time of each man for himself and God for us all. Only yesterday, the head of the army was busy deceiving people with military strategies and tactics and where is he now? Never trust these people! This is the second time we have been deceived. Our house is very close to both the parliament and State House, in a very strategic position so we'll face the brunt of the fighting."

•••••

I settled down to boiling the cassava, while the women cooked in silence, most of them on their verandas using stoves. I mixed the cassavas with the last of the butter we had. Tamia and Momodu had the appetite of hyenas! They were eating as if everything was okay. Brima could not eat. I tried talking to him once but he ignored me. I noticed that the landlord and his family had not opened their door since the chaos started. He had been very active in the recent days, mobilising youths for community protection, and since he was an ardent supporter of the Government, I guessed he was quite afraid of being attacked. I thought of making funny noises at his door to tease him, but reconsidered; this was no time for jokes. He was a nice person, and his wife, Miss Eku was the most loved elderly woman in the community. She cooked for the youth and would always have kind words for us when we visited or met with her.

The day went by with sporadic outbursts at different sections of the city. In the afternoon, we decided to venture out and walk around a bit, and whenever we saw a vehicle we would go behind a house to keep out of the way. By 5:00 p.m. we saw several trucks coming down from Circular Road, taking Fort Street towards State Avenue. There were men, women, and children on the trucks, wearing military fatigues, some carrying AK47 rifles, some with Rocket Propelled Grenades (RPGs), and others holding white flags. They were shouting, "Peace is here, peace is here, come out and celebrate with us!" They were in a jubilant mood, the tone of their cheers chiming with the word 'peace' lulled me into a warm safe space. This was a space in which I allowed myself to lift the pent up anxiety off my shoulders; I was reassured by the notion of 'peace' meaning the rebels would not harm us. People left their homes, carrying everything white from t-shirts to uniforms, to wave at them. We were all cheering, "Peace, peace, we want peace!"

Fort Street was rapidly transformed from its recently gained ghost town status to a bustling street. The rebels were throwing food and people were scrambling to get some. A packet of biscuits were thrown in my direction, I caught it. It was thrown by a boy who could not be more than ten. I waved to him and he waved back. After the peace parade by the rebels, we went home and Momodu admonished us, "We cannot trust these people. They are chameleons; they can change at any time. Today they will be happy, tomorrow it will be a different story. I believe we should avoid any contact with them. If there is a way we can get some food let's get it while we can." Kolorie gave him some money, and Tamia, who was staying in our room for the meantime, also contributed. Momodu went to the house opposite ours where our neighbour Makalay sold food stuffs. He came back with small bags of garri, rice, oil, pepper, butter, onions and maggi. Luckily for us, there was some milk, sugar, and tins of corned beef, which Kolorie had bought for the month of Ramadan. We had enough provisions for a week, the coming days seemed shrouded.

•••••

From stories heard, several Nigerian soldiers were killed when the rebels entered the city on the 6th. Coupled with this, homes were destroyed along the way with people killed as they were either used as human shields or caught in cross fire.

The 7th of January started like any normal day. Apart from a few gunshots heard, everything was fine. People were moving up and down the streets. I could feel my back aching from sleeping on the floor. I checked the time – it was 8:00 a.m. I had overslept, and the others were still sleeping. We needed the sleep; from the uncertain peace, it looked like there would be days with little or no sleep ahead. It was funny to see everyone sleeping fully dressed with shoes on - Momodu even had a hat on. I guessed it would make for easy running. Outside, to the west it was foggy, something was burning but I could not figure out what. I tuned in to BBC, where there was something on Congo and later Sierra Leone. The reporter said "Leaders from African countries and the West have been criticizing the recent attack of the rebels on the capital of Freetown, Sierra Leone. Leaders at the Organisation of African Unity (OAU) meeting in Addis Ababa have released a communiqué asking for a ceasefire, and a halt to all activities that will endanger lives and property. The Foreign Minister of Nigeria has said that their troops will be reinforced and they will launch a counter-attack as soon as they are ready. The meeting was mostly on Sierra Leone, a country that has suffered a decade of a very bloody, civil conflict. It is reported that the rebels are getting most of their arms and ammunitions from Liberia and that President Taylor continues to support the Revolutionary United Front."

From Sierra Leone, the news item (or agenda) switched to Zimbabwe and Robert Mugabe, another hot topic for the BBC. I decided to tune in to the FM 98.1, a local station also known as Radio Democracy, set up in 1997 when the government went into exile after a military coup. "This is the voice of the people, FM 98.1. Do not listen to any other station. They only fool you! The people of this land will be redeemed." "Reduce the volume, are you mad? If you're caught listening to this station, you'll be castrated!" Kolorie warned, so I reduced it but continued listening. "The president of our land will be talking to us this morning," the speaker continued, "and he will tell us what he is doing to redeem our motherland from thugs and bandits. Democracy will not die; the rule of law will prevail. We want you to know these bandits will be uprooted from our soil, and they will be thrown into the abyss of darkness. Stay tuned to FM 98.1, the voice of the people." Solemn liberation-themed songs began playing.

I liked the liberation song "We shall overcome" which we sang regularly to assuage our fears and anxiety:
We shall overcome
We shall overcome one day oh

Deep in my heart
I do believe
We shall over someday

Songs from Bob Marley, Peter Tosh, Joe Hills and other reggae stars all on liberation followed. At 10:00 a.m. the president started speaking, "Fellow citizens, as I speak to you today, I continue to be deeply saddened by the scale of personal suffering and the loss of loved ones and property inflicted on many residents of Freetown, particularly those living in the eastern part of the city, where the rebels have embarked on an orgy of atrocities, including rape, mutilation, and arson. On behalf of my Government, I would like to convey once more, my heartfelt sympathy to the entire population of the Western Area, and in particular, to those who have suffered injury, the loss of family members, loved ones, or property. I deeply regret that despite all the efforts made by my Government with the means available to us, absolute security was not available to all of you. Let me once more appeal to all of you for unity, in the face of this destabilizing event. Let us not allow the evil forces to overpower us. Let us resolve to stand firm in this dark hour, for the dawn will soon break. Let us all sum up the courage needed to persevere. Without this, the land that we love, our Sierra Leone will be doomed."

As he concluded his speech, heavy firing began with furious shelling of mortars. I hurriedly turned off the radio. It seemed as if the battle for the west of the city had begun. For over 6 hours we could hear missiles flying here and there; it was as if the clouds were raining bullets and bombs. I had never heard anything like it, not even during all the coups we had seen in Freetown. I was praying to God to make it easy for me, if death would have to eventually be my lot. I was shaking, and at that moment if anything or anyone had touched our door, I would have collapsed with fright.

•••••

When the fighting subsided, we ate what we could, took our bath, and dressed, waiting for what will follow. By midnight, the fighting started, this time with more ferocity. We decided to step outside to look where the fighting was going on, knowing that we would see the bullets flying since it was night. We were shocked when we looked towards the Wilberforce Barracks; bullets were flying back and forth by their thousands. Some people joined us; among them I was surprised to see our landlord. He just stood there, lost. I tried talking to him but he said, "My friend this is no time for talking, this is a time for one to try to stay alive. They say the toad likes water but not when it is boiling." He sat down with his hands on his head. I knew he was praying in his heart, calling on his ancestors to protect him. "Gorvie" Miss Eku called to the landlord, "The children are crying, and it is not safe to be down there." "We will meet in the morning," he said, and left.

There were vehicles moving up and down our street. I figured they were probably reinforcement going to the battlefront, or rebels moving around. We went indoors after a while. Kolorie asked that we pray together. He led the prayers, saying, "God, we are just innocent children of yours, who did nothing to bring war to this country but who are suffering today. We do not know what tomorrow will bring. All we see is uncertainty, hunger, and death. We pray that you guide us through this moment, take control of our lives and make us see the end of this. We pray for the entire nation. Bring solace to those who are hurt, those who have nothing to eat, and those who are dying at this very moment. Turn this war into peace and love. Thank you father God, for hearing our prayers."

Nervousness could be detected in his voice. I knew this was not an easy moment for him. He was now losing his cool. We all were. I decided to turn on the radio. There was only music on FM 98.1, so I tuned to FM 99.9, the official Government radio, but now taken over and being used by the rebels. "We have one thousand fighters moving in from upcountry and once they arrive, which will be in the next twelve hours, they will help those who are now fighting to take the West of the city and we will have the entire city under control." "How many fighters do you actually have on the ground?" "I cannot tell you," came the reply. "On BBC today, we heard that the Nigerians will be reinforcing. Do you believe that you will defeat even a reinforced Nigerian force? "Even if it is a reinforced bunch of U.S Marines, it will be no problem for us. We are prepared to fight at any minute or hour. We have proven that we are better soldiers and we are the only ones that the people of this nation should trust. We are their brothers and sisters. I have to go and fight, let us talk later." "That was Colonel Spare-No-Soul, who is leading the battle for the Western Area," the journalist said. Things were only getting worse, and I felt discouraged whenever I tuned on the radio.

•••••

Bang! Bang! Bang! "Guys wake up!" Brima was calling on us. In the next instance, Tamia opened the door. "They have announced that everyone should go out and celebrate peace, and tell the International Community that we do not want the return of the Kabba Government." "I will be damned to do that, I will go nowhere," Momodu said defiantly. "They've been announcing it and the street is full of people marching towards PZ, to show solidarity. We should at least go, even though we do not like them. They might search houses to look for those who refused to go," Brima interjected. I could see from the look on Momodu's face he was giving his decision a second thought. "Okay, I will go but I won't stay long," he said.

We started looking around for anything white that we could wear or hold. People of all ages were moving towards the centre of the town all dressed in white. We joined the queue with renewed hope. When we reached the Cotton Tree we saw masked devils and people

40

dancing, rebels on trucks and commandeered vehicles, some walking and shaking people's hands. Everybody was waving their white handkerchiefs or clothe, and chanting, "We want peace, we want peace!" A man with the flag of Sierra Leone wrapped around him was kneeling and kissing the ground. We decided to move towards PZ. As we approached Siaka Stevens Street and Wilberforce Street Junction, a sharp sound of a fighter jet was heard, and as most people dived for cover, as was normal practice those days, a colossal explosion followed. The PZ area was immediately up in flames. I went into a temporary coma only to wake up to a cacophony of wailing as if Armageddon was taking place. The sound from the explosion had left me partially deaf. A Nigerian fighter jet had just dropped a bomb. In my dazed state, I did the unthinkable. Instead of running from the PZ area, I ran towards the direction that the bomb fell. It wasn't to take a closer look but I had completely lost the sense to determine the road to my house. There were body parts I saw at least ten corpses and several injured people on the ground and white fabric pieces people wore or held in their hands few moments ago, were now soaked in blood. I felt a sudden tug at my shirt sleeve, and let out a blood curdling scream. With eyes full of terror I turned to see that it was Momodu and Tamia who had followed me.

"Let's go home before the jet comes again," Momodu said. Some had started collecting the dead and the wounded, loading them onto vehicles and taking them to Connaught Hospital. We passed by Lightfoot Boston Street, trying to avoid large groups of people. On returning, our landlord called us inside his house and asked what happened. From the house, he had also heard the impact sound of the bomb. When Tamia explained, the landlord asked, "Were rebels killed?" "People were killed but I think they were mostly civilians," Kolorie replied. We ate some plantain and stew prepared by Miss Eku, sat with their children Pa Kai and Keichloh, then went down to our room. The day was full of discussions about the bombing. We spent the rest of the day reading as we were getting used to the regular outburst of gunshots.

•••••

"Get out of your houses, you bastards and march for peace!" We heard someone kicking at one of the doors, and suddenly, there was shooting all over. We opened our door and met people outside, moving towards the street. To my surprise, three houses down the street were on fire. The rebels were burning houses! I sensed that something had gone terribly wrong. Probably ECOMOG had started their counter-attack. The rebels were all over, beating people who failed to sing and march. "We want peace, we want peace, we love RUF, we love AFRC!" Everyone was shouting. "Our house is on fire, it is on fire!" Tamia shouted. We all turned to see that the front section of the house was on fire. We ran towards the house, looking for buckets to fetch water. In as much as we succeeded in putting the fire out, it had done immense damage. "Man, it will be better if we stay close to the house; otherwise they will try to burn it again."

We went in and packed all we could carry in case we would have to leave. While packing, I thought of where we could possibly run to, if things got worse, but no place came to my mind. Freetown has two key outlets, the sea and Waterloo, when cut off from those two one is left with no choice but to wait for what fate holds for him or her. Aunty Joe was crying outside. The hair on my neck stood on end and I was really losing control. I could feel every part of my body shaking. The sound of gunshots intensified and afraid that the rebels would come and find us in the house, I went outside to sing. The whole place was lit with fire as several houses burned outside. A truck stopped in front of our house and a tall, fat man, who looked like the boss, came down and moved towards us. I wanted to run but I stopped myself. "What is happening here?" He asked one of the rebels who were forcing us to sing.

"Chief, those who are giving information to our enemies are living here. We want to teach them a bitter lesson." He turned to us. "Young men, are you not interested in contributing to the success of the revolution?" On hearing this, I instantly felt the warm fluid of urine trickling down my legs as I responded with a slight quiver, "We support the revolution, one hundred percent sir!" "Good. Then you will come with us and join the struggle. Move!" I turned towards Kolorie. "Move! If anyone attempts to run I will shoot," he said removing a pistol from his jacket pocket. Seven of us climbed the truck and were driven to the State House, the new base of the rebels. Once at the base, new orders were issued. "Come down from the truck with your hands up and move in a straight line." We moved quietly, with Kolorie and Tamia at the front with Momodu beside me. We were taken to what used to be the sleeping quarters of the security guards. We met young men and women there, some crying, whilst others were just seated quietly like prisoners awaiting death-row.

•••••

In the morning, we were taken out to the back of the building and the same man, the one who had brought us to the building, came to address us. He spoke for a while with one of his colleagues before addressing us. "My friends, today you will become soldiers of our revolution, the revolution that has the interest of the people of this nation at its heart. Together we will liberate this land from exploiters and reckless politicians. We will train you and give you guns." 'Train who?' I asked myself. I had always liked watching Rambo films and admired the valour and exploits of a soldier, but my love for the army was more for the US Marines than the Sierra Leone Army (SLA), or by now the "People's Army". "You, you, and you", the commander who looked like one on hunger strike pointed at two others and I. He turned to me, "You will be in the children's unit."

"Tiger" He called on one rebel who was smoking a cigarette, and said, "Take these boys. They'll be with you. Show them what it means to be a soldier." Kolorie tried protesting, but was kicked in the stomach by Tiger, and I was dragged away and taken into the building. There were more than a twenty children there, most of them my age, but some much younger. "You obey, we be friends. If you try otherwise, I kick your ass." Twenty of us were taken to the presidential helipad. "Have you ever handled a weapon before?" he asked. We all replied that we had never held one. "I will teach you the secret of a gun. It is my only buddy, and I eat with it, sleep with it, it is my baby, no parting. I will teach you how to use it." He took one of the boys and supported him as a shot was fired. The boy lost his balance but was held still by Tiger. He tried it with all of us. "You are all scared monkeys, why? You're chicken livered… You need the medicine given to cowards." He left and came back after ten minutes with two other rebels. They had a bag with small bottles containing a liquid. I wondered what they were going to do with them. They started calling us one at a time into a small room close to the helipad.

When my turn came, my wobbly legs somehow carried me to the room only to find the other boys on the floor, completely knocked out. My left hand was held down by one of the rebels as Tiger tied it tightly with a cord. He started looking for a vein, and as one pulsed in my arm Tiger injected the substance into me. A little while later, I started to feel lightheaded. As my head and world started whirling I heard myself ask in a faint whisper, "What have you done to me?" I was on the floor for a very long time until I felt cold water splashing on my face and a harsh voice command, "You ladies get up! Now you should be men!"

I slowly got up and saw that I had puked several times while on the ground. While it was still premature to fully comprehend what was happening, I sensed that my life had changed forever. Something potently evil had been injected into me and by it I had been robbed of my innocence. It was preparing me to join the evil world where Tiger and his likes belonged. As hunger seized me I asked Tiger for food. "You see my man, you are getting there. We have just learnt that one of the guys that came with you is your brother. He asked the commander where you are. I will put you to a test soon, to see if you are as strong as I would like you to be." He gave me his leftover food, which I greedily wolfed down while the other boys looked on.

"Now we go outside and we try shooting again before you get some food. March out!" We hurried out. I was blinded by the light, and I could not walk properly. We started the shooting lessons. I was surprised at the ease at which I was now handling and using the gun after being shown only twice. In the evening, we were told that each one of us, as a test of our courage and preparedness, would shoot one person or we would ourselves be shot should we fail to do so. By then, there was no trace (or ounce) of fear in me; I was prepared to do anything. When the time came, the others shot women and children, and then they placed Kolorie in front of me. An inkling in my subconscious was telling me that I knew Kolorie, but I was doped with the strange substance and the person before me looked different, almost unfamiliar. The impulse of the head combatting against the new me was pounding and the struggle of the head to give way to reason was lost. I pulled the trigger more than ten times. As Kolorie called out my name, recognition dawned subliminally and I felt some pangs from my conscience trying to reassert itself. It was too late, too late to withdraw my finger from the trigger. I looked at my bullet-riddled elder brother lying on the floor with in a pool of blood; I fell to the ground and lost consciousness.

•••••

"Wake up, wake up, we have to move, our enemies are advancing. We have to move out!" Tiger was shouting. There was heavy bombardment going on and tracer lights were all over. "Move guys, move fast." Tiger gave us guns. "Anything that crosses your path, you shoot. You understand?" "Yes, Tiger," we answered. We left in the very early hours of the morning. We took the Mount Aureol path as we began our long and steady walk to the jungle to begin our new lives as rebel soldiers. I looked at the city for the last time. There was smoke and fire everywhere as the houses burned.

The Call of War

Sitting melancholically with bloodshot puffy eyes, sleep a distant memory, and contending with being stuck between a rock and a hard place for what felt to be a lifetime, I cried as I reflected on my life. My past had been an unrelenting series of traumatising experiences, and my future from where things stood offered no glimmer of hope. Fatu sat staring at me as if we were from different worlds, I could tell from the expression in her eyes that she was wondering what was going through my head. "Fatu," I said, looking at her with weary and distressed eyes, "I cannot stand this anymore. We have to do something. I'm tired; if we don't do something now then we'll regret it."

"Adama, we are in a messy situation, but what can we do? Since I was a little girl all I have known is death, pain and war. Do you think I like giving my body to the rebels to stay alive? I'm 16 years old, like you, and I deserve to live like children in other countries do. Not abused, morning and night. I get beaten when they're angry, and have to cook when they're happy. Without a family, or home, I just don't know what to do." "Why can't we run away to a place where we'll be safe?" I suggested. "Adama, what are you talking about? Everywhere you go there is war, Liberia is in war, the Guineans are fighting with RUF at the Pamalap border, and if even we make it to Guinea, we will be accused of being rebels and killed. The Guineans have maltreated all those who have crossed the border from this area."

"I prefer being killed by the Guineans than by the rebels, at least I will know I died seeking freedom. These butchers we have here are not human beings, you see what they do to people, look at what they do to us." I said. "Tell me what freedom is. Do you know what freedom is? We've never tasted it; we know nothing of that name. I cannot remember a day since I was eleven years old, when I haven't seen or thought of death. Death is all around us, it's written on us, and it's just a matter of time before it catches up with us" "Fatu, you are scaring me. I don't think about death! Death is for someone else; I will live through this and tell my future children about the life I lived." I thought for a second after saying this, did I really believe what I just said or was I desperately trying to reassure myself? I could feel fresh tears streaming down my face. I felt lost and hollow; I couldn't crawl my way out of this hell. Even my body was not my own; it belonged to others who exploited it when they feel like it, and that is my price for staying alive.

Kailahun used to be a very beautiful and peaceful farming town, with coffee and cacao crops. Even though I was very young when the war began, I can vividly remember my father taking me to cacao exhibitions in town. Those were happy days, with farmers making profit and enjoying life. My father owned a very big plot of land and he had several relatives and friends working for him.

The war ended our happiness and destroyed all that we ever had. My father was out of the country when the war started and I did not know how to reach him. When our town was attacked, my panic-stricken mother fled, leaving me all alone in our house. I have since been taking care of myself, often resorting to harsh survival approaches, moving from village to village on foot, with people I do not know. I have eaten worms, cockroaches and lizards; I have begged for the head of a rat; I have drank water from a gutter and from a stream with waste in it. But I was determined to survive, and I knew I must. Sometimes I came across a deserted school and tried to imagine what the lives of the school children had been like, before the war. There was one time I had tried to copy the words I found in a book on to the blackboard. When I finished, I cheered, then hastily looked around to see if anyone might have heard or seen me. Reassured that I was alone, my joy turned to sadness as I felt that I should know how it felt to be attending school, not foraging for survival.

•••••

I once took interest in two priests who were hiding with us in the jungle. They prayed all the time and I sensed the emotion and faith they put in their prayers. I asked Father Albert, the older of the two, "Father, you are always praying and you put your faith in God. Why hasn't he saved you from this, why has he left you here to die in the hands of the rebels he created." He was surprised by the question, but gave me a lecture in understanding how God functions. He said, "Adama, there is nothing or none as powerful as God. One does not question the actions of God. God tests the faith and resolve of his servants. This is our test and we will pass it. Even the prophets of old had trials they had to endure." The answer didn't ease my confusion, in any way. It only deepened it. "But father, if he is all powerful, he can save us all and make the rebels stop fighting. What does he say when you talk to him?" He smiled and said, "Even you yourself can tell him, He listens to all of us, not just me. Pray to him and he will answer. The war is the work of the devil; Satan does not want the children of God to live in peace and happiness. He breeds destruction and evil, and turns brothers and nations against each other. He has polluted our land and driven us to killing ourselves." "Father, what brought about this war?" I asked. "My daughter, it is selfishness. People want everything for themselves and do not want to give space to others. People think power and money are everything; I want you to know that it is not true. Seek the Kingdom of the Lord and all shall be well with you, pray every day of your life and ask God to forgive even those who hurt you. That is the key to salvation, never give hate a place in your life. The moment you do that, you become like them. Never be like them." He exhorted.

After that dialogue, I prayed every day. Sometimes I got lost in thought as I prayed, not knowing what to say. My friend Fatu sometimes prayed with me. I found comfort in praying, even if the comfort was short-lived. Father Albert and I became friends after that conversation and he would often talk to me about everything from religion to politics, and life. He was a father figure to me and I missed him deeply when we were separated after an attack on the village we were hiding in. He was the first person that was like a family member to me after losing my own, and now I had lost him too.

•••••

"What do you think about us becoming part of the rebels, and fighting with them? Things would probably be better for us. Now they see us as slaves, but if they see us as part of them they will respect us." I said. "Go ahead, join them! For me, I would rather die than become part of them. In fact, there is no difference." "Look, if we join them, they will train us and give us guns, which we can use to protect ourselves, and even save some people. We will become feared and we will not be raped again." "We will get killed in battle, or caught and taken as prisoners." "We might also escape, and we will be free! Don't just look at the negative side of it. We can't go on like this forever. Joining them gives us the best possible chance of survival." "It would mean we would be given food". The discussion with Fatu about joining the rebels caused extra nervousness and anxiety.

"Let's do it, let's join them. Then we can find a way out of here." I looked at Fatu and she looked happy with the idea. She had become like a sister to me and there was no way I was going anywhere without her. The idea of joining the RUF had been lingering on my mind for a long time, but I just hadn't had the courage to tell Fatu, as it felt so wrong. War is the culture here, nothing else functions, the gun is the final word. As I thought of us enlisting in the rebel movement, I was momentarily distracted by the stench from my body; I had not taken bath in a week, and my only clothes were those I had on. Every now and then, I washed them at night and waited, or slept, in the nude while they dried enough to put them back on. "We'll go and bathe, then go down to the camp." I suggested to Fatu as I got up. The stream was not far from where we were sitting. It was in the early hours of the morning and the weather was good. Usually there were rebels walking around the vicinity, but by now they knew us and were happy to let us go about our business, unless they wanted something from us. The cold water eased my stress and hopefully washed off some of the grime from my body. I hadn't felt the clean feeling of washing down with soap for as long as I could remember but nevertheless, the water was refreshing. We sat on the grass quietly singing Mende songs, while waiting for our clothes to dry. The songs shut off our situation, songs of beauty and love, something we could only imagine but had not experienced.

"Let's go before it gets late." Fatu said. We dressed and began our journey to the rebel camp to pledge our allegiance to the cause. I was nervous but determined that this would take us closer to freedom. On our journey in, we witnessed a number of soldiers raping local girls in the bush; we kept our eyes straight ahead of us and made every effort to avoid being conspicuous. We were stopped when we reached the gate; though petrified, we derived strength from our determination, and objective. A rebel with impish looks screamed from his sentry post, "Halt! You idiots! What are you doing here? Did anybody send for you? It's not yet night; we will find you when we need you." "We've come to join you. We want to fight alongside you and support the revolution. We want to see the commander." I shouted in response. He seemed surprised and looked at me for some time, "OK, stay where you are, I will be with you shortly." He looked at us again and called on one of his colleagues, "Cobra, keep an eye on them, I'm going to see Papay." "No problem." Cobra replied. Cobra came out and stood beside us; he was carrying a machine gun and looked like a trigger-happy guard. We stood beside him, nervously awaiting the return of his colleague. After ten minutes, he returned with two other rebels to escort us deep into the camp. "Papay wants to see you two." Before setting off however, he practically stripped us naked and then put his hand into our private parts, searching for what, I do not know. "They're clear, let them in," he said to Cobra. He turned to us, "My friends will take you to Papay. If we suspect any game, you're dead." We nodded and entered Papay's compound.

The camp was a whole city in itself. It had everything one could imagine: schools for fighters, living quarters, an ammunition store, a garage, a food store, and a medical centre. The civilians of Kailahun built the structure for the rebels; most were killed in the process. This was the headquarters of the RUF. I had never seen the head of the RUF, only the second in command; a skinny man with a black beret and glasses. He was feared by all but I never heard him speak, and was seldom seen out of the camp. Papay was the commander of the camp and he was known to have an insatiable sexual appetite, his preference was young children. He was said to have come from Burkina Faso. When we reached the bungalow of Papay, we met him comfortably seated outside, eating plantain. Papay spoke, "This is good for a man, I like it. It makes me feel strong and ready." We gave pretentious smiles to make him feel good. "Leave them with me; I

52

will decide what to do." The two rebels saluted and left. "So, what's up? You say you want to join the RUF. I like babies like you, I will make you good fighters, no stress. You are going to be the best we ever had. I will show you how to kill and avoid being killed. My killer machines, we will make you killers of men." I felt anger rising inside me; if I was carrying a weapon I would have killed him. He was talking about killing as if it were some sport one would enjoy playing. He suddenly lost interest in us and continued eating his plantain forgetting that we were standing there. After a few minutes he turned his attention back to us and asked, "Tell me the truth, what made you want to join the RUF? Don't tell me it's because you like it, I won't buy that. There must be a reason, and I want to know." He was wearing a stern face that scared me into silence. Fatu spoke, "Papay, we are tired of living in the bush like animals. We want to be part of a group and have people to call family and friends. We want to do something and the only thing around here is war and we need to have food and avoid being raped." Fatu caught me completely off guard; I have never seen or heard her so bold.

"Look, I want to warn you, the path you are choosing will be very bloody. You will regret you ever came here. I've been doing this for over 30 years; I have fought in six wars: in Guinea Bissau, Congo, Angola, Mozambique, Liberia, and now Sierra Leone. I do not know how I got into this business but I guess poverty and having nothing to live on or for, played a part. I will be doing this until I get unlucky one day and catch a bullet. I will ask you again, do you really want to do this? I have never asked someone before, I am always happy to get volunteers. It makes my work easy. What I see in your eyes is not a willingness to kill, but the desire to survive. It is different from what we do here; we kill and expect to be killed." We were completely taken aback by his sincerity and I saw the look on Fatu's face change. I gripped her left arm and said, "There is no turning back. We will do this. We have no choice." She nodded her head in agreement. "Papay, we want to join, our hearts and minds are made up, we are aware of the consequences and we do not mind." He smiled, pushed aside his plate and hugged the two of us and said lasciviously, "Welcome my girls. Why don't we go inside and test the potency of the plantain? You will like it." We entered into his apartment with him.

•••••

I stood gripping my gun, an old AK47 that had changed hands many times. I handled it like a professional. Having undergone three weeks of training, I was now a trained fighter, part of the RUF. Fatu seemed relieved that we had food to eat, clothes to wear, and we were no longer used for sex by the rebels. A soldier from Liberia was our training instructor, 'Captain Jones', as he was called, was a smart man who knew the art of guerilla warfare. We learnt a lot from him. Fatu seemed stronger than me and was faster crawling in mud and climbing walls. "I think we should help the women to cook while we wait for our assignment, it is better if we get acquainted as fast as we can," Fatu said. She was always looking out for things to do. "You go ahead, I'll catch up with you. I'm having stomach cramps; I'll join you when it passes." I was lying; I simply did not want to go to the kitchen. I did not want the men to see me as fit for the kitchen; I wanted to be a fighter. That is what I signed up for; if I get sent to the kitchen I would never have the chance to run away. Dragging me as she spoke, she said, "I know you don't want to go. What do you want us to do? At least we can go there and see what they do; we do not have to cook with them.

"All right, I'll go with you, but you know I don't want them to make us stay in the kitchen. I want to do something else, not cook." We went to the kitchen section and I was amazed with what I saw, I had never been there before. I saw over 30 women and girls with about 40 massive pots in which you can cook an entire cow. Everybody was busy in the suffocating heat, fused with a nauseating smell of sweat and uncooked meat. Several pairs of eyes fixed on us with suspicion and I put on a smile that seemed to disarm them as we walked up to them. We introduced ourselves and told them that we will occasionally be stopping by to help them out with their work. They were surprised, and looked at each other and back at us as if we had broken a taboo. Breaking the silence, Fatu asked, "Is there something wrong?" A fat lady with a round face and a few grey hairs said, "No, it's just we're not used to being helped. We appreciate your offer, and will be happy to be seeing you around." As she spoke, she gave us huge chunks of fried meat. It was really juicy and very spicy. "I'm Yeanoh, head of the kitchen. You need anything, ask for me. I have been here for seven years, these are my girls, and this is our department." I immediately came to like her. She looked like someone who had seen the best and the worst of life, and had completely surrendered to her fate. "Where are you from?" I asked her. "I am from Koidu, where I was trading when the war broke out, and I have never returned. For me, this is home. I don't know if I would survive anywhere else." She turned around and saw that everyone was looking at us and had stopped working, "Get back to work girls, I will talk to them." They immediately turned and continued with their work.

"You command a lot of respect." I was surprised by how they obediently responded to her. "To the girls, I am a mother. I'm all they have. They look up to me for leadership, when they get harassed, I plead for them. When they are sick, I treat them. When they want clothes, they ask me. Even the men come to me when something is wrong. I have not left the camp in seven years, I'm always trying to help those inside. We're one big family." I asked her, "Do you normally hear from your family?" "No, I have not heard anything from them, I only pray that they are safe somewhere. I asked Papay to look out for them when he went there, but he could not find them. I see them in my dreams and I miss them so much. My girl should be your age by now." She was so open and friendly that I began realising why she was respected and loved. She had a certain tranquility about her that was very comforting and assuring. "Do you believe in the revolution? Do you think it will succeed?" Fatu asked.

She looked around her, took us to a corner, and in a lowered voice said, "Please never ask that question again, it will get you killed. The revolution will succeed by the grace of God. When I was abducted, I was very angry and always praying for the Government to come and free us. I then had the RUF letters engraved on my legs." She raised her skirt to show us the letters RUF imprinted inscribed on her legs. We had those too, on our backs. It was stamped on us with a hot iron during the training. "Now tell me where will I go, where will I be safe, if not here? You will not understand, since you are young girls. Be careful what you say, in here, the walls have ears." Someone was coming towards us, and she quickly changed the discussion. "I heard you were here and undergoing training. I wish I were as young as you are, I would have been a fighter too, but you see my size and grey hairs, I will easily be killed in a battle. It is only in the kitchen that I can be of use," she said laughing. "My advice to you is to be careful in all that you do, listen more and talk less." She took us on a tour of the rest of the kitchen, their living quarters, and the food store. She told us stories of people who had been in the camp before us. We ate in the kitchen with her, and around midnight we said goodnight, "We will be passing by every day. We're very happy to have met you and thanks a lot for the good food." "You are welcome any time, and God be with you my children." She stood by the door of her quarters watching as we made our way back towards ours.

•••••

A little room had been given to Fatu and I, all we had in it were two mats and two sheets to cover with. Some clothes had been given to us by Papay. He said we should get all we need for ourselves. The room was very dark but I was accustomed to the dark. I was so tired that immediately my back touched the mat, I fell asleep. The night was not peaceful; I was disturbed by horrible dreams.

My first war experience came a month after my training; information reached the camp that Government troops were planning to retake Segbwema. Two hundred of us were lined up, but Fatu could not come, because she was sick with malaria. I was nervous despite the training I had undergone. No amount or quality of training can sufficiently prepare a soldier for his or her first battle. Anxiety easily sets in and leaves one shaking. The black beret commander came out for the first time to talk to us. His quarter was closely guarded and no one was allowed to go within two hundred metres of it. When he came out of his quarter, soldiers picked themselves up as a sign of respect. He walked slowly towards us smoking a cigar, with about fifty rebels guarding him. He seemed tough and his bony face showed years of hard, if not miserable, life.

We had been lined up in the sun for one hour waiting for him to address us. He moved between the lines looking at us in the face, but saying nothing. When he reached the end of the line, he turned towards Papay and said, "You believe they are ready for battle?" "They are as ready as the word itself. They will face any force and defeat it." The commander, with Papay, and two others, spoke aside for about fifteen minutes before turning to us again. It felt like hours while we stood waiting in the heat. "Soldiers!" "Yes, sir!" We replied. "I am General Mosquito. I am the second in command of the RUF, and I have been briefed as your training was going on. I am impressed with what I heard from my lieutenants. We are facing the possibility of an attack at Segbwema, one of our strongholds. You are going to serve as a support force to our boys on the ground. I rely on you to keep Segbwema free from government forces, losing it will be a major blow to us. Do you get me?" He shouted at the top of his voice. "Yes, sir!" we shouted. "The RUF is known for its successes. We started with two hundred and fifty fighters. Now we have over fifteen thousand, we have more than fifty percent of the country under our control and we want more. Losing any ground is unacceptable. When you fight, you fight as a true soldier and you win this war for the country, I will not accept any other result. I have been told you are all properly armed and you will go with support weapons that we just received from our friends in Liberia. Papay will lead you into battle, and I will be monitoring your progress. If they attack, make them run for their lives! Kill all of them! I want no prisoners, if you come with a prisoner; we will give the prisoner your ration. Are you getting me?" He screamed again. "Yes sir!" We replied. Papay and General Mosquito exchanged salutes and he left with his guards.

Within thirty minutes, we were on our way to Segbwema which was not very far from Kailahun Town, but strategically located. It needed to be under RUF's control at all times if Kailahun was to be a secure stronghold. We were loaded in eight trucks with guns, ammunition, and food. I was dressed in military attire provided by Papay. I wished Fatu was well enough to travel with me. There were about ten women in the group, and we hardly spoke as we travelled. Unlike me, they seemed seasoned in the art of war, and were desperate to reach Segbwema. I tried to keep to myself. Papay was at the head of the convoy sitting on top of a truck with an anti-aircraft gun. He had a red scarf around his neck and was wearing a t-shirt with the image of Che Guevara, the Argentine revolutionary legend. Papay was fascinated with him and frequently spoke about Che Guevara as if he were a close friend or brother. The only book I had seen him with, was about Che Guevara. He referred to him as the godfather of modern revolutions, and swore he would have served him if they had ever met. I was happy that Papay was leading us in what was my first battle.

•••••

The rough journey to Segbwema took several hours and one of the trucks developed engine problems and had to stop, to be fixed. We waited together before moving on. The RUF at Segbwema were happy to see us, it was a ghost town and not even a dog could be seen roaming. We passed the night in trenches, fully prepared for action. I was nervous, with every little noise catching my attention. There were four fighters in my trench, two of the guys slept for a while, as we took turns keeping watch, but I was very tense and nervous. In the morning, food and water were distributed and the local commander briefed us. He told us that they expected the soldiers to attack at night since that was their usual modus operandi. Papay got up to talk to us and there were cheers from everyone, he was popular among the fighters.

"I am happy to be with you at this moment and I will remain with you until this is over. We will give the enemy the decisive blow; let us look out for them with the eyes of an eagle. Let us be ready for them if they come at night, let us be ready for them if they come in the morning. My motto is: Ever Ready". No one should ever take us by surprise. When that happens, you do not live to tell the story, and you will be lucky if anyone survives to tell it for you. Be brave and strong, and we will remember you in the day of victory. In the coming hour you will move to strategic locations, where we are expecting the attack to come from. You will be in those positions until you are told to move. If you are caught out of your place, you will be considered an enemy. Am I clear?" "Yes Papay!" We replied. There was a smile of contentment in his face. "Now fall out." I was sent with five others to a check-point, on a road that led in to the town. We had two rocket propelled grenade launchers, grenades, and a whole crate of machine gun ammunition. One of my platoon mates, Alhaji had earned himself the reputation of the worst drug user. While we were comfortable with the normal wraps of marijuana that was passing around, he was busy injecting himself with cocaine. There was rash all over his body and he was as pale and lifeless as one could imagine.

•••••

It was on the third day of guard duty at the checkpoint that one of our spies in Kenema communicated to us that the Government troops were moving towards Segbwema. At that moment, my initial verve and excitement took a nosedive with the dawning realization that I was not fully ready for this. However, I had no choice but to go through with it. I said a silent prayer, kissed my gun, and wished myself good luck. We laid a five mile long ambush, moving completely away from the town. There was no way we were going to miss them when they came. If possible, we would take every one of them down. The period of waiting was stressful and I was restless, we lay in ambush positions for twelve hours before we got the sign that the enemies were coming. There were seven trucks full of soldiers, moving at a slow pace. We let them enter approximately two miles into the ambush before opening fire. Over seventy rocket-propelled-grenades were launched at the trucks simultaneously, and as soldiers jumped from their trucks in confusion they were taken down. Some braved it and started fighting back; they were taken out one by one. It was a harrowing sight. The strike was intense and decisive, and within two hours we finished off the last of the Government troops. We searched the bodies of the dead, collected their ammunition and food, and set fire to the destroyed trucks with the remains of the soldiers in them. That night was a happy night; an orgy of alcohol, drugs, and wild sex ruled it. I spent the night with Papay whom I had been gradually falling in love with.

•••••

When we returned to our base, I spent most of my time narrating to Fatu what happened and she was sad that she was not there. She was now feeling better, and told me how Yeanoh helped her during her illness. I went over with her to Yeanoh, to thank her for taking care of her, and also to share my Segbwema experience. She screamed when she saw me, "Hey, my daughter is back!" Everyone immediately rushed to me and I was hugged several times. "Victory is sweet, and I thank God for it. Those soldiers came close, I was worried," she said. "I don't believe they will attempt it again. Those who came did not live to tell the story," I said, very proud to be the only one among them who had gone to the battlefield, and shot at enemy soldiers. I did not know if my bullets killed any of them, but I felt confident enough after that experience to face any other battle. I ate and drank with the girls, and then went in search of Papay. I could hear voices in the room as I got close but when I knocked no one answered. I knew Papay was busy with another girl. For the first time, I got jealous and wanted to open the door to see for myself but I stopped. Papay had never told me he was in love with me. Even though deep within me I knew the sex he was having with me was just for pleasure and nothing else, I had nonetheless allowed myself to become emotionally attached. With the pangs of jealous gnawing at my heart, I realised my fondness for him was not healthy and resolved to put an end to it.

I went to my room and wept uncontrollably from a broken heart for several hours. As a sixteen-year-old girl, you have crushes on people easily, and get hurt just as easily. I did not want to become vulnerable to Papay. I wanted to continue living as we did now; falling in love only brought complications I couldn't cope with. Fatu found me crying, knelt beside me, wiped my tears, and asked why, "Nothing," I said, "I'm feeling sick, and I believe it's from the sleepless nights and the mosquitoes in the trenches. I will get some medicine and should be fine." I lied. "You'd better, or you'll be knocked off your feet if you don't treat it now. I was helpless when it attacked me," she advised. "I will go to Yeanoh in the morning, and get some medicines. Don't worry, I'll be fine; I just need some rest" I knew I must have sounded unconvincing, but I just wanted to be left alone. Why was I feeling this way for someone who did not even know I was in love with him? During all the period of the war, I had been sad, scared, and lonely, but now to be affected by this new thing; even though I knew it would be foolish and pointless, I decided to have a talk with Papay in the morning.

Unfortunately for me, in the morning we were called to go and secure a small town about 10 miles from Segbwema, a precaution in case the Government troops launched a counter-attack. Fatu went this time, but Papay did not come, and I felt like I had left my attention behind. I saw him briefly in the morning, heading towards the commander's camp. I spoke less as we went, trying not to let Fatu notice my sadness. I answered her questions and tried talking when I could. At Segbwema we rested a bit, had sugar cane juice and marijuana, and then we moved in. We had a whole bag of marijuana in our truck and I drowned my sorrows in puffing marijuana, and was not myself by the time we reached the town. The town was deserted as its inhabitants had run to neighbouring villages. The chief, we were told, was a strong supporter of the RUF. He was in the army with the head of our movement, whom we only knew as Chief. We were told that he was arrested in Nigeria for carrying a pistol to the airport. The local RUF commander in the town, a man who came from my town, was happy to see me.

"I knew when you were a small girl that you would do something great one day. Your dad would have been happy to see you become a fighter." I thought he had gone mad; my dad would never had wanted me to join the rebels. That same night the counter-attack took place, it was a long and bloody battle that lasted eight hours. The soldiers came from all fronts, but we fought gallantly until they finally retreated. We lost twenty-eight fighters, and they lost forty. There were several wounded on our side, Fatu was shot in the leg and I had to drag her to safety. In the morning we buried the dead before handing 10 captured soldiers to the local commander. The sight of blood and dead bodies was awful, but I suddenly had a strange thought. I looked again at the bodies, lying on the ground, they looked peaceful, not conscious of what was happening and would never know pain or suffering any more. They only had to give an account to their maker on how they spent their lives. Two of the girls I had trained with were killed during the battle. One had had her head completely blown off, and the other shot in the breast while we were fighting. I was worried about Fatu, who was bleeding profusely. Her leg was treated and bandaged, and luckily for her no major damage was done. The bullet went through the flesh and did not touch the bone. We spent two more days in the town before going back to base.

•••••

In the ensuing weeks, I took part in several battles, some taking me to faraway places. My new life made me whole again; I became popular and liked by those around me. The commander made me join their war council meetings, where I was called 'Fearless Cat.' I killed ruthlessly. Strangely though, I had come to find finality in death, so that when I took a life it did not weigh on my conscience. Fatu was transferred to Makeni, to prepare for a massive move on Freetown. I was to join the group later when they entered the city. In the meantime, I had my talk with Papay, and told him what I felt for him. I broke down while talking, and sobbed like a baby. I only stopped crying when I realised tears had welled up in his eyes as well. He opened up to me about his past life, about how a bomb blast in a market place killed his wife, and changed his life completely. He had closed his heart since then to avoid falling in love, lest he gets hurt again should anything happen to the person he loves. After that discussion, he asked me to transfer to his flat. We were married six months later. It was a joyous moment, Yeanoh made special dishes, and the Imam in the camp blessed our marriage. I had never known such happiness before; it was a rebirth for me. We went to battle together and became inseparable. I got pregnant three months after the wedding; I thought of the child inside me and wished that I would have had it under different circumstances. I knew my child would face the life I lived, and become a warrior like me. Papay was very caring, making sure I got all I needed. Instead of fighting, I spent time in the kitchen with the girls and Yeanoh. I was advised each day on what to eat, drink, and do, to make the baby healthy. I spent time talking to the baby inside me, hoping he or she would hear me.

•••••

After seven months of the pregnancy, the attack on Freetown took place and Papay was called to go with a support force to Waterloo, where he would join up with General Kamzo, who had moved from Makeni. Everybody was there to see them off. It was a huge convoy with over thirty trucks. I kissed him goodbye, wishing him well and asked him to look out for Fatu. I waited anxiously for his return counting the hours, the days, and then the weeks. After three weeks the commander came to me with Yeanoh and two elderly women. Upon seeing them, I realised something was wrong, and fell down crying. The women helped to sit me down while the commander told me that Papay had died in the battle for the Congo Cross Bridge. He said he died bravely. As he was speaking, all I could do was look at my stomach and ask myself how I was going to tell our child that his father had died. Even then, I knew I would not talk of how he died, but how he lived and loved the two of us. I will tell of the hero his or her dad was. I made up my mind at that moment that I would never leave the movement. I would dedicate my child to it. For the sake of Papay, we would continue the course. I turned to the commander and said, "I will be fine, do not worry about me. I need some time to rest but I will be okay." They shut the door as they left me to mourn the death of my husband.

Naked I Stand

The entire city was in a state of panic, following the rumour that Kono had been attacked by the rebels, and that fighting had been going on there for over twelve hours. I called the local radio stations in Freetown to find out if it was true, but having received no news from Kono they were unable to confirm. Left with no option, I hurriedly made my way to the police station in our neighbourhood, to see if I could find out more. Sprawled on a camp bed and smoking a pipe, Sergeant Kanu looked like someone who had no interest in what was happening in the world. His radio was crackling out songs from the sixties, and as I walked up to him he said, "These songs are the songs of our days, when men were men and boys were boys. Those were the days when no one went to bed hungry and children used to respect their elders. Sit down sister, how can I help you?"

I sat down close to him and with my head between my hands. I said, "I just heard that Kono has been attacked. Can you please tell me if it's true or not?" He was very surprised. I could see that he did not have a clue about what I was talking about. He got up and called to the other policemen in the station, "Have you heard? They say Kono is under attack. Someone please radio Kono. Find out what is going on. I never thought the rebels would make it there. The Executive Outcomes were hired to protect the area. What are they doing? If the rebels get Kono the war will last forever: That is the bread basket of the country." They tried reaching Kono directly, but to no avail. No one was responding. The Kenema station was contacted and they gave confirmation that indeed the rebels had attacked Kono, but reinforcements were on the way from Teko Barracks in Makeni. I cried out, "What can I do? My daughter is there with my mother. Oh God! What can I do?" The officer tried to console me but I was inconsolable. I said, "Teko is far from Kono and the road is so bad, the rebels would have killed everyone in the town before the soldiers reach them. Also, there's no guarantee that they will be able to get them out of the town."

A corporal said, "The war is taking a nasty shape. The Government should try and do something. This military Government is only good at making promises. It is all about talking and nothing else." Sergeant Kanu said, "These guys only care about themselves, I told you when the coup took place, soldiers should never get involved in politics. Now we even hear stories of them buying dogs in Europe, saying the dogs in Sierra Leone are not good enough to keep as pets or guard dogs. They are also chasing the wives of others, and lavishing money on girls, while people die of hunger and starvation. The regime is full of young, naïve and arrogant idiots. They call themselves Secretaries of State, passing with big cars and prostitutes. God save us." The young corporal who seemed to share the views of Sergeant Kanu said, "The military sees us like enemies, they don't respect us. While they are doing fine, we go months without pay. The rebels attack police stations and kill policemen; we're sitting targets. This war will never be won with the barrel of the gun; they should negotiate and reach an agreement that everyone will be happy with. With all their might, America failed to defeat the Vietcong in Vietnam. Russia also failed in Afghanistan. Rebels are animals, the more you kill them the more they recruit. So, no one ends up winning."

"I feel sorry for our head of state. He is young and inexperienced and has recycled politicians around him who use him like a tool," Sergeant Kanu said in a low voice. I was listening to what they were saying but it was not sinking in, I was not interested in political discussions. So I changed the topic, "What should I do now Sergeant?" He exclaimed, "Sister, there is nothing you can do except trying to reach those coming from Kono and see if they have any information on your daughter and mother, and to pray for them." The weather was humid but I was having chills. I knew that until I heard word on the safety of my daughter and mother, handling this situation was going to be tough on me. But I had to be strong; otherwise things would only get worse. I thanked them and left for home. Lost in thought, it wasn't till after I was almost run down by a car that I realized I had strayed and missed my way home. The driver expressing his anger blasted, "Take your trouble elsewhere; I will not even stop if I kill you." My house became like a funeral parlour, everyone was crying and even those who came to comfort those crying joined them in crying. The house was full of people who had relatives trapped in Kono. It was one of those moments where one would want the world to end. I told myself that it was a bad dream and I would wake from it.

•••••

The days following the Kono attack were very traumatic as all incoming news was centered on the nefarious atrocities that the rebels were committing. I spent the day going around looking for people from Kono, but heard no news of my child and mother. Moseray, a boy that stayed in the same street with my mom, said to me when he arrived in Freetown, "The rebels came like rain pouring down from the sky. They were all over the town; soldiers as well as civilians were running for their lives. We didn't have time to look for each other, as we were all trying to get to safety as fast as we could. I walked for a hundred miles to Magburaka; some people couldn't make it, and died on the way from exhaustion. I am lucky to be still alive." My nights became sleepless. I felt I was losing my mind, praying fervently that nothing bad happen to my family, as I would never forgive myself. I promised myself I would bring them from Kono in August, now it was September. As time went by I got caught up in trading activities yet every time I thought of them and what could be happening to them, I cried bitterly.

•••••

After two days without news I decided to go to my daughter's father and tell him what had happened. It had been three years since I last saw him. I took custody of our child when we divorced. He was initially reluctant to let me take my daughter but decided not to fight me over her. However, he told me that if anything happened to the child I would regret being born. The look on the face of his niece when she opened the door bespoke how unwelcomed I was. His family was very unhappy with our divorce and the blame was placed on me. How unfair they were. I could not sacrifice my happiness for the sake of being married; I walked away and never looked back. My husband was a Muslim who believed that having more than one wife was normal. I on the other hand do not believe in polygamy, and I was not willing to put up with it. I had made this clear before our wedding that that was unacceptable. Since he wanted to be with me then, he put my mind at ease by indicating that he was in full agreement with me. I thought all was fine and that particular issue would never surface in our home, but a year after having the child, I was at home preparing food for him when I saw a well-dressed delegation composed of the local imam and some elders from the mosque. They came to the house and showered my child and I with prayers. The water and cold drinks that they hurriedly gulped did very little to reduce the intensity of their prayers. I was confused; I thought something bad had happened to my husband Saiku.

The Imam started, "Amie, we are here to tell you that today Allah has blessed you with a helper. It has pleased Allah to give your husband another wife. We have joined their hands in marriage and tomorrow the new wife will visit and pay obeisance to you the senior wife." I could not believe my ears, I felt rage growing in me, but tried to remain as calm as I could. The Imam and the other people continued to talk and advise me on how I should run the family and treat the new wife as a sister. They said she would be staying in a flat already rented for her, by Saiku. I had never felt so disappointed in all my life. I was betrayed by someone I loved so much, the father of my only child. He promised me he was not going to have another wife. He lied to me. Surprisingly, rationality set it. I knew then that the end had come for me and Saiku. My thoughts were interrupted by the Imam, who asked, "Do you have anything to say? We have done all the talking and we need to hear from you."

I opened my mouth to speak, paused briefly and said, "I am fine. I'll talk to Saiku when he gets home." I thanked them for coming and let them out of the door. Immediately they left, I packed two bags, one for me and one for the baby. I left late that night for my family's house on Ambrose Street. I was not going to live with a liar. I had seen my friends and sisters suffer in the hands of their husbands, I had seen how devastating a family made up of different wives and children could be. I was not prepared to accept it. I preferred to be alone and happy, than married and unhappy. After a fruitless endeavour by my family and community elders to bring us together, I filed for a divorce, which the court granted. My baby became the closest person to me, my only companion, until she reached seven years when I started traveling around the provinces trading food stuffs. My mother suggested taking my daughter Aisha to her for the holidays, so I would have more time to move around. I also planned to move my mom over to Freetown since the war was slowly spreading across the country.

As I entered the house, I met Saiku's wife Mma, coming down the stairs. I had only met her once. She recognised me, greeted me gently and told me that Saiku was praying. I waited in the sitting room as I scanned the house, which was neat and clean. I observed that Mma was pregnant and I was happy for her. I heard that she had been having problems with her mother-in-law who was demanding to see another grandchild since she no longer considered my child to be her grandchild. In our society, after marriage, if the woman did not get pregnant, she was put under immense pressure. During arguments or brawls, she was even insulted by relatives of the husband as unproductive. Mma would have seen hell if she had not become pregnant. In our society, the woman was seen as an object to be owned, used, misused and abused. The aspirations, feelings and needs of the woman are not respected. Pam, a friend of mine, got shunned by her entire family because she said she did not want to marry and have babies before finishing school. Her father said she had made a deal with the devil and probably was in marriage with an evil spirit. She was kicked out of the house and asked never to return again. I could not understand our people and their vaunted subscription to customs. Since my divorce I was told almost every day to look for another man, as I was getting older. I relentlessly responded that I was comfortable with my life and I could take care of my child. My family organised meetings to advise me on this, which only left me feeling annoyed.

I once told my aunt, "I have listened to all you've said, and I want to speak on this issue. I have been silent in all previous meetings and I believe that silence does not help. Let me make myself clear enough so we will understand ourselves. I will never remarry. People say that one cannot tell the future, but this one I can tell, for I know deep inside my guts that I do not want to do it. I know what I went through with Saiku, and it left me empty inside. Now I am full again. I am happy with my child. No one will steal that happiness from me." From that day I was never called to a meeting again but I always overheard them talking about it when I was in my room and they thought I was out.

Saiku came out after praying. We greeted each other and sat in silence. He had grown fat and had developed a bulging stomach. He was starting to go bald too. I broke the silence explaining to him what had happened and how worried I was. Saiku was always a calm character no matter the situation. He asked me what I wanted to do and I told him that I would keep looking and if in the coming days I heard nothing from them, I will go to Kono. He said, "I don't think that will be a good idea, you might get hurt there. I advise that you wait until the fighting is over and then go when it is safe. Otherwise you will get into trouble. You should have informed me about this from the first day. No matter, I am still Aisha's father. I care for her as much as you do. I will be trying to get news from Kono, and then I will see what I can do. Try to get some sleep, you look tired." He went into his room, came back with some money for transportation, which I refused to accept. He drove me home because it was raining, but the silence during the journey was deafening. I had a restless night and was woken up by my aunt who told me I had been crying in my sleep. I knew that all would only be fine when I had my baby in my hands, when I could kiss her, and tell her that I would never leave her again.

·····

Ten days after hearing of the attack, I heard that Government troops were making progress in Kono, and that they were pushing the rebels to the suburbs of the town. I had an idea in mind and decided to seek the advice of Amara Kallay a friend of mine. When I walked into his office, he was recording the details of a transaction so he beckoned me to take a chair. He was like an elder brother to me. He was experienced and good hearted. He was one of the few people who really understood me and I had sought his advice when I was facing my marriage problems with Saiku.

"I went to your house yesterday but you were not in, any news?" he asked, after he finished what he was doing. "Amara I need to talk to you, let's go outside." When outside I said, "I want to go to Kono and find my people. What do you think? I can't wait any longer." He seemed appalled by my suggestion; "I don't think that is a good idea. Anything can happen; I have seen what the rebels can do to people. We can go to the military headquarters and pay any soldier going there to look for them. I do not want you to go." I thought for some time and asked him, "If you were in my shoes, what would you do?" "Sincerely I don't know. I guess I would be pretty much confused and would do things I might regret. I am a man and a retired officer, I can bear the heat. You are a woman, and you have never been under attack. Let's wait a day or two more since there are reports that Government troops are making progress. I will go to Cockrill later this afternoon to look for soldiers going to Kono. So please don't do anything that will jeopardise your life. "But I feel like I am not doing much to get them out of that place, I should do more, not just sit around here, having food to eat and water to drink, when they might not, and may be killed if they go out looking for food. My mom suffers from diabetes and one of her legs is bad, so she cannot walk long distances. I'm afraid that if she tries, she will not make it." I suddenly looked at myself and realised I had lost much weight, I seldom ate and when I did the food was tasteless in my mouth. I could see the strain in Amara's face as he tried to dissuade me from the thought of going to Kono, "Try to understand, there's not much you can do now. You do not have to hate yourself for that.

There are several people like you who are going through the same situation. You have to control your emotion. I really understand what you are going through. Try to take it easy." I looked at him, "You don't understand, you think you do, but you don't. I have suffered a lot to raise up that girl. She is all I have. She is the reason I live. So I am prepared to sacrifice my life for her, I believe nothing will happen to me. I will return as soon as I see them."

"What if you do not meet them there, what if they have moved to a more secure place, probably the surrounding villages? What if they got out of the town before the attack but they do not have a way of reaching you? Think for a moment, don't just act." He held my hand as he spoke, and continued, "I know this is weighing you down but it will pass and you will be happy again with them. Have faith in God, He who gives life is the only one that can take it, no one else can. Things can only go wrong if you lose faith in Him. Always trust him." I cried out, "I have faith! I am just confused and not finding answers to my problems." Amara hugged me, and asked me to have patience. I felt better when I left his office. Later my aunt summoned a meeting of over twenty of our relatives based in Freetown. My aunt began, "It's good to have you all here today. The last time we all sat like this, there was a wedding. Today our happiness has been stolen; the land of our people is under attack. I called you so we could decide what to do."

Saa, my mom's younger brother spoke, "I am really worried for Sister and the little one. I hope Bakarr will be able to reach them from Tongo. Bakarr was supposed to go visit Sister when the attack took place. I don't know if he went. I tried calling him yesterday, but his phone was off and this is not normal with him. No matter what, his phone is always on." "When last did you try calling him?" My aunt asked. "I will try calling him again now" he said as he dialed his number; we all moved nearer to him in anticipation. Instead of the dial tone we were all hoping for, we heard the phone operating system's automated voice say, "The customer you are calling is presently out of coverage area, please try call later." Initially I felt disappointed that we could not reach him but a glimmer of hope rose in me. If he were with them, then at least they would have someone to help if anything went wrong. He was quite a strong and courageous person who had survived several rebel attacks. We had warned him countless times to stop traveling in the provinces until the war was over but he never listened and as if by some cruel twist of fate he always seemed to run into rebel attacks. He said his business was thriving and that was what was important to him.

Saa continued, "I have made arrangements for a place for Sister to stay when we get her out of Kono. She is never going there again. We should not let her risk her life, even though she is always saying that she was born in Kono, raised in Kono and will die there. That makes little sense. We were all born there but we are now living in Freetown. I stepped in, "Uncle, I spoke with her when I took my daughter to her last month, she agreed to come to Freetown and actually should have been with us by now had it not been for the fact that I was delayed because of my trip to Guinea." The sense of guilt washed over me again. Everyone was looking at me in silence. Uncle broke the silence, "Well I for one I'm happy to hear she was prepared to leave Kono finally. It makes things easy for me. So now we have to concentrate on how to get them out." I told them of my intention to go and get them from Kono. My aunt screamed "You must be crazy. No way. No one leaves here. My daughter, you are going nowhere. We will get one of the men to go for them. We hear from the Government that Kono has been retaken, so no one moves, don't even think about it. Please! I think you want to kill me with grief. I am worrying about my sister and your daughter and you want to be an addition? Please spare me that. Saa please talk to her, she is very stubborn.

I do not want her to even continue thinking about it." My uncle said to my aunt, "She was only making a proposal. She wants to know if it makes sense. Now she knows you do not want her to go, so she won't." Even though a part of me could somehow understand her cause for concern, I was fuming with rage and could not contain myself. I hated it when my aunt talked to me and made decisions for me like I was a little child. "My child is there. My mom is there. I should have taken them out before the attack, but I didn't. Now I want to go and get them, and you're saying I'm crazy. Sensing that I was losing my temper and was about to start shouting, she responded softly, "There is no way you could have known that there was going to be an attack on Kono, my child. No one thought that would happen. We know how much you love your daughter and your mother. Remember, she is my sister and I am the grand-aunt of your daughter. I love them too but I do not want anything to happen to you. That is why I am trying to stop you." The anger disappeared as suddenly as it had come, and I apologised for raising my voice at her. After the meeting, I bought some sleeping pills and took one more than the prescribed dose. I had not slept for more than two hours straight since I heard of the attack. I could feel my body protesting. Despite the overdose, sleep remained elusive and only came after several hours of twisting and tossing in bed.

The following Thursday it was announced that the rebels with the help of mercenaries from Burkina Faso and Liberia had finally taken over Kono. I could not move out of my room, could not eat or drink or even listen to the news. My aunt came to my room late in the afternoon but instead of talking to her, I turned my face to the wall. It was obvious that I was not in a talking mood so after sitting on the bed in silence for thirty minutes she left. By evening time, my mind had been made up as to what my next course of action should be; this time around no one was going to talk me out of it. I was ready for the consequences, no matter what they might be. Passivity was eating me. Late that night, I packed a small bag, took enough money and planned my journey to Kono.

•••••

The first crow of the cock met me on my feet, all prepped up and ready to leave. I left a note on my bed that read, "Aunty, I cannot wait anymore. I have to go look for mama and my daughter. I am sure nothing will happen to me and I will find and bring them to Freetown. Do not be angry with me, please pray for me. Amie."

After failing to find any public transport that would take me even near Kono, I eventually found a mini bus filled with resilient traders and people also going in search of their relatives. I gladly joined them and on our way, some of us shared our individual experiences of the previous days. "My daughter and mom are there and I need to get them out as fast as I can. The situation is getting worse," I explained. A passenger had heard that her brother had been shot in the leg and wanted to get him to the hospital in Freetown. Everybody was busy giving account of relatives in Kono, which gave me a sense of relief that I was not alone. I decided to try convincing the driver to take us as close to Kono as possible as he had indicated that he would drop us off at the outskirts of the township. Since everyone was trying to reach Kono, we raised the transport fare, which he accepted. He agreed to take us as far as Bada Bandasuma.

The highway was deluged with checkpoints where soldiers openly harassed people for money. Their unkempt and frail looks worried me as they looked exactly like what a soldier should not look like. By their scrawny looks, I wondered how they could possibly offer any form of redemption for the people by keeping the rebels at bay. In a bid to step up the offensive against the rebels, the military regime had recruited thousands of young idle people into the military. These hungry and impoverished youth saw their involvement in the military as the means through which they were going to overcome their poverty. There had been reports of some soldiers collaborating with rebels to launch attacks on innocent civilians and at the end share in the spoils of war. This negative perception of the army quickly eroded the public confidence they had won during the early days of the military coup and they became widely known as Sobels, essentially meaning, soldiers by day, rebels by night. The public outcry against them was echoed in the media, which was lashed out by the military. In a press conference, the head of the military threatened that authors of such articles would be severely dealt with for spreading false rumour. However, such experiences as soldiers' regularly extorting money from us only reinforced popular suspicions.

I initiated a dialogue with one of the soldiers at a checkpoint to understand why they do what they do. "We are not supposed to pay at check-points. We are Sierra Leoneans and the Government pays you," I taunted him. "You do not know what you are talking about. The Government is in Freetown, and we are here dying for you and you are talking nonsense. How much do you think they pay us? Look, I will reshape that your mouth that looks like a beak, if you do not shut the hell up." I stood aside and allowed the others to pay and pass. The soldiers had established a 'conveyor belt' system through which the money flowed, the soldier collecting passes the money to another soldier who counted it and passed it on to their boss, a lieutenant who was busy working on a calculator. He had become an accountant, trained in stealing from those he was supposed to protect. Because their superiors in Freetown cared little about the welfare of their officers, the officers were resorting to exploiting innocent civilians to meet their needs.

Not one to give in easily, I goaded the soldier further, "If I do not pay, what will you do to me?" He answered, "You won't go; you will sit here with us watching as the others go. You think we are joking?" Then one of the women I was travelling with, Nadine, retorted, "What you are saying makes no sense." After some time of casting aspersion on each other, we reluctantly paid, mounted the vehicle and threw dirty words at them as we departed. "God save us, these thugs turned soldiers are devils. They would sell their mothers for money!" The driver said, "This is what they do to everyone that passes through any of these checkpoints. We drivers pay more than you do. It does not matter how many times one passes here." The poor road conditions made progress painstakingly slow. Our ability to endure was pushed to the limit; when we got stuck in mud, we the passengers had to get out every time to push. It appeared that journeying to Kono required us employing previously untapped stamina.

•••••

Anxiety and uneasiness filled the car as we approached Kono. Villages once filled with people were completed deserted; only dogs and vultures could be seen. This puzzled me for I thought that only Koidu town and the surrounding villages were attacked. I became seriously troubled, and for the first time since the start of the journey I was beginning to entertain second thoughts about my coming. I however quickly reassured myself not to panic, for if I had come this far, I should continue to my final destination, Kono. I hadn't planned how I would go through the rebel-held territories and how I would get out. It was only now that the short-sightedness and naïveté of my decision to come to Kono was giving way to reality. To encourage myself and not buckle under the strain of uncertainty and panic, I reminded myself that the two most important people in my life were facing the possibility of death, and that I had to as a matter of urgency reach them. I should stop at nothing and face this courageously. Besides once we all got back to Freetown, this would be water under the bridge, a bad dream from which we would be awoken. As I reined in my thoughts and became conscious of my immediate surroundings, I heard some passengers praying, reciting the Lord's Prayer and verses from the Quran.

•••••

On the road leading to Bada Bandasuma, we saw a young girl crawling on the road. "Driver stop, stop, there is a girl on the road" we shouted. The driver stopped the vehicle and we came down to see if we could help her. She must have been around 10 years. As we touched her forehead and started looking for wounds, we saw several young boys and girls coming from the bush with guns, sticks and machetes. What surprised us most was when the supposedly wounded girl got up and jubilantly shouted out to the mob of youngsters "I told you this would work! These bastards fell for it, wow older people are stupid!" Realising we had been ambushed, we quickly made a dash for our vehicle but before we could make it, the eldest of the children, who appeared to be in his late teen years, fired three shots at the vehicle, daring anybody to enter it. I was scared to death. I stood behind the driver, not knowing what else to do. One of them suggested, "Let us move off the highway, we do not know who might pass here. The older boy looked at the girl who had been lying on the road and said, "You really impressed me, as from today you are my second-in-command. You are tough and I like that." We were moved into the nearby bush, while the rebels offloaded all our baggage from the vehicle to the bush. They were about twenty in number and all appeared below the age of eighteen. They lined us up. We were nine in all including the driver and an old woman of about sixty years, who was going to look for her grandson.

The older boy spoke, "We are taking you to our camp, some of you might make it, and others might not. You should do all you can to make things easy for us. Each of you will be carrying some load on your head, and you will be naked. Now undress and be very fast as we are out of time. You try any trick with us and you will be sorry." I looked in the direction of the old woman and felt more ashamed for her than for myself. We undressed as fast as we could. One of the ladies was in her menstrual cycle and when she pleaded that they save her from undressing, she was hit in her stomach with the butt of a gun and she threw up.

•••••

We walked for over three hours, stopping twice to drink water. The load was unbelievably heavy; under normal circumstances there was no way I could have carried such a load. At the outskirts of the camp, we met other rebels, who were much older. The head of the group that was with us said to them after they had exchanged greetings, "These ones are ours, no one goes near them. In fact, they will be staying with us, I will tell the commander." One of the older rebels answered him, "Look, we have so many in our possession that we have started reducing them, No one is interested in yours." They looked us over, spreading open our legs and fondling our breasts. One of the older rebels continued, referring to our naked bodies, he said "I took fresh young girls, these ones are expired, no one will even look twice. You should see some of the ones I have and you will jump at them. Tonight you can visit me. I will let you taste any one you like and you will understand what I am talking about." "I'll be there. Where are you going now?" the boy asked. "Just routine checks, I will be back at camp in an hour, so meet me after 8 p.m." We took the path that led us to the camp.

When we reached their camp in Kono, I was stunned by the amount of work I saw people doing. You could see that the rebels had started building a very big base, indicating that they were there to stay. Most of those working were abducted civilians. Armed guards were all over the place, supervising as the workers laboured. The eyes that fixed on us as we walked through the camp brought back the acute consciousness of my naked state.

There was no way to cover any part of our bodies however, because two hands were needed to balance the loads on our heads, fearing punishment if it fell; thus we just had to suffer the humiliation in silence. Our captors were cheered with outbursts of gunshots. We followed them obediently, trying to be as close to each other as possible. We were led to a big room, where we met about forty well-armed boys and girls. The other armed youngsters and our captors were very happy to see each other again. We were taken to a corner and made to lie on our stomachs. "Lying this way relaxes the body. When I am ready for you I will come", said the head of the group that captured us as he joined his colleagues who were so high on drugs that they were oblivious to us.

By this time I was not thinking about my daughter or my mother, I was thinking about myself, and how to get out of the mess I was in. I thought of all the advice given to me in Freetown. I didn't listen, and now here I was, lying naked with the fate of my life at the mercy of young children. Nadine was whimpering. The driver's eyes were closed, and I felt guilty as I had been instrumental in persuading him to bring us to Kono and now he was facing possible death. I started asking myself what sin I had committed that God was trying to punish me for. I prayed asking God to deliver us from the rebels. We lay face down for close to four hours, with nothing to eat or drink. The rebels meanwhile were coming in and going out, drinking, smoking, and babbling on and on, yet paid no heed to us. It was as if we did not exist. I assumed that by some stroke of luck everything would be all right. I was mistaken. Late in the afternoon, they descended on us like locusts. We were mixed with previously captured people and as we awaited our fate, the rebels started chanting war songs, as they led us all outside.

One of the rebels we met at the camp looked at the old woman that was with us and asked, "Sir J, why did you bring this one? Old bones like this are of no use. They only occupy space and eat our food. These are the ones that destroyed our country. While the politicians were stealing our money and building houses overseas they kept quiet and were their girlfriends back then. Today you will pay for that." Sir J said, "Whatever you do is fine, I didn't have time to look at them properly, and also I wanted to be off the highway." They dragged the old woman from the crowd of the captured, pushed her to the ground not far from where we stood and shot her twice in the head despite her pleading. That was the first time I saw a human being struggling to die. I shuddered with fear. Her eyes were wide open with her blood forming a small pool. Her hands were clasped in the pleading manner she had before being shot. She had asked that her life be spared and that she had committed no offence against the RUF. She was denied her right to life, and there she was lying dead before us. As we travelled the arduous road to Kono together on the bus, we didn't realise that death would arrive in our midst within a day.

Everything that was suggestive of the word bravery, courage, and strength, died within in me at that moment. I sensed a similar state of despair in those around me, as we stood naked, expecting death. The young girl that had the main actress in our ambush moved towards us. Everyone avoided eye contact with her, but it seemed that she already had her target in mind. She called the driver forward, who immediately fell on his knees begging to be spared. It was a pitiful and eerie sight to see a heavyset full-grown man kneel before a child who could pass for his child and beg for his life. She laughed sinisterly, "I do not want to kill you; we are only going to play a little game. If you win, you'll go free; if you lose you'll be killed. I do not like losers. I will play with your dick, but if it gets hard, I will kill you; if it doesn't then you're free. Let's begin!" All the rebels laughed and Sir J said, "I love your dirty tricks. Make him enjoy it. Make him piss on himself and after that we cut it off! Ha! Ha!

Ha! She took his penis and started playing with it with her small hands. I was terrified for him. While this was going on, eight of the boys beckoned me and a young lady brought to the camp that afternoon. We were taken back to the room where we had been all afternoon. They shoved us to the ground glaring down at us lasciviously. They however became angry when I fought back, knocking one unto the floor. Immediately, one of them drew a long machete saying if I did not lie down quietly he would decapitate me. They eight took turns raping us; four more entered and joined in.

After they had satisfied themselves, most were in a jubilant mood, but the rebel I had pushed came up to me and said, "You pushed me when I tried touching you. Who do you think I am? You think I am one of the brats you are used to pushing around? You did not realise that I was only trying to help you by giving you pleasure, making you enjoy my dick. Woman, you are doomed, you are certainly doomed. No one steps on me and goes free." I pleaded, saying I will do anything he wanted me to do, but he did not listen. He went out for a while and came back with two very strong boys and two machetes, "Now you will get what you want, since you showed me that you do not like the advances of men, even a good looking one like me who is stronger than all the men you have had in your life. After dealing with you, no man will ever look your way again. Hold her for me!" He shouted.

I was put on a table and braced by several of the boys. He then told the boys, "I am going to cut off her hands, nice and slow, like I did for that soldier. I'll enjoy this, she insulted me. I will show her who I am." He took the machete and started slicing the flesh off my right hand, I screamed in excruciating pain. "Tie her mouth. Tie it tight. This one is a parrot." My mouth was gagged. I could feel another rebel putting his hands inside me, as his colleague continued using his machete, "Let me teach you this," he said to the boys that were with him, "When you slice the flesh it makes your work easy. I have chopped off over 30 hands. I am the best at this, so while I am still here you boys had better take the opportunity to learn. I want you boys to watch and learn. In the morning, you will do some practice." He was slicing the flesh from my hand as he spoke. I could feel my heart palpitating so hard I thought it would burst. The ordeal felt like a horror movie, only that this was real. Both my hands were chopped off, and I was dragged back out, leaving a trail of blood on the ground. The rebel who had severed my hands urinated on my face, and left me in the open to die. Nadine and the others rushed to me and used the rags they could find to tie what was left of my two hands. I fell unconscious from blood loss, trauma and shock.

•••••

When I opened my eyes I saw shadows moving around me. After some time I realised I was in a hospital; my horrible experience started coming back to me. I looked at my hands and saw two bandaged stubs. I sobbed silently, too weak to cry aloud. I saw a nurse coming towards me and I wanted to stand up and run away. "I am going to get the doctor; I will be back in a second." I wondered how I found myself in a hospital. She returned with a doctor. Still crying I asked them, "Why didn't you let me die? I cannot live like this. Look, I have no hands. What am I going to do, how am I going to live?" The doctor sat on the bed as he checked my temperature and said, "I am very happy that you're still alive. You have been here for four days. Our visiting time is until 4 p.m. but your family is on the way. "Where am I?" I asked him. "You are in Freetown; you were brought in here four days ago from Kono. I am Dr. Yumkella; I have been treating you since you arrived. Now get more rest. I will come back to see you when your family is here."

He gave the nurse a prescription of medicines to be administered to me. The medicine was pumped into an intravenous drip that I was taking. I thought about my family coming and I became depressed. I looked at the stubs, called the nurse and asked her, "Why did they not let me die? I am useless now; I will only be a burden to people. I do not want to live. Help me end this? I have suffered so much. I do not want to continue suffering, please." She looked at me with tears in her eyes, "Sister, you will survive this and you will live a normal life. We have had several people who have been amputated, who thought all was lost but today they are alive and moving on with their lives. Let me get you some food."

I thought of my daughter and mother as she fed me, I wondered what had happened to them. After what I had experienced, I had little hope. My pain and my hurt were killing me. I never anticipated that I would become a human wreck. As I was fed, I thought about my life since my childhood, the things I had gone through and the desire to be happy, no matter what life brought. The challenge I had to face was larger than life, bigger than my strength could contain. In these shoes, death must feel better than living. I didn't want to see any family. I didn't know what to say to them or what they would say to me. At that moment, I didn't want anyone to feel sorry for me for that will only add to my pain. As these thoughts consumed me, the nurse came to me and told me that they had come and would be seeing me in few minutes. I was helped to sit up and I waited, listening to my palpitation. The door opened and my aunt, Saiku, Uncle Saa, and two of my friends Janet and Sophie entered the room. Everyone was in tears, and I cried uncontrollably. The doctor came in and said to them, "I understand this is a difficult moment, but she has been crying a lot, and needs rest." I saw the nurse wiping her face, turning to the window so she could not be seen crying. Saiku was reciting verses from the Koran cursing the devil for the evil he had brought to me. I asked Uncle Saa if he had heard anything about Mama and my baby. He said, "Bakarr called the day before yesterday to tell us that they are safe in Kenema. He was able to take them out. They will be coming to Freetown tomorrow." I could not stop the tears, but was happy that my child and mother were safe. In that moment, the concern I had felt for my own life was lifted.

"Please tell me, how did I get here?" I pleaded. "When your aunt realised that you had left for Kono, she called me immediately. I left the next day to trail you. I reached Kenema, spent the night there and was getting ready to go to Kono when I heard of a massive counter-attack taking place there. Helicopters started bringing the wounded and dead to the Kenema Government Hospital. I found you there, and brought you to Freetown so you could be properly treated." Saa spoke for the first time, "I'm so sorry. I'm so sorry. You will be fine; we will take care of you." He was crying as he spoke. The official visiting hours came to an end at 5 p.m. I was then left alone with my thoughts.

Two days later my mother and child arrived. My daughter ran to me, when she saw me, she hugged me but I could not hug her back. She looked at me, saw what was left of my hands and asked, "What happened to you, mama? Where are your hands?" I did not know what to tell her. My mother collapsed when she saw me and was taken to recover in a nearby room. I wanted to explain to my baby that it was my love for her that took me to hell. I now lay in the hospital useless and uncertain of my future. One day I will explain what happened to me, when she was old enough to understand, she was only seven and could not understand yet. I will tell her about my journey to hell and back, and my encounter with the devil. For now I had to concentrate on how to learn to live as an amputee, for the sake of my child.

Facing the Past

"Please, I don't want to die, don't do this to me, I'm a foreigner, I'm innocent. I'm only here because of work. Please!" The woman screamed as I started rubbing the knife against her left breast, her hands tied behind her back. "If even you are from Mars, I do not care. People like you have been exploiting our country. When you were enjoying our money you were a Sierra Leonean, now you are a foreigner. I'm going to give you a choice of saving one of these balloons you have. Which one do you want to keep?" I was talking in a cold-blooded manner, with my eyes as red as hot coals. She cried, "Please, I do not want to lose either, I will give you whatever you want. I have money at home, just take me there and I will give it to you. Please!"

"You do not seem to understand what I'm trying to do. I'm cutting one of these balloons, whether you like it or not" I said, rubbing the knife on her breasts as I spoke, "So, I want you to tell me which one. If you do not tell me, I will cut off both. However, if you like the two, I will leave the one I am going to cut off with you, so you can sew it up again. Or, if you ask me nicely I will sew it for you. Now, which one should I cut?" The woman was Lebanese, around forty years of age with curly long black hair and blue eyes. She tried dragging herself away from me as I laughed, "There is nowhere to run, nowhere to hide my dear; not even the angels can save you today." "I will give you anything you want, please take me home and

I will give you money and jewellery. Everything I have!" "This is the problem; you people believe that we can be bought with money, that we are all poor and useless. Keep your money; you will need that for a surgery." I took the knife, sat down close to her, tore off her dress and reached for the nipple of the left breast. Blood spilled out as I sliced it off. The deafening scream from the woman caught me off-guard and my instant reaction was to kick her, and then proceeded with cutting off the rest of the breast. I drew rings around portions of the breast and surgically cut them off piece by piece. The resistance from her lessened as she lost her strength, she was in a state of shock. I looked at her as I sliced the last bit of her breast off and said, "Sweetie pie, I will not kill you. I only want your husband to have one breast to suck, instead of two." She had passed out by the time I was done, so I gathered the pieces of her breast and laid them on top of her belly. I wiped the blood off the knife, picked up my gun, and as I walked out I said to myself, "More people, I need more people to practice surgery on."

•••••

Going down to the centre of the town, where we held our captors, I came across two boys in my unit ferrying two women and three men that they had captured. "Boss, these ones were caught trying to escape from the town. What do we do with them?" "Kill them and make it painful. What did I tell you the last time?" "Spare no soul!" they shouted. I moved on, but on second thought, I returned to them. "Come with me." I took them to a building that was close to us. "Now give them what they deserve." I sat on the verandah, watching them unleash terror on their victims. The eyes of the victims were plucked out with bayonets. They were then shot on the neck. Then I told them, "You guys are slow learners. I need to teach you more tricks. When you kill people by shooting them, they feel nothing, within seconds they are dead. It appears then as if you have done them a favour.

Death has to be painful and it should come at a very slow pace. When you look into their eyes, you see fear, you see pain and they beg and scream and that sounds like music in your ears. You own the power of life and death. Make use of it."

One of the boys said, "Boss, you should have seen the fear in the eyes of these people when we caught them. They were all on their knees begging!" "When you make someone older than you cry, it shows that you are stronger than they are. My business is to make them cry, I introduce pain to them in ways they hadn't imagined. Now go and get some more, but avoid shooting them. Use your knives; you know we're running low on bullets. Let's meet at the centre of town when you are done. If you get to see any creature you think I will like for the night, bring her. You should know my taste by now." Choe, the smartest boy in the unit, said "Boss you know we are here for you, whatever you want is yours."

I really liked Choe, and I always had him around me when I was on a mission. Sitting down at the river that afternoon, I thought of the people I killed that day and felt a sense of satisfaction. I killed a total of twelve, all of them above 30 years. And whenever I killed people, I saw in them the image of my dad, and the hatred I had for him was transferred to them.

•••••

I was born into a large family in Makeni town, in the Northern Region of Sierra Leone. My father had four wives and twenty children. At a young age, I realised that of all the women, my father disliked my mom the most and he treated her in an abysmal manner. Domestic violence was the norm in our household; my father conducted himself like a monster, beating my mom and her children whenever the opportunity presented itself. One day, my dad came home and realised that my mom had not cooked because she was suffering from typhoid and had no stamina to get of her bed. He jumped into a catatonic rage and carpet-bombed my mom with kicks and slaps. In the process she hit her head on a wall, and passed away two weeks later from the injury sustained. I developed a raging flame of hatred for older people, as those who were close to our family were hypocrites who knew that my father was responsible for my mother's death and yet said or did nothing about it.

After my mother's death, my father treated me like a stranger. I had to stop going to school because he refused to pay my school fees. I was always lonely and alone, as my elder brother (of the same mother) had moved to the city even before our mother passed away. Denied a plate at my father's table, I had to live off the left-overs of my half-siblings. I endured and adapted to living without affection. However, there was one of my sisters who liked me and would always secretly keep some of her dinner aside for me, until her mother caught her and scolded her. The words she told her daughter would ring in my ears for the rest of my life, "If I ever see you with that dog again, I will treat you like I treat him. You are very different people." "And you!" she said, as she turned to me, "If I ever see you coming close to my daughter I will kill you. Now get outside!" I walked away with shame on my face. After that, I wanted to write a letter to my brother, but I didn't know how to write. Even if I did, I didn't know how to get his address in the city.

At the age of nine, I started pickpocketing in the local market, as a means of survival. On the few occasions I was caught, I was given the worst beatings of my life. Once I was brought to my father, who told the people to take me to the police station because I was not his son. I stayed in the police cell for four days. Even though the police told me that a child should not be kept in a cell, they still kept me there saying there was no other place to send me and others like me. There I met a man called Saidu, who became a good friend of mine. He spoke to me about the world, and different things that interested me.

He was the first person since the death of my mother who was ready to answer all my numerous questions. In one of our conversations, I asked him, "Why are people so wicked in this world?" He answered, "My son, the world is a beautiful place, but monsters have overtaken it, and they treat others like animals. Let me tell you why I'm here. I was brought here because I couldn't repay my younger brother some money I owed him. I paid his way through school, and he is now a civil servant. I took money from him because my son wanted to go to college in Freetown, and I could not afford it. I didn't know he would have me arrested for struggling to repay him. Some people are harsh while others are more forgiving. I believe your mother was a nice person." "Why are some people rich and others poor? Why do some people have so much to eat and others, like me, have nothing?" I asked him all the questions that I had always wanted to ask someone, and he answered as best as he could.

He carefully explained, "I wish I knew more, these things confuse me too. This world is not a fair world. There will always be rich and poor, sick and healthy, slaves and masters. Once I was rich, now I am poor. People used to respect me but now no one does. This is the world and our reality." That night as he slept, I thought of all the things we had talked about and my young mind could not fully comprehend them.

I saw the police cell as a comfortable place, as I got food to eat and a place to sleep. In our community, the market place is the home for children and young men with no accommodation of their own. One has to claim a place before 10 p.m. otherwise others would take all the best stalls with no leaking roof on them. One night, I got into a fight with an older boy who asked me to get up so he could sleep in my stall. I stoutly resisted but the brutal blows rained on me, convinced me to quit. In spite of me deciding to look for a new spot, the boy rather than let me go, grabbed me and sliced through my back with a blade. I could take it no more. I grabbed a beer bottle that was close to the stall and with the speed of light, the bottle found its place on the back of his head. I did not wait for the scream, I took off in full flight, like a gazelle pursued by a lion.

I moved to the bus-park, where there were even tougher fights for a place to sleep. News of my fight with the bully circulated and I gained the reputation of a fearless boy, who wasn't afraid to hurt anyone that stood in his way. The reputation allowed me some space and even those stronger than me tried to befriend me. I do not know why they were not told of how I fled the scene. This would have lessened the respect they had for me.

On the night before my release from the cell, I asked Saidu, "Do you believe in revenge?" Saidu was stunned, "Why do you ask such a question?" "I hate my father. If I have the chance one day I will kill him." He replied, "When I was a young and happy man, I did not believe in revenge. I thought it was a thing for people who do not have faith, or people who have no love in their heart, and believe in an eye for an eye. If you ask me today, I will tell you that I would cut off the balls of my brother given the chance. When people hurt you, do not let them go free, they should pay for it." I had come to trust Saidu, and the things he told me helped to shape my idea of life and what is good and bad. "What do you want your son to become in the future?" I asked him.

"My son is a brilliant young boy who wants to become an engineer. He performed brilliantly during his Selective Entrance and Ordinary Level Examinations. While his colleagues are busy playing football or running around, he keeps studying. Whatever he sees in the street that has writing on it, he will pick up and read. When he got accepted to the college in Freetown, I could not pay his fee and that broke my heart. I sold the little stuff I had but the money I got wasn't up to the amount required to send him to Freetown. I then went to my brother who gave me the money and asked that I pay him back with a 100 percent interest rate in three months. I knew it was crazy to accept that, but at that point I had no option; I could not bear to watch my son sitting at home, when he deserved to be at the college." "How is he doing in Freetown?" I asked. "I guess fine, he sends letters and messages regularly. I eagerly look forward to receiving his letters. He is the first member of my family to go to a college; I am so proud of him. I know he will make a great engineer one day, and will achieve all the things his father failed to." "Why don't you ever speak of his mother?" I asked. I was always interested in hearing how mothers treat their children, and comparing it to memories of my own.

"I hate speaking about that woman." I was shocked. Saidu continued, "She abandoned us for a rich businessman. When hardship hit our family she started going out with the local businessman who had a big shop full of provision and was living here. She later followed him to Guinea, and they got married there. I almost committed suicide from the shock and hurt. It was at that time that I made up my mind to give my son the best education I could, and make his mother regret abandoning him. I am the only parent he knows, and that is why I do not want to let him down." We continued talking, even as Saidu used the bucket in the cell to answer to the call of nature. "I would like to be a soldier one day; I want to have a gun. With a gun, people will be afraid of you. They will not disrespect you, if they do, you shoot them," I said. "There are laws for soldiers, you don't just take a gun, and go around shooting people. If you do, they will kill you too. A soldier is there to protect people, not to hurt them. At the moment, soldiers are fighting to stop rebels from harming innocent civilians." Saidu responded.

That was the first time I heard that there was a war going on in the country, or heard the term 'rebel'. I became curious, "What war?" I asked. "I think we should get some sleep, I am very hungry and if the little that is in my stomach is spent, then the night will be a long one for me. We can talk in the morning." But I persisted with my enquiry about the war. Saidu gave up, and tried explaining to me, "The front is where the rebels and the soldiers are fighting the war, people get killed there. The rebels came from Liberia and attacked our country, but they have a Sierra Leonean who is their leader, and they have been fighting for over two years. We are all tired of it, and want it to end. Can I get some sleep now?" Within minutes, the snoring of Saidu could be heard all over the police station. I sat watching him sleep peacefully. In the morning, a police officer came to the cell and took me out. "We are letting you go but make sure we never see you here again." I thanked him, and asked to say good bye to Saidu before going. We shook hands, and I promised to visit him. I was blinded by the sunlight outside, having been in darkness for a long period; it took some time for my eyes to adjust.

•••••

I spent the day roaming around the town, and washing dishes at the local restaurant for food. That night I was given a hero's welcome at the car pack. One of the boys called Josie said to me, "Now you are a prison graduate. We are all used to that place, sometimes when we are tired of the streets; we commit a crime so someone will take us there. It is the only hotel where you don't pay."

One of the other boys told me, "I have been there more than ten times and all the officers know me. When someone takes me there now, they keep me for a night and they tell me there is no place for me and they ask me out." Josie asked, "Did you like it?" "I do not know if I liked it, I met a man there who was very friendly to me." Josie laughed, "With the kind of life we are living, that is the first place you should like. If you do not like it, then you should quit the streets. It's our second home. The first time I was taken there I was horrified and could not stop crying but after two days when they went to get me out, I begged them to leave me there for two more days, I wanted to rest. The streets were not too friendly at that moment, and sometimes I missed the cell." The other boy called Sullay gave me some meat that was in a paper. "Where did you get that?" Josie asked. "This is rat meat. I hunted them this afternoon, and roasted them." I spat out the meat I was already chewing, "Rat meat? Why didn't you tell me?" Everybody started laughing at me. "Do you mean to tell us that you don't eat rats? Here we eat everything from earthworms to bats. You do not choose; you eat what is available. It won't kill you, now take the meat and eat it." The voice of Josie changed, and became sterner, and I knew that making Josie angry was not the best thing to do. He was a fearful character; I took what looked like the leg of the rat and closed my eyes as I chewed it. It did not taste that bad after all. I had two more pieces after that.

"Now guys, I have a programme for tonight. The maize at the farm by the market is ready for harvest. Tonight we are going to take our share before they are harvested." Josie told them. I remembered the boy in the market, whose head I had smashed the bottle on, and I was afraid. "Josie, if I go there I will be beaten. There is a boy there I fought with when I was there. I do not want to meet him again." "You see this coward! Do you think anyone will dare to attack you when you are with Josie, that person will kiss goodbye to this world. I will eat him raw. Don't you have any balls? Are you a man? I think we should check to confirm this. If you aren't coming, you won't taste the corn, I want to assure you. You will sit watching as we roast and eat them." Josie seemed to be getting very annoyed with me, so I told him that I would go with them, although I was still afraid that the boy at the market would see me. "As a man, you should never be afraid of another man. Stand up and fight whenever someone threatens you. If they realise you'll fight back, they leave you in peace. If they realise you are afraid of them, they always go after you. That is how you survive here. There is no brother or sister in the streets." Josie advised me.

•••••

We went to the farm very late that night. We took two cups of sand with us. Breaking the maize from the branch causes a lot of noise, so while breaking it we poured sand on the branch to reduce the noise. We had a full bag of maize. Half of it was roasted and for the first time in a long time we had spare food at the end of our meal. The maize was very juicy, and we extended our generosity to the other boys in our park. The remaining pieces were safely hidden and the peels were gathered and taken to the garbage site. We sat late into the night telling stories and talking about our lives in the street. The street became a permanent home for me. Seasons came and went, and I grew in size, and in thoughts. I became a hard-core street boy at the car park, and had two more encounters with the boy I fought with at the market, and won, making him avoid further contact. I was more intelligent than most of them, so they soon started looking up to me for leadership. However, whenever I saw any member of my family, I would dodge. Once, I almost ran into my father.

The boys I associated with were now my family. They cared for me and I cared for them, we were inseparable. The year I turned fourteen, I was a full grown man, and no longer the little baby that came to the park five years ago.

•••••

One afternoon, after a meal of rice and potato leaves bought at a stall close to the park, Josie said to me, "I have some people I want you to meet. They have been talking to me for some time to get me to join them, and they promised that they will make my life better. I told them about you and they say you can come with me." I asked him, "What do they do?" Josie stuttered while trying to answer, and I sensed he was withholding something from me. "Tell me, I want to know. You can't just go and meet with people you know nothing about. What if you are trying to sell me?" We both laughed. "To be honest, I don't know what they do. One of the guys met me last week and told me that they only want young boys to help them with what they do, that is why I want us to meet with them and find out." "I hope it's something good they want us to do." "Whatever they make us do will be better than what we are doing now. For the first time in our lives we will do something different and better, which will give us some money. I'm getting tired of being a load carrier. My neck and back ache constantly." He said, trying to convince me as I was not as optimistic as he was. But I promised to go with him.

That afternoon I took my bath under the only street tap in the town, wore one of the three shirts I had. My wardrobe, which was stored and transported in a plastic bag, was slowly increasing. When I had arrived at the park, I went through the whole year with the t-shirt and shorts I had left home with. However, I was able to secure three shirts and two pairs of trousers, and that for me was an impressive wardrobe. Like me, Josie had dressed neatly and it struck me that with a little bit of cleanliness he could look normal. We began our journey into the unknown. As we started going out of the town I stopped Josie, "Where are these people staying?" "We're almost there. We'll be meeting one of them at Makasi, and he'll take us to their place." Josie was quick to reply, not wanting me to change my mind. Ten minutes later, we saw a huge guy, sitting on a slab near Makasi; a bar that Josie frequented, which was full of prostitutes and drug dealers.

When I had asked him one day why he loved the place so much he replied, "That is where I ease my stress. You know keeping tension inside you is never good. May be you should try it someday." Out of curiosity I asked, "Try what?" "Prostitutes, we call them Kolonkos. I have a girl there, and I am her best customer. Sometimes I go to her two or three times a week. Now, if even I do not have money on me, I can have what I want and pay later. Open your eyes my boy, you are still in darkness!" Though I had seen prostitutes all over the town, the thought had never occurred to me to sleep with one. When I continued asking Josie about prostitutes, he got annoyed and told me, "The only way you can know what I am talking about is this: find some money, follow me one night when I'm going there, I will get one for you. Sometimes you ask questions like a small boy, try to grow up. How do you think I started going there, or I came to know about women?" "Hey!" the man called out to us, "Why are you so late? I've been here for one hour, and the boss is waiting. No one keeps the boss waiting." The giant of a man told Josie. "We had to get some food and that took some time. We will never be late again." Josie replied. "So, this is the friend you spoke of," he said turning to me, "I'm Jack. You are?" He asked, shaking my hand.

"I am Haroun." "Let's get going, the boss doesn't like waiting for people." We moved further out of town, taking various bush paths; the constant change in direction left me disoriented. I had never ventured that far. In the middle of a bush, Jack stopped and said to us, "Now, we are going to our base and anybody who enters there will be treated as one of us. What you see there and what we say there should remain there. Our secrecy is our strength. We kill anyone who tries to show someone else our base or tell them about our activities. We are a secret group. I'm only telling you so you know. When the boss is speaking, no one speaks, and when you are told to do something, you do it, no questions asked. If you obey the rules, your lives will be easy and you will enjoy working with us. I should not be telling you this yet, but since I'm the one bringing you in, I wanted you to know before you enter the base." I held Josie's hand, trying to signal to him that we should run away. Josie however paid no heed to me, and continued following Jack obediently. Left with no choice, I followed the pair.

•••••

We approached a cave, and at the mouth we met three guys smoking and drinking alcohol. We exchanged greetings after which one of them said, "So these are the smart rats we have now. Welcome boys!" They shook our hands, then one said, "The boss says you should see him immediately." The cave was massive, partitioned with different sections serving as rooms and stores. It was well lit with kerosene lamps. The boss who was lying on a mat, reading a book got up as we entered what appeared to be his room. He was short, well-built, and as hairy as a gorilla. He was wearing shorts, and was bare-chested. He asked us to sit down with him as he placed a straw in the book as a bookmark and closed it. He welcomed us and asked us to tell him about ourselves. I was so shaky and could not help but look around, not knowing what we had gotten ourselves into. Josie told him of our lives on the street, and how we had managed to survive all the hurdles. "Tell me about your families." he said. That was the first time I heard Josie speaking of his family, "My father died when I was young, then, my mom got hit by a car and is now paralyzed, she is in Freetown with my aunt. I was staying with my grandmother, but when she died no one wanted to take me in, so I ended up on the street."

When asked to speak, I told the boss about my family, their dislike for me, and my dislike for them. I told him about how my father killed my mother, and how I ended up on the street. The boss then said to us, "You are the kind of boys I have been looking for. Boys with no strings attached to them, no family they'll want to go back to; boys that will look up to me as if I were all they have in this world. I will now add value to your life, and you will never cry for food, clothes, money, or a place to sleep.

Here is home for you and we are your new family. However, you will be told about the secrecy of this place and what we do, so from today you are staying here, you cannot go back to the park. You will be given some food, and in the morning your induction will start." As we got up to leave, the boss said, "One more thing, feel free to let me know when you face any challenge." He then waved us away. Amara took us to the kitchen, where we were served with food we had only imagined eating in our dreams. They had huge chunks of chicken, goat-stew and rice, with coca cola, my favourite drink. That was the first time in my life I had a full bottle to myself. As I ate, I wondered what kind of work we were expected to do that allowed us such first class treatment. As I gulped down the coke, it drowned all my worries, and there was a smile of satisfaction on my face. It reminded me of the poster in the park of a woman smiling with a bottle of coke in her hand. I felt relaxed for the first time since I entered the base. A little room was given to us with mats spread on the ground and blankets to cover ourselves with. We slept soundly.

•••••

The following days were full of activities, but also horrible realities. We were trained to be armed robbers. We took lessons on how to operate guns, how to sneak through windows, what to look for when we entered a house, and where to look. Initially, I was initially uneasy about it, but after a while I warmed up to the idea because, among other factors, it offered me a clear chance to make the selfish rich people suffer; I could even make my father suffer. Food and drinks were everywhere and Josie and I really took full advantage of these resources. We indulged ourselves to the point that after the third day, Josie developed some stomach problems as a result of overeating.

Two weeks later, we were assigned to our first mission, which was a success. We attacked a vehicle along the Makeni-Magburaka highway, and made away with a lot of goods. We took millions of Leones from the passengers, majority of whom were business people going to buy goods. Josie and I were impressed with the precision with which the mission was executed. The passengers were pretty shaken up, and gave up all they had. After robbing them of all their possessions, mostly money, the driver was asked to drive off.

Everything we got from our raid was handed over to the boss who would give some money to everyone and keep the rest in his room. He was quite fair with us; with the exception of himself, no one had more than the other. For the first time in our lives, we were rich in our own way and could buy nice clothes and shoes. On one occasion, we went to town and gave some money to our friends at the park. One of the boys asked us, "You suddenly disappeared and you returned nicely dressed with money to share. Why, are you working for a witch doctor?" Josie made up an excuse, "You cannot believe this. We have been adopted by a rich man. One day you will visit us. The man's car broke down and we helped him fix it. As a sign of gratitude, he took us to his home to have lunch with him. While there, he asked us to stay with him since he has no children." To make the story convincing Josie told it with a stern expression on his face, but I was unsure if the boys fell for it.

One of the boys told us, "We were worried that something bad had happened to you. We looked all over town for you. If what you say is true, then we're happy for you. Remember that you left us here, if this man has friends who want people to stay with them, please tell them that we are here." I felt sad for my friends and for a moment I wanted to stay, but I knew that was impossible, no way was I going to give up my new good life. We had to go, as there was a meeting that night. After the meeting, I said to Josie, "I want to go to Makasi tonight. I feel like dancing and having cold drinks." We had been given our share of money from the previous day's work, and rather than saving them I was feeling quite thriftless. We informed Jack who was a popular figure at the Makasi, and Jacob, who managed the operations of our plans, and they decided to go with us. Jacob, a former soldier who deserted the military after fighting in Liberia was now the close confidante of the boss. So he told everyone what to do.

•••••

Makasi was full that night. Saturday was the day everyone went out for fun and in a town like this one, Makasi was the right place to find it. Beautiful girls of all ages, in mini-skirts, or tight jeans with legs like those of roasted chicken, streamed across the place, some smoking cigarettes and drinking beer, looking out for customers. Josie had told me that there were rooms at the back of the club where the girls took their customers. The cleaner the room the more expensive it was. When we entered Makasi, girls who already knew Jack and Josie immediately surrounded us. I didn't know how to react at first to a girl who came and sat on my lap. Josie said to me, "Come on relax! She won't eat you! Go and talk with her!" The girl led me to the back of the club where we agreed a price and within a few minutes I found myself on top of a woman for the first time. I screamed as ecstasy overwhelmed me; I was experiencing something new, something I had only been hearing about. My euphoria continued until the girl threw me off. After that, I lay satisfied, with a broad smile on my face. The girl laughed at me as she dressed up.

•••••

"How did it go?" Josie asked me. I looked away not knowing what to say, "Let's go home, I'm tired and I want to sleep." I said. Josie laughed, "Now you are a big man, I know you'll be coming here every day. You have to wait until I see my girl; she must be busy with someone." As we were speaking, a girl of about sixteen years came through the back door, and Josie called her over. She was the most beautiful girl I had ever seen in my life. Light skinned, small mouth, round buttocks, and firm breasts. She walked with grace and charm over to Josie, "Have you been here long? I was with a customer" she said. I could not take my eyes off her. She would make a perfect woman if only someone could get her out of the life she was in. "Take a beer on me." Josie told her. I asked Josie, "Would you mind if I have my way with her?" Josie laughed, "Why not. She's not my wife! You can have a million turns as long as you pay her." I had sex for the second time that night. Her name was Martha, she was a year older than me, but I really liked her, and got jealous whenever Josie talked to her.

•••••

The war was spreading all over the country and Makeni was about to fall into the hands of the rebels. The boss, sensing that there was no way his trade could thrive while the town was under the rebels, considered joining them. When the town finally fell to the rebels, the boss called us to a meeting. "Now that the rebels have taken Makeni, I want all of us to come up with ideas as to what we should do now." Jacob spoke, "For me, I think we should join the rebels. That is the only way we will succeed. We can store whatever we have here, and after the war we can return here and continue with our business." Jack supported him, and it could be seen that the boss was also buying into the suggestion.

"Is there anybody here with a different point? For whatever decision we take now, we will execute as a group. No one will do otherwise." He both asked, and instructed. Everyone supported the idea that we become rebels and we were all ready for it. After sealing off the mouth of the cave, our boss pledged his loyalty to the rebel commander who was in charge of the town, and we entered our new lives as rebels. After weeks of training and a few missions, Josie and I became famous, as we had a group of boys under our control, and we were fearless fighters. Our boss grew steadily in prominence among the rebels as he was a tactician, who thought strategically, and easily gained loyalty and trust among those he commanded. We travelled across the country, fighting in different places, and against different forces such as the Kamajors, the Sierra Leone Army, and the Nigerian troops within Sierra Leone. Jack was killed massacre a battle in Kono, and we dearly missed him. Dosed with cocaine, we could kill several people in a day.

•••••

One day I returned to Makeni, and decided to go in search of my father. I knew the time for revenge had come and I did not want to postpone the inevitable this time around. I told Josie who had come with me to Makeni. Josie thought over it for a moment and asked me, "Do you really think you want to do this? Can you stand the thought of you doing it, and can you live with it?" "I'll never be happy as long as I live, if I don't kill him. I see my mother in my dreams, asking me to do it, and I want to make her happy. That man doesn't deserve to live, and this is the only chance I have. I don't know what tomorrow will bring." Josie said to me, "I cannot advise you on this. Do what you must, but don't ask me to go with you. I won't." He turned his back on me and walked down the street. This confused me because Josie had never denied me anything. But I knew that I wanted to have my revenge and would have it that day. I went into a house that had been broken into, and took from my bag 'the powder of life', as the Boss called it. I sniffed it and checked my gun and knife. Nothing mattered now; my mind was made up.

The gate to the house was locked, so I jumped over the fence and looked to see if anyone saw me. I then moved on to my father's apartment. My father was eating with his second wife when I opened the door. The spoon fell from his hand, and his immediate reaction upon seeing me was to draw a machete from under his pillow. I shot him on his left foot, and he fell down. My step-mother, who did not remember me, ran towards the door, but I kicked her to the floor. I felt adrenalin rush inside me, and I was incandescent with rage. I had been waiting for this moment to come for a very long time. I had to do it in a way that all those who would witness, would remember the day for the rest of their lives. I wanted to torture them and also their children. However, even in my madness I was not oblivious to the fact that although their children were made to hate me by their parents, there was one who liked me and had even been punished for that.

I dragged my father out of the room. By then neighbours were coming out to see what was happening. My father sat up holding the foot I had shot. I asked him, "Do you remember me?" He looked at me for some time and said, "Yes, you are Haroun." I shouted at him, "The Haroun you treated like a dog, the Haroun you deprived of a mother, the Haroun you deprived of a childhood. I have been looking forward to this day for a very long time, today you will pay the price for treating me like a dog." I said to both my father and stepmother, "Now you bastards lie on the floor, if you move I will shoot you. Do you know me?" By now, I had also ordered my step-siblings to gather around and join their parents on the ground. Most of them, some slightly older than me said they did not remember me when I asked if they knew who I was. Only two remembered me, I had grown tall over the years and my face was full of scars I had gotten from fights during my street days. "I know you will not remember me. I am Haroun the brother you treated like a beast, the brother that was not important enough to enter the house. The brother that had no place to sleep in his father's house, the brother that had nothing to eat when there was plenty of food in the stores for all of you. You created a monster, and now the monster has come to hunt you. I will kill all of you." I kept my eyes on my father as I spoke. I turned to him, "Why did you kill my mother? Why did you hate her so much? Why?"

He moved closer to me as he spoke, "I never hated her. If I hated her I would not have married her. I was looking all over this town for you when you left; I have been restless ever since. You are my child, why should I treat you like a beast? Please, I am your father, don't kill me." I hated him all the more as he lied. "Shut up, you liar. You killed her and no one spoke up for her. You were beating her like a drum and thought that it was all over and that you would always have your way. You killed her but you failed to realise that she had children and that I was seeing what was happening." My father's already bulging eyes were protruding as if they were about to fall out. "Wicked people are the greatest cowards in the world. You thought you were powerful and could do whatever you wanted to do. Now you are here, a scared parrot. I wanted to make it painful and slow but actually I will make it fast because I can't stand the sight of your face any longer." I saw the sister that had been nice to me and I told her to get up and go inside the house. She stood up, looked at her brothers and sisters, and begun to cry, paralyzed with fear, not knowing what to do.

"Don't be scared M'balu, I won't hurt you. You were the only one that showed me love, and gave me food when I was hungry. Go inside, don't be afraid." She went away slowly, turning frequently to see what was happening. When she was close to the building, she bolted inside. I shot my father's other leg, thereby disabling him completely. I then took my knife and started surgically cutting off each and every one of his fingers. "You used these to beat my mother. You will never use them again." I felt nothing inside but rage whilst doing it, and the urge to make him suffer the more. The children and their mothers were shrieking and sobbing as my father cried from the pain being inflicted on him. I told him, "Now you will know that whatever evil you do comes back to haunt you. I wish you burn in hell." I cut off his ears and shot him five times in the face. It was a nasty sight.

I turned to the rest of the family, indecisive as to what to do to them. I wanted to shoot all of them. I raised my gun, pointed it in their direction, and stopped. "I'm letting you go for just one reason, which is M'balu. You should be grateful to her, or else you would all have been dead today. I do not want her growing up hating me." I moved out of the house kicking my father's lifeless body as I left. The children and women ran to the dead man screaming. Their screams engendered a deep sense of satisfaction in me. My dreams had finally come true. I had laid my childhood nightmares to rest. I had done what my mother wanted me to do. Someone had paid for being evil. I suddenly thought of Saidu and all that we spoke of, and wished I had a way of letting him know that the revenge had I sought for my mother's murder, had finally been realised.

•••••

After the incident with my father, I became a complete monster, killing every grown up person that crossed my path. In them, I saw my father. I could count close to one hundred people who had become my victims. Josie was concerned with what was happening to me. One day after we had returned from a mission, he took me to a hill and we sat and talked about our past. He was looking for a way to bring up the topic. He braved it up, "Haroun, I am concerned with what is happening to you." "What do you mean?" I asked. "I do not like the way you have been behaving recently. You changed completely since you killed your father." Josie paused, waiting for a response but none came, as I rather turned my face the other way trying to avoid eye contact. Josie continued, "I think the time has come for you to move on with your life. You should let go of your past and try to move forward. When we entered this movement, it was not to have blood on our hands. I am getting tired of all this, I hate the life I am

108

living. I have never been a decent person all my life. I spent some time thinking about this, but I don't know what to do. You are more than a friend to me; you are my brother, my only brother in this world. I don't want to see anything happen to you, I want to still be strong after the war. I want to try to live a decent life. I am begging you to let go of your past, I saw the women whose breasts you cut off and I was not happy. Please promise me that you will never hurt anybody in that way again." Josie held my hand and when he saw that I was crying he was moved to tears as well. He stopped speaking, hugged me and we cried together; two people who had been victims of circumstance, lives transformed beyond all possible human recognition.

Twisted Inside

It was at the age of twelve that I first came to hear the word 'war'. I was in the second year of secondary school, and my history teacher was explaining the history of the Second World War. "Katimu, spell war for me" He had caught me talking to my friend and had done that to embarrass me. I said, "I'm sorry sir, what word?" "War." He repeated. Even though I had never heard that word before, I spelt it out, slowly, "W... A...R" "Correct, but learn to pay attention in class. Next time, I will punish you." He was an albino, with patches all over his arms and face and he always wore long sleeves to hide the patches. One of my friends told me her parents had said that Mr. Saffa was badly burnt during the forest fire that spread to the village, before we were born. The fire killed eighteen people, and destroyed most of the village. Students called him 'the black and white dimension' and made several jokes about him but not to his face. Sometimes I felt sorry for him, for he was very nice to us, and was a good teacher.

"The Second World War led to the death of millions of people in Europe, Asia, parts of Africa, and America. When I say "America", my friends normally say I am wrong, but they forget the attack on Pearl Harbour, which led to the death of Americans on American soil." He was going too fast for our young brains and we could not understand what he was saying. Jeremiah asked him,

"What is Pearl Habour?" "I see you are not following what I am saying. Let me start all over again." He said. I sat up straight and tried to concentrate since the topic sounded interesting. I liked history. "From 1914 to 1919 the world suffered from a very brutal war called the First World War. A student from Serbia called Gavrilo Princip killed the Archduke Franz Ferdinand (and his wife) who was the heir to the Austro-Hungarian throne. Germany backed the Austro-Hungarians and Britain, France and Russia backed Serbia as they believed that the death of the prince was only used as a guise to begin a war in Europe. You have to understand that there were several treaties existing in Europe and countries had pledged to protect their allies should they come under attack. For instance, Russia had an agreement to protect Serbia if she came under attack."

The introduction to the First World War was very interesting and the whole class was paying attention. "After the First World War, Germany felt the punishments she was subjected to were unfair. So the leader that came to power in 1933, Adolf Hitler, stated that 'Germany was not defeated, she was stabbed in the back.' Consequently, he prepared Germany for another war and this time they wanted to win. Their technology had improved, and their air force and navy were very strong. Germany started making claims to lands and took over Austria and Czechoslovakia in early 1939. The British did not want another World War so their Prime Minister Neville Chamberlain tried to satisfy the greed of Hitler by letting him hold on to some of the lands he claimed for Germany. This was meant to encourage Hitler not to take the path of war but Hitler was determined and the German invasion of Poland on the 1st of September 1939 finally sent the world into the Second World War. This time with many more casualties, and the price paid by the world was very high."
That day when I got home I asked my father, who was also a teacher in my school, about wars and what we had

been taught in school. "My child, never pray to witness a war. It will be the worst thing that you will ever see. During wars, parents abandon their children and some get killed. Everything bad happens. That is what has started in Liberia. Only God knows if it will affect Sierra Leone." "Will you abandon me if there is a war in Sierra Leone?" I asked him. He hurriedly answered, "Why should I do that? You are my treasure. You are my princess, I will go nowhere without you."

"But, Papa, why do people kill each other?" I further enquired. He responded, "When you grow up you will come to understand that there are different kinds of people in this world, and they do things for different reasons. Some kill others for selfish reasons, others because they want to revenge, some because they do not like seeing others happy. There are also big and powerful people who make others fight for them because they want to be President. This is the case in Liberia. You will never get one answer, for everyone behaves in a different way." "Mr Saffa said Adolf Hitler was a powerful man, and he caused the Second World War?" "That is true. I was born after that war. Your grandfather fought in Asia, for the British. He would have loved to answer your questions if he was still alive as it was his favourite topic. He always wanted me to join the army instead of going to college. You have to understand this: Hitler was a powerful but also an evil person. Only evil people start wars. Did your teacher tell you that he killed himself, and his bones have still not been found?" I asked my father "Are the Liberians fighting for the same reasons Hitler went to war?" He answered, "Liberia is not as powerful as Germany was. There is a rebel group called the National Patriotic Front of Liberia (NPFL). Saffa should be telling you these things. I will remind him tomorrow. They want to remove the President Master Sergeant Samuel Doe from power. They say he is corrupt, and is not working in the interest of his people." I said to him, "But that doesn't make sense.

More people suffer because of war. If you want to help them, it is not by killing them." My father patted me on the back and said, "Now you're getting what I'm saying. You are a very intelligent girl; it comes from your father's side." My mother, who was busy sewing all along, became offended. "I knew you would say that! You can never say it comes from the mother's side, you men. Everything good is from men, and everything bad comes from the women."

•••••

One year later, war seeped into Sierra Leone through the Liberian border. Fearful rumours were coming from every angle and they were causing panic. However, after two years without any attack on our village, life continued as usual. We started thinking that the war would never come our way. One of my friends in school said to me, "They say the rebels are only interested in the mineral rich areas, not poor villages like ours. They will never come here." I asked Mr Saffa that day, "Are rebels only interested in mineral-rich areas like Kono and not areas like the one in which we are living?" "Katimu, why do you ask a question like that?" I responded, "I would like to know?"

"It is difficult for one to know exactly what the rebels are interested in. They will for sure want mineral-rich areas more than they would want other areas. The minerals will help them buy guns and ammunition, to keep the war going on. With the minerals, they will even be able to get significant support from people in other countries who are interested in minerals. Some areas the rebels take for political reasons, and some because of their strategic significance for winning the war." The word strategic was big for me. "What is strategic?" "In this context, being strategic means prioritizing the things that are important and necessary, for example, if the rebels want to cut off Government troops from reaching an area like the one in which we are now, they will take and secure Makeni, and the Government troops will have no way of reaching here." "Do you think they will ever come here?" He looked at me for a while before answering, "Let's pray they don't."

•••••

Few years later, it appeared our prayers had not been strong enough to keep the rebels at bay, because our worst fears came true. We came to know first-hand what the rebels were capable of doing. That day brought darkness, affliction, and unhappiness into my life. The cacophony outside woke us up as it was in the early hours of the morning and my mother opened a window to see what was happening outside. She saw several men, women, and children, carrying guns.

My mother quickly closed the window and checked that the doors were properly locked. They were definitely rebels. How was this possible? We had never suspected any rebel activity in the area. Even though there was no soldier or police in our village, we had never been attacked during the entire period the war had been going on. But today, the war has caught up with us. My mother asked my father, "What are we going to do now?" He was overtaken by fear, and we could sense this as he spoke, "What do you want me to say? I don't know. We can only wait and see what happens. No one is going outside, we stay here, and whatever happens we stay together as a family. I never expected that war would come our way at this time." "What if they come here? They will kill us! Do you want us to wait for that?" My mother asked him. I wanted my mother to keep quiet so we could listen to what was happening outside. I knew my father did not like her questions and was trying to avoid a dialogue on what to do at this time. However, he didn't have answers.

"If you want to go outside and get shot, then go, but my children and I are not leaving this house. I do not want to talk at this time. Do whatever you want." He opened the window slightly, trying to look outside again. It was dark, so he could not see much, but we could hear activities clearly going on, and a shot or two were heard in the distance. My mother ducked for cover when she heard the gunshot. That was the first time I had ever heard a gunshot in my life. I was terrified, but my younger brother Baba who was eight was still sleeping, oblivious to the threat outside our home. I sat closer to my mother, fully understanding her worry and fear. We had heard a lot of people talking about the war, the rebels, and the destruction they were unleashing across the country. I could not fully comprehend why Sierra Leoneans would pick up guns and start fighting each other. Initially, I thought the people telling us about the rebels were lying, until we saw the people travelling through our village as they fled their homes. Some even stayed for few days in our village before moving on.

My mother started packing our clothes into a bag, while tears ran down our cheeks. My father grabbed her arm and stopped her. "If they meet you doing this, they will think you have something to hide and they will hurt us," he said, "By behaving this way, you are putting all of us in danger. Just sit quietly and let God take control."

My younger brother woke up. My mother took him into her arms so he would not cry. He was still sleepy, and looked at us with eyes partially closed. My mother tried to rock him back to sleep. The rebels were going around breaking down doors and bringing people out. They were shouting that they were looking for Nigerian soldiers hiding in the houses. My father re-opened the window to see what was happening outside but quickly closed it; his eyes wide with terror as he turned back to us. Whatever he had seen out there had clearly horrified him. His reaction shook me inside, for my courage laid squarely on him, and if he, my source of courage and protection, was scared, then I was doomed. The noise had completely woken my brother up and he started crying. I felt like my life was coming to an end. My father brought us together and asked us to pray. We held each other's hands as we normally do when praying; my father led the prayers:

"Lord, we call upon you at this moment of need to come to our aid. We are your servants. You said in times of need, ask and it shall be given to you, seek and you will find. You told us that unless you keep the city, the watchman will watch but in vain. Your slaves are calling on you for help now, Lord. Answer us, answer us! We are doomed, and only you can deliver us from the fangs of the serpent."

It was at that point that the rebels smashed down our door. I ran into our bedroom and hid under the bed but the rebels saw me entering the room. Two boys between fifteen and sixteen years entered the room after me and shouted that if I did not come out from my hiding place, they were going to shoot. I came from under the bed and stood before them, shaking. "Where were you running to? No one can run from us, no one. When we want to get you, we get you; we want you to live, you live; we want you to die, you die. Now get out." I was pushed out of the room.

My parents were kneeling down as they were when we were praying. There were two adult rebels in the room together with the two that had come after me. One of the rebels was saying to my father, "The entire country is falling into our hands now. Ha! You people have always supported the Government. We wanted to attack this village on Election Day but other missions came up and you were spared. You people voted when we had said that no Sierra Leonean should vote. You villagers who know nothing said you wanted democracy. All democracy brings is pain and death. Now you have a Government, but that Government cannot protect you. We protect only those who support us. Tell me where the Government people in this village are. We want to see all of them."

My father answered him, "Only our chief is here. No Government person lives here. This is a small village, government people live in the towns." "You mean to say that I am stupid and I do not know what I am talking about? There are Government people in every village in this country, or are you one of them?" "I am only an innocent teacher. I teach at the school here," my father replied, his voice shaking. "And that is the school where the voting took place. So you know what I am talking about!" The rebel was becoming furious. "I was not in town when they voted. My brother was sick, so I took him to the hospital in Makeni I do not even like the Government, I have always supported the RUF," my father lied hoping that might help. The rebel laughed. "Those who tell us that they like us when we attack their villages are the ones that do not like us. We know." The other older rebel said to him, "We have other things to do, let's not waste all the time here."

He beckoned to the boys and ordered them to take care of us, as he turned and left the room together with the other older rebel. "No problem, we'll handle them," one of the boys said, grinning like a Cheshire cat as he spoke. He looked devious, which scared me. The other boy asked my parents, "Where is the money? Bring it out fast!" My mother went into the room followed by one of the boys. She brought out the small box where she kept the money she got from selling goods at the market. The boy took the money and pocketed it. The other boy, who was shorter and skinnier, said to us, "You see, all we need is cooperation, nothing else, and everyone will live. Cobra, which one do you want, mother or daughter?" "Ah Tormentor, how can you ask me such a question? Will you take an old blood when there is the option of a younger blood? You can have the old one, I want the sweet baby." My parents were looking at each other not believing what the rebels were saying. My father begged them, "Please do not hurt them. I beg you in the name of God."

"Who says we are going to hurt her. We are going to see what she is made of. You should be glad that we are interested in your daughter. Other people sometimes ask us to have their daughters instead of them. You are not grateful that we want to do something with her. We are cute, she'll like us." He let out a small snigger as he spoke. "Please! I am begging you, please let her be. Don't touch her, please." "Don't listen to this old fool, Tormentor. We don't have all the time in the world." He called to me; I did not get up, but looked up at my parents. He pointed his rifle at me and said, "Move or I shoot. If I can't have you alive, I do not mind having you dead. It will be easy for us." "Get up, I am saying it for the last time!" I got up, and as he moved to grab my hand my father lunged at him and he was shot in the leg by the other rebel, called Cobra. My mother covered her mouth in disbelief.

Tormentor, who tore my clothes from my body, forced me to the ground. I was very weak, overcome by fear, and did not have any strength to fight back. Tormentor started poking his fingers inside me. I felt great pain as he did it. I tried to hold his hand away from me. But he slapped me across the face so hard I could see stars. "If you try stopping me, I will use a knife instead of my fingers. You are enjoying this and you are pretending not to. Try something stupid again, and you will regret it." He continued inserting his fingers inside me. He then unzipped his trousers, climbed on top of me, and forced himself into me. The pain was unbearable. I cried out loud. I heard my father shout, "Let her be, please, let her be." There was a brief scuffle, then a gun went off, and I knew that they had killed my father. I could hear my younger brother and mother sobbing. Something died deep inside me and at that point I surrendered wholly to the rebel's forceful thrusts, all hope lost.

I was in excruciating pain when he finished. Thinking it was all over I forced my eyes shut, waiting for him and the others to leave us alone. But that was not to be. Despite my obvious agony and the blood that was on me, he called on Cobra. "Get ready, I am finished." "Bring your ass out so I can go in." Few seconds later, Paul was on atop me, ramming himself into me, overly excited with what he was doing, hurting me every second, and forgetting that he was dealing with another human being. The pain was unbearable. It was like my legs had died. When he finished, he said that my vagina was too big for him, so they should use a stick insisting they want me to feel satisfied too, as he claimed that only a stick could help me get the satisfaction I wanted. He went outside, and came back with a stick he had broken from a tree that was nearby, while the other one was pointing his gun at us. He shoved the stick into me, twisting it in different directions. I screamed so loud; there was so much blood coming from me that I fainted.

•••••

I recalled waking up the next day and seeing my mother wiping my face, and other faces gathered around me. They were happy to see that I was recovering. My mother's eyes were so sad, that I had to ask her, "Where is papa?" But I already knew. She turned away, hiding her tears. I looked at the other people but no one could answer me. I knew he was dead. The memories of what had happened the previous day came back to me. I tried sitting up but I could not. I was weak and still in so much pain. My Aunt Seray came to my side, "Don't push hard. Try to rest for now. We are trying to see how best we can help you go to the town for treatment." I asked her, "Where are the rebels?" I asked, suddenly remembering that they could still be around, which filled me with more trepidation. "They left the village after burning houses. We do not know if they are coming back. We can only pray that they don't." Mr Saffa was also in our house. "We have to get this girl to a hospital in Makeni, before things get worse" My mother cried, saying, "There is no vehicle or anything now. What are we going to do?"

"We will do what the people of old did before using vehicles. They walked, and so shall we. Magburaka to Makeni is about 26 miles. So we will make it before the day ends, but let's waste no time." Arrangements were made for my mother, Mr Saffa and my uncle Daniel to go with me to Makeni. Boys from the village were to carry me to the outskirts of the village. Mr Saffa and my uncle would take turns carrying me to Makeni. Everyone was crying in the village as I was carried to Makeni. Some people were about to bury their dead loved ones. The attack had destroyed the village completely. Some waved at me, and others came close to wish me well. I was still bleeding and it was looking really bad. As we left the village, Mr Saffa took me from Cyril, who had carried me the last round from the village. My mother thanked them as they left.

The journey was a difficult one, for the sun was not friendly on that day. It was very humid. As the men walked and carried me, each movement caused me pain. I slipped in and out of consciousness several times. In between taking turns to carry me, we took time to rest. Four hours later, we had covered a significant distance. We were afraid of meeting rebels along the way. But after walking for such a long time and not running into any, we came to believe that they were not on the Makeni road. I tried walking twice but could hardly make three steps. In the evening we reached Makeni. There were soldiers everywhere. We were stopped at a check-point, "Where are you from?" A soldier asked us. "We are from Ratok, in Magburaka, and we are taking this girl to the hospital in Makeni. Our village was attacked yesterday and she is seriously hurt." I was put down so the soldier could see me properly. "Are the rebels still in your village?" "They left after destroying everything." "That is what they do now; they cannot fight us so they attack civilians."

He felt sorry for me and called on one of his soldiers. "Take them to the hospital." "Yes, sir," the junior soldier saluted him and led us to a military vehicle standing close by. "May God bless you for this kindness," my mother thanked him, but he cut her short. "No need to thank me, it's my responsibility. I am working for the state, and for the people."

The hospital was full of people, some lying on the ground. The soldier led us to the emergency room where the doctors were cutting the leg of a lady who had stepped on a land mine. Her mouth was tied to stop her from crying out. I could see her eyes wide open in torment and disbelief as the doctor sawed through her leg. The sound of the sawing process was horrific.

The soldier asked one of the nurses, "Why did you not put her on anaesthetic before doing this?" "We are very low on supplies. We have not been getting anything for the past five months, so this is the only way we can do it. We know it is painful but we have to help her. It's the best thing for her." After Mr Saffa had finished explaining to the nurse what had happened to me, she took me to a small room where a doctor later joined us. I was examined and cleaned by the doctor and the nurse. When I was brought out, the doctor said to my mother, "She needs to have surgery; otherwise her condition will worsen. She might never give birth. Take her to Freetown as soon as you can, and get her to a surgeon."

My mother cried when she heard this. "We have no money, doctor. We cannot pay for anything, not even the transport to Freetown. Please, help us, please!" "There is not much I can do, as you can see, the situation here is terrible. I have been doing all I can to help, and now we do not have any supplies. I will help you by getting you onto the Government ambulance, which is heading to Freetown tonight. In Freetown you can figure out what to do. I am sorry, that is the only way I can help. The ambulance leaves in 2 hours. Come back and see me in one hour and thirty minutes. I will be here, I work all night." We went to the hospital waiting room and my mother asked Mr. Saffa and my uncle what was to be done.

"I am prepared to go with you all the way as long as it is for this girl; I owe it to her and her father. Her father would have done the same for my daughter, he was my best friend. My wife will take care of the boy, so we have to focus on Katimu now. Let's go to Freetown and see what will happen there. My brother stays there; we can stay at his place while we try to get help." "I have forty thousand Leones with me. I do not know how far that will take us, but we will see when we reach there." My mother said, "Saffa, I won't begin thanking you now. I will wait until all this is over." He hugged her as she began crying. I regretted then laughing at Mr Saffa behind his back at school. I felt ashamed of myself. He had come all the way for me, and my family, and acted as a father in my father's absence.

There was sufficient space in the vehicle for all of us. The doctor gave my mother some painkillers which she was instructed to give to me twice a day. This was my first journey to Freetown. Under normal circumstances I would have been excited, but now I was a physical wreck, a burden to be carried around by three people. I was given water and bread, as we set out on the journey. I drank the water and tried eating the bread, which I swallowed with great difficulty. The journey was not smooth as the road was full of potholes. It made the journey more difficult, and uncomfortable, as the vehicle bounced and jolted around. The city was very dark and engulfed in graveyard silence when we arrived. We went straight to the Connaught hospital, which had electricity. The ambulance driver called on two workers to carry me to the out-patient department, where I would stay until a doctor could see me the next day, since there were none available at that moment.

My uncle and Mr Saffa sat with the night watchman, and shared the floor he slept on until the next morning, while my mother slept on the floor by my bedside. "We would like to treat her but you have to understand that this costs money. It cannot be for free. We are not running a charity here. We are running a hospital. I am sorry." The doctor was almost shouting at my mother as she spoke. "We have only 40,000 Leones, and we will give it all for her treatment. Please, help us! She is in so much pain in this state, it was rebels that did this to her." "I have to go and check on my patients, come back when you are ready." My mother pleaded earnestly as the doctor walked away. All the pleas fell on deaf ears. So Mr Saffa took us to his brother's house in the city, where we stayed for a week while they tried to find the money needed to enable me go through the required surgery.

•••••

After a week, my uncle sat down with my mother and said, wearily, "We have tried everything we can think of, but nothing seems to work. Let us take her to the hospital for another treatment and buy medicines that she can use in the village until we can get the money for the surgery. We can stay here forever and the situation will not change. At least when we are in the village we can start looking for money." My mother saw some sense in what he was saying. After further discussions with Mr Saffa and his brother, I was taken again to the Connaught hospital where I was cleaned and given medicines that they said would help fight off infections and heal the wound inside me.

The nurse, who treated me, said, "If the surgery is done as soon as you have the money, she will have the possibility of having children. Please, try as hard as you can, for her sake." I cried, hearing her say this. How could the system be so cruel? I might never have my own children, which until now I had never really thought of. I had always assumed that one day I will have a big and happy family. I felt sorry for myself and I also felt sorry for the stress my mother was going through now. She had grown old in just a few days. She wanted me to live, to be healthy, to be strong, but poverty like a giant boulder in her path was obstructing. She had done all she could and was frustrated by a system she had trusted, a system that had created a war which had rendered me useless, a system that couldn't help her, a system that is not functioning.

We began our journey back home, to an impoverished land, where my mother, and her family and friends, were expected to come up with money to help me survive the atrocity that had befallen me. My pain was great, and I was very ill, but I put on a brave face to save my mother from more distress. I laid my head on her lap as the vehicle jolted in yet another pothole. My emotional pain eased off a bit and my heart warmed as my mother started stroking my head. Overcome by her love, I shut out my pain and determined to get through the predicament, at least for her sake.

The Trials of Hawa

"Foday come here, bring your brother with you, your father wants to see you." I called on the children, who were playing in the sand with other children, who were also in the camp with us. Unisa, the younger child could not easily be taken from the football he was playing with. At four, he had developed so much love for the only sport he knew. I saw Foday pushing Unisa towards me, "Stop it. Why do you do that to your brother?" I had noticed that Foday would always find a reason to hit or punish his younger brother, and I didn't like it. I wanted them to get along and look out for each other. I had struggled to keep them alive, so I was greatly affected when they were either happy or sad. I had promised myself that I would ensure their safety and wellbeing, and one day after the war, we would live a normal life. I kissed Unisa as he came crying, he was such a sweet kid. "I will beat him, don't worry, I will also let you beat him, do you want to beat him?" "Beat him mama, beat him." He looked just like his father, with whom I have been for the past six years, travelling across forests, mountains, rivers, villages and towns. My life as the wife of a combatant had been difficult, full of near-death experiences, pain, and grief. Maada's call brought me back from my musing.

"Come to papa!" He called the kids, kissing them as he took both of them into his arms. I was happy that, after two months in multiple battles, he had returned alive. He was the man I once hated, but came to love, my husband and the father of my two boys. "Tell me about your journey?" I asked him, wanting some attention, now that he had seen the children. "We are making steady progress and I'm sure by January we will be in Freetown. My first battle was in Kambia, then Port Loko, which was not easy to capture. I left our boys at Rogbere Junction, we are taking a break so I decided to come see you. In the coming days I will join them, but for now I need to be close to my family. In Port Loko, I almost got killed when a mortar hit the house we were in." I felt a sharp pain in my heart. That would have been my end too; he meant the world to me. That night, as I lay down hearing his breathing as he slept, I rolled closer to him, laid my head on his chest, and thought of our past and of how thin a line separated hate and love.

•••••

"The refugees coming into our community are rebels, I do not trust them. Liberians are people you should not trust." My mother was telling my dad who was one of the border guards at the town of Bomaru. We had been there for over twelve years, and it was the only place I knew as home. I was three when my father got posted there. My father had served in the army for more than twenty-six years, and always said that if I were a boy I would have joined the army, to continue the family's military tradition. My grandfather and great-grandfathers had been soldiers who served in the colonial army. "They're not rebels; I've been telling you this. They are refugees running from the war in their country. What do you want us to do with them? Turn them back and close the border? They will get killed. More than 20,000 people have been killed in Liberia and the war is said to be very bloody. That is why Sierra Leone and other countries came together and sent troops there, to stop the war. I don't understand how you think at times" my father reproached her.

"Say what you want to say, but I know that there are rebels among those coming in. I don't like seeing them walking around this town. They should stay in their camps and not mix with us." My mother was very adamant on her position. "Well, go and ask them to leave" my father interjected sarcastically. I noticed that he did not like the subject and always got angry when my mother brought it up. My mother shouted back at him, with a serious face, "Maybe you have a Liberian girlfriend, and that is why you are defending them. The day I see you with one, I will kill you." My father laughed, "Haja, so this is why you do not like them. You are jealous. Please leave those people alone. It was the Government of this country that let them in. Just pretend they are not here and go about your own business." "O.K! I will not talk about this again but one day you will tell me that I was right. I am not happy with what is happening in their country but I am only scared about what they will do to our country. The dreams I have been having these past weeks are not good. God is telling me that we should not trust those people. My dreams never fail me." My mother was a superstitious person and was always talking about dreams and evil spirits.

My father replied, "Dreams always confuse people. Do you know how many times I've dreamt that I died but I'm still alive? Do you know how many times I've dreamt that I have millions of Leones, only to wake up and continue my life of poverty? Please do not speak to me about dreams. Is the food ready?" As we ate dinner, my mother tried to bring up the subject again but my father stopped her, "Please Haja, let's talk about something else. I have to go to work tonight. I can't be spending all my time discussing refugees. I'm not the one that brought them here. I cannot send them back. I'm just an ordinary soldier working for the Government." And with those words, my father walked out of the house, his food half eaten. The following months saw more refugees coming into our town. Most of them got moved to other

127

areas, as the town was too small to take all of them. Their movement intrigued me and I watched everyday as they queued for rations of the food distributed by the people who took care of them. It was in one of such queues that I saw for the first time, people with white coloured skin. So enthralled by these strange human species, I ran all the way home to tell my mother who laughed until tears streamed down her face. After she had had a good laugh, she sat me down and told me about white people, "We are not the only people in this world. There are people with different colours living in different countries. If you go to the capital you will see many white people. They are normal human beings like you, so don't be afraid of them."

I started going to the camp every day to see the white people working. One day one of them tried to talk to me. "What is your name?" she asked, handing me a piece of the bread she was eating. The words rolled out so fast that my ears could not catch up to the words. I knew even my teacher would have difficulty understanding her but at least I got the word "name" and I answered, "I am Hawa."

My mother did not want me to ever go near the camp so when she learnt that I was going there frequently she became furious. My stubbornness made me defy her and I continued going and playing with Emily, my new friend. I showed Emily our town and taught her to play our local girls' games with me. She liked them. She also taught me to play ludo, a game I came to like. I also often braided her hair. I met most of the people she worked with. I took her to meet my mother. There was a scene the day we went to my house. Every person, young and old, from our neighbourhood came out to meet or catch a glimpse of her. Some children were scared of her. Others braved it and came up to touch her. They relaxed after they realised that she was just a normal human being. I felt great that day. Unfortunately, Emily did not stay long in Bomaru; she was transferred to Guinea where there were also refugees. She left me clothes, shoes and money. Although she was much older than me, we were of the same height and she was quite petite so her clothes did fit me. We were both unhappy as we said our goodbyes the day she was leaving.

•••••

Our town was attacked on the night of 23rd March 1991. My father was not at home as he had gone to work. "Lie on the floor. Don't make any sound." I could tell my mom was panicking as she whispered these words to me. I lay on the ground while she checked to see if the doors and windows were properly closed. I prayed for my father to come home safe, knowing that he was part of the fighting that was going on. Several hours went by like minutes and in the early hours of the morning the shooting stopped. I got up and sat on the bed as my mother looked around for food. She was talking to herself, "I told Gibril those people are rebels. He would not believe me, now see what is happening." She slowly opened one of the windows looking to see what was happening outside. Our neighbours were all outside talking. "I think they're gone. There are people outside." She told me. We opened the door and joined those outside. "Mr. Kamara, do you know what was going on?" She asked our neighbour, a man with a large head and eyes as small as peas. Cigarettes, and cola nuts had taken their toll on his dental cavity, and his teeth were as brown as dust. When he opened his mouth, most of those around him often turn their face to the opposite direction to avoid the odour. I wondered at times how his wife coped with that. "I need to go and find out. This was too much. I believe they must be rebels. I have never heard so many gunshots in my life. If it were Freetown, I would have said it was a coup d'états going on, but this is Bomaru, and we are close to Liberia."

"These people should be sent back to Liberia. They are bringing us trouble, I smell it. Only God knows how many people have been killed. Gibril has not returned."

My mom said to Mr. Kamara, putting her hands on her head. "Ah! Don't worry, Gibril is a gallant soldier. They must have chased the attackers out of the town. I will go to the army post to see what happened" Mr. Kamara said, trying to reassure my mother. "You are not going anywhere. Someone will come and tell us." His wife Marie said. "You women are easily frightened. What do you think will happen to me? I will be back within an hour, no need to worry." Marie addressed her husband, "When did you become a journalist? You do not even know what's going on and you want to go there? What if there are people waiting to harm others? What if the attackers are not yet gone but lying in wait in the dark to attack? Don't even think about it. You will stay with us here and we will all wait till morning." She instructed. Our house was at the outskirt of the town so it was not easy for us to know anything that was happening at the centre of the town unless we went there. I could not stop worrying that something might have happened to my dad.

An old woman, Aunty Sally, who was known to be a rumourmonger said, "Yesterday the clouds were very dark and I suspected that something was going to happen." My mother beckoned to me to listen, as Aunty Sally the know-it-all spoke, "That was a sign from God, I should have told you yesterday. There are always signs when something is about to happen, we just don't notice. The clouds yesterday were as dark as the ones I saw the day before Sir Milton Margai died in 1964." Aunty Sally was a widow. Though we saw her as someone who always wanted others to think she knew everything, she was still the sweetest adult I had ever met. She cared a lot for us the young children in the neighbourhood. She was an old nurse, and treated us when we were sick. Also, she told us nice stories. "I hope these people never come again. I am very scared." She was talking to herself because no one answered. "I have to go and see what is happening in the town, Marie, you cannot stop me now." Mr. Kamara was really desperate to go but his wife was insisting not to.

"Kamara I am not trying to stop you. I only know that you are not going anywhere. I heard that when death is calling someone, the person becomes stubborn. It will wait this time. You won't leave me and these little children." My mother joined her in talking him out of going, "Kamara, listen to her, you never can tell what will happen, especially when she has advised you in front of all of us. Let's be patient." Mr Kamara asked my mother, "What if someone does not come?" My mom replied, "That is a sign that we should stay close to our house." Mr. Kamara was quite an impatient fellow. I could see that he was really finding it difficult not to go. But in the end he agreed with his wife and my mother and stayed. Later, Marie and my mother cooked together for those in our neighbourhood. Even though I consider my mother to be the best cook in the world, and so was in no doubt that what they cooked that day was properly done, it was tasteless in my mouth; anxiety about my dad was gnawing at me. "Evil has descended in our midst. It must be stopped now before it grows. Children will suffer, women will die, and men will eat men if this continues. What is happening in Liberia should not be encouraged in Sierra Leone. We do not know fighting. We only know peace. However, there are those who say 'if wah no cam, dis country no go betteh' because they believe that only war will wash away the corruption and bad governance in this country." As Aunty Sally spoke those words, I became more frightened. I had never heard of war or fighting before. I only started hearing of it when the refugees arrived in our town. Now Aunty Sally was making it sound very frightful. I turned at every sound I heard, hoping to see my father.

"I believe the attackers are gone. If they were still around we would have heard more shootings. Our soldiers must have driven them out of the town. Probably they were all killed." I believed Mr. Kamara was still building his case to go and see what was happening or to get information as to what happened. "Let's hope they are gone and will never come again." My mom answered, very worried that my father had not returned. We heard vehicles moving towards the town. Everyone stood up. The movements continued for thirty minutes followed by silence, which also left us in silence, everyone trying to figure out what was happening. "Something strange is happening. This town is becoming something else." Mr. Kamara said. "God will definitely protect us. He won't let anything bad happen to us. They say trust in him, and he won't let you down." My mother prayed.

•••••

My father came home a bit later than usual the next morning and everyone was overjoyed to see him. He was in full military gear and was covered with mud. I ran to him, "Yes! Papa is here!" Questions flooded him, and he stood looking confused as to which one he should begin answering. "Which one do you want me to answer first?" He asked as he pulled off his helmet and sat down. He explained what happened as everyone crammed around him. "At 2 a.m. one of the guards came and told us of some unusual movements ongoing at the border. Seven of us went to see what was happening and immediately we reached there we started hearing gunshots coming from the direction of Liberia." My mother interrupted, "I told you!" "Do you want me to continue or not?" He asked, annoyed with my mother's interruption. "We then pulled back to radio Daru and inform them of what was happening, and also request back-up. An hour later, we had a full-scale attack on the town. It was not an easy battle; there were about 250 rebels from Liberia, well-armed. They initially overpowered us, but we were able to push them back into Liberia. We lost some soldiers and they lost some combatants as well. I should have come home then but there was no way I was going to leave because we were anticipating another attack. Now we have re-enforcements from Daru, if they attempt it again, they will be sorry for it."

My mother, who was a pessimist, still stood by her convictions that there were rebels amongst the refugees, "The only way we can solve this problem and avoid any such future incident is to get the refugees out of this town. As long as they are here, more rebels would come again. I am sure those here with us might have buried guns around this town, waiting for the right opportune moment to take them up; I have been saying this but no one is listening." Mr. Kamara supported my mother, "Who says no one is listening? If it were up to me they would have been removed from this town a long time ago. Those people never liked us. The Government does not know what it is doing." My father, ever an optimist and advocate for the vulnerable, stepped in their defence, "Where will they take them if they are removed from here?" Mr Kamara answered, "Let the Government take the refugees to Freetown, so they will be close to them, not with us who cannot defend ourselves. I will never feel safe as long as they are here." "If those attackers had succeeded in taking this town, the refugees would have been hunted and gutted. They would have massacred them. Probably they were even coming to hunt them, no one can tell. I also think that they might have run out of food and they came here to get food and money." My father was still holding on to his point, not wanting people to believe that the refugees were responsible for what happened.

Aunty Sally who had been silent all this while spoke, "You touched on a very sensible point, and they might have been here because of food. I see no reason why Liberians would attack our country when they are already at war. I believe they wanted to steal and run back into Liberia. Now since they have started this, the Government should warn them by making serious statements and protecting our borders. They will never try such a thing with Guinea; they would be crushed at once. They know we are a small country and that is why they came here." "Don't worry. We are now fully equipped to deal with any attack. More than 300 soldiers, well-armed, already arrived here from Daru. They are taking positions across the town. I do not believe they will come again" my father remarked. "You easily believe anything. We never thought that we would be woken by the sounds of gunfire when we went to bed that night. We are lucky to be alive, anything could have happened. Now you say they will not come again. As for me I am sure they will come back or even those already here will try something, but I do hope you are right." My mother told my father who looked at her with indignation as she spoke. I thought he was going to explode in front of the neighbours. Fortunately, he said nothing. I always wondered how the two had come to marry when they practically disagreed over every issue. However, I knew they loved each other. My mother was someone who would not let her beliefs be kicked out. She was always seen as pushing her ideas whenever the opportunity presented itself. My father on the other hand was a soft-spoken character who did not like to quarrel. Whenever my mother was in a quarrelling mood, he would leave the house and return when he thought she had calmed down.

Unsurprisingly, I had never seen him raise his hands against my mom as our other neighbours did to their wives. Unfortunately for Mr. Kamara however, his wife was stronger than him. Once they had a fight and she lifted him up. In his lifted position he shouted, "When you put me down, I will kill you!" Some of the neighbours pleaded with her to put him down, "He is your husband. You should not be treating him like this in front of people." When finally she put him down, he rushed into their house as if he was going to take something to hurt her with, but never left the house until the next day. That fight became the gossip of the week. Everybody was laughing about it, young and old. Marie was a no-nonsense character. She was a wood-seller who spent most of her time lifting heavy objects. She had a bad temper, and easily picked up fights with those who crossed her path. Known for this, she was left alone when angry. Her best friend was my mother who was the only person that she could listen to when angry. Whenever Mr. Kamara felt offended by her, he asked my mother to intervene.

•••••

Discussions about the attack continued for a while. By then more people had come from the other houses to hear my father narrating what had happened. Desmond who had lived in Liberia during the initial stages of the fighting said, "These are not just bandits but rebels who are determined to enter this country. When rebels in Liberia captured me, I frequently overheard them say their next destination will be Sierra Leone, and then Guinea. Now I see that they were telling the truth. I believe that the attack was a strategy to assess how Sierra Leone will respond. Once they know that the response is not too strong, they will continue trying until they succeed." "God forbid, succeed where?" Aunty Sally interrupted him. "Mammy, you should not underestimate them, I was in their captivity for three months. I know what they are capable of doing. Rebels are the most troublesome people I have ever known. Let's pray that they turn their attention elsewhere, otherwise we are in big trouble." Desmond said. "Well we are securing the borders at the moment and will respond to any other attack with full force so they know we are not here to joke. They seemed to be highly trained. They fought us like professionals and we initially found it difficult to get them out of the town. At one stage they almost pushed us back. I don't know who is training those guys" my father remarked.

"They are getting full support from Burkina Faso, and Libya. Most of them are trained there. Some of the fighters are even Burkinabes and Libyans. I don't know why they do not just keep the fighting in Liberia. Why do they want to spread here? I believe there is high politics in this but we just cannot understand it. The Libyans are using West Africans for very selfish reasons. Now we have sent soldiers who are getting killed in a war they did not start or know nothing about. Our soldiers should be brought back to protect our country now that they have started attacking us." Desmond continued. He seemed to know a lot, and people were listening to him. "When I came back I told my relatives that the rebels wanted to attack Sierra Leone too. They thought the war had affected my mind and made me go crazy. As soon as I heard the shots I knew that it was a rebel attack. They are trained to create panic and use that as their weapon to do what they want to do. I believe that the time has come for me to move to Freetown, I do not want to witness another attack." That statement frightened me, but I felt reassured when my father spoke.

"We have the best army in the Mano River Basin; you do not need to worry. During a massive attack in Liberia, it was only the Sierra Leone Army that was able to push the rebels back. The rebels were more than us but we were better fighters. We are not like the Liberian army, the British trained us, and you should remember that. If we were having more ammunition like the Guineans have, no army in the region could stand us, not even the Nigerians." "The Nigerians loot like rebels. For them everything is about profit; they do nothing out of genuine reasons. Everything is business for them. If you have them in your country you should be worried. I saw them at work in Liberia and I was surprised" Desmond said. "I should take my bath now. I need to get the mud off and catch some sleep" my father said, looking tired as he moved towards the house. The next day, journalists and soldiers flooded every quarter of our town. My father came home every day telling us what the soldiers were doing to protect the town. After some weeks, the journalists left, and the soldiers reduced, but few people took notice of this, as life had virtually returned to normal; the attack was less spoken about in the town. It was then that the rebels attacked again.

•••••

My father left that morning for Daru to collect ration for the unit in our town. My mother was not feeling well. Aunty Sally had decided to sleep at our house that day to tend to my sick mother. I was dreaming when the sounds of the gunshots penetrated my dreams. I woke up with a start and saw that my mother too had gotten up but Aunty Sally was sleeping. "Wake up, they are here again, wake up!" The shooting, though not in the vicinity of our neighbourhood, was very heavy. I could hear bombs exploding. My mother who had earlier wrapped herself with a blanket, stood up, forgetting completely that she was sick. "Don't stand like that! Lie on the floor." Aunty Sally, now wide awake, pulled her down. I was relieved that Aunty Sally was with us, I would not have known what to do with my mother. The fighting and sounds of gunfire went on and on. No one dared to go out. I prayed that it would all stop like the first attack did. My mother told Aunty Sally, "After this one, I will take my child and go to Kenema; I do not want us to die one day from these attacks." In the afternoon, the fighting started coming closer to where we were staying. I could see my mother praying, as she lay with her face to the ground. Suddenly we heard gunshots in our neighbourhood.

"Aunty Sally, they're here. Can you believe this?" My mother cried. Aunty Sally didn't say a word. She closed her ears, trying to shut out the sounds of the shootings, which were growing heavier every second. We could hear the movements of people with heavy boots. I prayed for them to be soldiers. 'Bang!' The sound was followed by the soft thud of a bullet landing on the bed my mother had been laying on not too long ago. I could not believe my eyes. I moved closer to the wall feeling that it would be safer. Five minutes later, our door was broken by a rebel's kick. Three of them entered our room and ordered us out, "Out! Out, and move slowly!" One rebel commanded us. We moved outside where we saw that our neighbours were also being ordered out of their houses by heavyset dishevelled young men with moustaches shaped like Adolf Hitler's. Two had dreadlocks. Only one was in military fatigue. As we came out of our houses, one of the rebels who had a gallon in his hands doused our houses with petrol and set them ablaze.

We were split into two groups, the men and boys in one group, and women and girls in the other. "Now tell us, who are those hiding Government soldiers and policemen here? If you don't tell us, we will kill you one by one" the rebel who broke into our house shouted. Aunty Sally spoke, "There is no soldier here. We are all farmers and traders. That is what we do for a living." I admired her courage. No one else dared to speak. "Liar! This town is full of soldiers and their families. I know what to do if you do not tell me" the rebel threatened, pointing his gun at Aunty Sally. I closed my eyes thinking he was about to shoot. "I will count to ten, I need answers, one, two, three," Aunty Sally, oddly not fazed by his threats, spoke again. "I am telling you the truth, we have no soldiers here. If they were here obviously you might have seen them by now or they would have defended us against you. Our houses are burning now, so where would we keep them? If they were hiding in there, wouldn't they have run out by now?" "Stop lying. Some of the men here are soldiers" he said, turning to the men.

"Who among you is a police or a soldier?" he asked. "It's true, we are farmers, we have never joined the army" Mr. Kamara said in a shaky voice that betrayed his fright him. "Scorpion, tie them, we need them." Turning his attention to the women and girls, he looked through the gathering for a while and said, "Tie these two also," pointing at me and Boima (the daughter of Mr. Kamara who was my age) "and kill the rest." I held on tightly to my mother who was screaming, pleading, crying and holding on to me all at the same time. I was however snatched forcibly from my mom. Similar thing happened with Boima and her mom. Then in the full glare of everyone and amidst the screaming and crying, mainly from the women and children, one of the dreadlocked rebels tore off the clothes Boima and I were wearing, exposing our bodies, and tied our hands behind us. I watched as eight people including my mother, Aunty Sally and Mrs. Kamara got shot more than three times each. I watched on helplessly as my mother struggled to die, her eyes fixed on me. I was screaming and writhing in agony as they shot them but there was not much I could do. The rebels laughed as we cried, and the men seethed with impotent rage. They poured petrol over them and set the corpses on fire. Through teary eyes, I watched my mother's body go up in flames. It seemed almost surreal to think that it was just yesterday I was hugging her as she lay sick in bed with malaria, today she was in death's embrace, killed by people she did not know and had never offended. I was beside myself with grief and cried my heart out, as we were dragged away; the horrors of my mother's death still before my eyes.

One of the rebels continuously poked my breasts with a stick as we moved, but I felt nothing. My sense of being had died along with my mother. I thought of my father and cried out for him. As we walked through the town, I saw several dead bodies lying in the road; most of them soldiers. Rebels were coming from every direction with people they had captured. One of the rebels said to the other as we passed the corpse of a soldier, "They thought we were not coming again. They failed to realise that we never give up." "I told you that they could not beat us. They were running like dogs. I would have been happy if we had stayed the last time instead of retreating. They thought they had defeated us. When I came to the town dressed like a car mechanic, I heard what some of the people were saying. They made me laugh. They were so stupid. Today they have paid for their stupidity." "I was afraid for you. I thought someone might recognise you." As I listened in on their dialogue, I felt goose pimples all over my body and wished someone had taken my mother's forecast of doom regarding the rebels' return seriously. The two continued speaking as they led us to where the other rebels were gathered.

The town was glowing red with houses on fire everywhere. In my heart, I was reciting the prayer my teacher had taught us to recite when we were in trouble. 'The Lord is my shepherd; I shall not want. He maketh me to lie down in green pastures…' I needed such a prayer at this moment to keep strong and hopeful and so I particularly kept stressing and repeating the portion that said 'Yea though I walk through the valley of the shadow of death, I will fear no evil: for thou art with me…' After the first encounter with the rebels andwith what I had seen so far, I was convinced without a doubt that they were capable of every imaginable evil.

•••••

We joined with other victims of all ages captured from all over the town; men and women, boys and girls, some much younger than me. Mr. Kamara tried taking Boima along with him as he and the other men were taken to the post where my father worked. She was jolted from him, and made to join the women and girls, as we were taken to a house close to the frontier, which was to become our cell. That night, rebels came in one after the other, picking out girls and young women. I could not understand what was going on until a lanky, malnourished rebel with reddish and frightening eyes came, and after looking at all of us, took my hand, and dragged me along. I was almost naked, with no blouse on and my skirt torn in different places. He took me to a room, ripped off what little was left of my clothing, forcing me to the ground as he unzipped his trousers. I cried out begging him not to touch me and that I was only fifteen, and a virgin. He was deaf to my pleas. He pressed me to the ground, prying my legs open. I could not fight back since he was much stronger than I was. He forced himself into me and I could feel my vaginal walls tearing apart. My body was trembling. I was in the greatest pain I had ever felt. I closed my eyes as he rammed himself deeper into me. I had always said that I would wait till I was married before having sex and in any case I would only have sex with the man that would marry me. That moment and savage act killed my childhood, my innocence stolen by a rebel. I cried from physical and emotional pain as he continued his evil act, gratifying his manly sexual appetite. From that day, everything resembling hope was snuffed out in me; in a single day I had suffered multiple traumatic experiences including the loss my mother and getting raped by a vicious stranger.

When he was done, he wiped himself of his sweat with the tattered remnant of my skirt. "Get up and let's go!" he said. I felt weak, and could not get up. I was choked with pain and my legs cramped. I cried as he pulled me to my feet; I could barely stand and when he let go of my hands I swayed a bit so that he had to reach out and steady me. "Are you okay?" he enquired. Him asking me at that point if I was okay, I thought was rather belated and misplaced and thus didn't bother to reply. To his second question however, I did answer; "What is your name?" he asked. "Hawa" I muttered.

He took me back to the cell where I lay helpless with other girls who had suffered similar fate. The older women among us told us that the pain would soon pass off, and we would be okay after a little while. A 'little while' took a very long time to arrive. I tried standing up but could not make it without support. One of the women in the cell walked up to me and asked, "Are you not the daughter of Haja?" "Yes, I am" I replied, recognising her as the woman who normally sold fish to my mother. I cried as she kneeled down. "Look what they did to you. Where are your parents?" she asked. "My mother has been killed. My father was out of town when the attack took place. He must still be in Daru." "I am so sorry; your mother was a good woman." She sat down close to me and stroked my head, singing slow traditional songs, which lulled me to sleep.

I was woken up by the creak of the cell door being opened; new captives were pushed inside. That morning, the rebel that raped me came to our cell and gave me some food. I gave some of the food to Boima, who was also feeling sick, and to Rugiatu, the fishmonger. We ate every bit of the food. I felt guilty eating, as I thought of my mother lying burnt and dead, and I threw up as thoughts of her intensified. I started feeling sick all over again. I noticed that Boima was bleeding; I took a rag that was near me and handed it over to her. I turned my face as she wiped herself, and Rugiatu went to her aid. I tried to shut out the world around me and allow my mind to drift to thoughts of my parents. I started thinking of things we had done together as a family. I thought of my dad returning home from work every morning and me rushing to greet him, and of words and stories my mother usually told me. I thought of all the arguments she had with my father and how many times my father would tell her she was naive. I couldn't believe my mother was now meat for vultures and dogs. I cried uncontrollably as these jumbled thoughts ran through my mind.

That afternoon the rebel whom I had come to know as Maada brought more food for me. The regular food was distributed later that afternoon to everyone. That night, the young women were once more picked out one by one by the rebels. Maada took me again but this time did nothing to me. He rather gave me some clothes and made me bath. I felt slightly refreshed after the bath, since I hadn't had one in a while.

142

"Tell me about your family and your life." I did not speak. I was wondering why he was asking me a question like that. I remained quiet, expecting him to ask me to lie down so he could have his way with me as he did the last time. "Don't be afraid of me, I will never hurt you again, I am sorry for yesterday, I should not have done it, I was a little bit high." I could not believe what I was hearing, a rebel apologising. I told him about my mother in tears and he told me how sad he was to hear this and that he will go to the house and bury the corpses there. He took me to the cell after about an hour, giving me more food to eat and paracetamol. That night Maada was asked by his colleague Anthony, whom he had trained with in Liberia and had been fighting in the same units ever since, "You seem to be interested in this little girl, I see you taking food to her. Tell me what is happening, you are becoming soft, this is so unlike you, why now?"

"Ah, my man, there are times in one's life when you meet people you like, no matter the circumstances. I feel sorry for her and that had never happened to me. She is so young! I want to help her, but I do not know how to go about doing it." "You are not meant to think like that, you know the commander will be angry if he realises you are getting soft. I know you are also a very senior fighter. Take it cool, the euphoria or whatever it is you think you are feeling will pass away. Take some beer and find another woman, and you will stop thinking about her. We are expecting a counter-attack. That is what you should be thinking about, not some little girl. Now get over this and let us move on." Anthony patted Maada on his back as he spoke. "You cannot understand but I am going to help this girl, I cannot leave her here. She will be my wife. I like her and I do not want anything to happen to her. She has suffered too much already. I will talk to the commander about this tonight." Maada said determined.

He said I was the first person he ever saved. There was so much blood on his hands. He had never cared about life or even thought of death. To him, killing was normal. It was a game he was experienced in, and was well trained to do. The verb 'save' was not part of his vocabulary before he met me.

•••••

The next day Maada came to the cell, took me out and told me what had happened, and that I was now to live with him. He told me that all the corpses found by my house had been buried that morning. I was happy that he remembered to bury the corpses, which made me trust him a little bit. He took me to a house he and his colleague Anthony had transformed to their quarters. The floor was full of guns and grenades. That day I became a bush wife, the wife of a fighter. I travelled with Maada across the country as the war intensified, fighting along with him, cooking his food and washing his clothes. Maada became the closest person to me and with time I started forgetting about my loss, and came to love and trust him.

In 1994, I became pregnant with our first child. We were very happy but thinking about the difficulties we were going through, I felt sad for the baby. When the pregnancy got past six months, I started spending more time in the camps set up after a town had been taken. On occasions Maada would leave me for a couple of weeks. During those moments I felt insecure, that someone might hurt me, or that we would be attacked. I begged him to stay closer to me as the time for delivery grew closer. He asked his commander, who agreed, and I was very happy.

•••••

In July of 1995, I gave birth to a baby boy. The older women in my camp assisted me during delivery. I held my baby in my hands and thought about how my mother and cried. Foday was a strong boy. He was a child of the bush. When he started eating, he ate anything given to him. He seldom cried, thus making my life easier. I was very happy with Maada, and the child. One day Maada asked me, "Do you ever think about how your life would have been if there was no war and you had continued living in your town?" I could not answer him. I opened my mouth twice to speak but could not find the right words. When I finally found them I said, "I would probably still be in school." I could see that the answer impacted him, and he changed the subject. As more and more Government soldiers were killed and some captured during battles, I wondered what had happened to my father. I wondered if he knew that my mother had been killed. I described my father to Maada and asked him not to shoot a soldier that looked like him. I was just being naïve. I knew that in the battlefields, if you did not shoot the enemy, the enemy would shoot you. Either way someone was bound to die. My son told me once that he wanted to be a fighter like his father. His favourite toy was a gun his father brought for him from Kono.

Two years after having Foday, I became pregnant again and gave birth to Unisa. During this period, Maada got shot on the arm and relocated to undergo treatment at the camp in Kailahun, so we went with him. The camp was beautiful and very far away from the fighting. It was a hard life I was living, and I knew my children were also finding it difficult. But for them, that was all they knew. They never complained because they didn't know better.

One day we came under attack as we were going from Makeni to Magburaka. We thought that we had secured the area not knowing that there was an ambush planned by Government soldiers. Foday was with me. As soon as we were attacked, I tied him to my back. I was able to fight for two hours, helping to clear the ambush. At one stage I had to crawl with him on my back. It was not easy but I had to do it, to save him and myself. After that encounter, Maada became worried and anxious as the fighting traumatised Foday who continuously cried and becomes restless at night. He asked me to stay at the camp in Kailahun and take care of the children there, not wanting anything to happen to them.

The camp was full of life. The children were very happy to meet children their age. They were always playing football, or acting as soldiers, running after each other with guns. My heart leapt for joy when one day I asked Unisa what he wanted to be when he grew up, and he said a musician. Music was a source of love. I wanted my children to know love, not hate. From that day I started singing to him. I also asked Maada to find a tape for him so he could be listening to music. When we got the tape, the only cassette available was Michael Jackson's 'Thriller' album. So day-in and day-out he listened to it when he was not playing football. Songs like 'Billie Jean' and "Wanna be Startin Something" could regularly be heard coming from our hut. Within days people started calling Unisa, 'Unisa Jackson'. "Why are you smiling? You have something on your mind. Please tell me." Maada asked me as we sat in our little world. Maada was a very gentle person especially when he was not fighting.

"Nothing" I lied. Then I kissed our children, sending them to go out and play. They were now our only source of hope, and the products of our love. At times I thought of the irony of Maada being a killer, like I had become, contrasting with the caring father and husband he was. I pushed the thought away and concentrated on being not only a bush wife but also now a bush mother, with two bush babies to devote my life to.

Don't Stop, Just Run

"There is no way we can try to escape without being caught. There are rebels everywhere, and even if we end up escaping from the ones that are holding us captives, we will be captured on the way again. And if we running away, where will we flee to? The village is now in the hands of rebels. We need to think through this instead of getting ourselves killed for doing something stupid." Sahid always shot down my breakout plans and it was frustrating. I had made several attempts to convince him to join me, but he was always coming up with different reasons not to. He was convincing the others also not to take a risk as big as the one I was proposing. It was really getting on my nerves but rather than take any action alone, I decided to remain calm and do all the talking to convince the others to see reason in my great plan. "If we stay here we will be used, and when the rebels are tired of us they will kill us. Look at me! I am not going to die here. Many people have escaped and they have never been caught. The only way you can acquire freedom is by trying. The security here is not tight as most of the rebels have gone to the battlefront. This is the time to do it, and we have to do it. It will be impossible to run-away when they return. If you are not coming, I will go alone. For how long will I be a load-carrier? My neck is almost stiff from years of hard labour. If I do this for one more month, I will die so at least let me die while trying to be a free man."

I looked at the others as I spoke to see if there was anyone who would support me. Everyone kept quiet, so I continued my preaching. "I know you are all afraid to take this risk, I am afraid too, but we do not have an option. It will be better if all of us take it together and watch out for each other. We cannot make it to Guinea even though it's very close, because the Guineans have secured their border. They will kill even a fly that tries to cross it. We all heard what the rebels were saying last week after they went close to the border. Our only chance is to head for Freetown. Though it is far away we can reach there and be safe." "Let's be real here. You think Freetown is like going to Bamoi and back? Freetown is very far away from here. We will never make it. I have only been to Freetown twice and I cannot even remember the way," Sahid protested, again. I wondered why the others were not taking part in the discussion. I countered, "I know the way. You need not worry about that. I know every forest route from here to Port Loko. Once we reach there, getting to Freetown is easy. You can never get lost, no matter how stupid you are." Kofie asked me, "How do we leave here?"

"When they send us into the forest to get wood for the kitchen, we go and never come back. It will take a long time before they will notice that we have not returned. By then, we will be a long way from here. No one will have the time to go looking for us." I was confident, and I wanted them to know it. "Initially they were sending someone to watch us when we went to get wood, remember, but now they let us go by ourselves. So they must believe we won't run away. Tomorrow we have a chance to leave here. We go with nothing, just the machetes and the ropes to tie the wood, so they will not suspect anything." "Do you think it will be as easy as you are suggesting? There are rebels crawling all over this area. If we are caught we will be as good as dead," Sahid objected again. I then realised that he clearly did not like

148

my idea. I asked him "O.K. Sahid tell me exactly what you want us to do. Continue staying here? We are as good as dead here too." "I am not saying that. I am only trying to say we have to be careful." "Sahid, you are older than all of us. The way you are speaking should reflect that. Saying we should be careful does not suggest anything. What do you want us to do?" He answered "I want to go but I am scared."

The tension that had built up in me subsided and I relaxed for the first time since we began the conversation that afternoon. We were in an open field, where we sat when we had nothing to do. The rebels saw us as part of them and they were never bothered when they saw us sitting and talking together. I went through the plan a few more times with everyone, and finally we were set for the next day.

•••••

We were five in number. Sahid was the oldest at 18. I was 17, Jack and Raymond were 16 and Kofie was 14. Sahid, Kofie, and I were from the same village, Rolal, in Kambia district, while Jack and Raymond were from Kychom, also in the Kambia district. We had all been captured in Bamoi, where people from the neighboring villages meet to trade their farm products. We had taken some of the rice our parents had harvested so we could sell it. The rebels chose that day to attack the town. They descended on the town in their hundreds. There was no escape point as the rebels had surrounded the market place and hundreds of people were killed, and scores more suffered from bullet wounds that day. We were lying on the ground beside our sacks of rice until the rebels reached us. They were very brutal as one of them hit my face with the butt of a handgun. There was blood all over my face.

"What are you doing here?" one of the rebels asked us. Sahid answered, "We are here to sell our rice." "So you are farmers. You will be useful to us. Come." We followed him. He saw that we had left the rice behind.

"The rice is more useful than you. If you do not pick those bags up, you will find yourselves dead beside them." He watched as we lifted the heavy sacks. "Lazy boys, you eat a lot but do nothing. Carry the bags before I kick your asses." There were rebels loading onto the trucks, scattered goods left by traders who took different directions. Even though this was not the first attack I had witnessed, it was the first time I had been caught. We kept up with each other as we followed the rebel, who had found a pack of beer and was drinking it as he walked. There was a happy smile on his face. I wondered why he was smiling.

There were dead bodies scattered around us and our captor stumbled on one, caught his balance and said, "He is jealous, he wants my beer." Then he poured some into the dead man's mouth. "You see, he is drinking. He is not dead." He shot the corpse twice. "That is for drinking my beer." After seeing this I became utterly afraid. I realised he was a mad man who could do anything. I wondered why he had not turned on us yet.

Together with the rest of those captured and their captors, we made our way to Kambia Town, which had fallen by the time we reached it. There were simultaneous attacks on the two towns. The soldiers that were stationed in Kambia were either killed or taken captive. As we reached the town, our captor told us, "You will be my slaves while I am here. I love this place. This is where I was born. I promised some people here that after several years, they would see me again. I told them that when they saw me, it would be the last time that they would ever see anything. I am back, and this time they will pay." He sounded crazy and was repeating himself as he spoke. He was talking mostly to himself as we walked. "I was driven out of this town because they said I was a thief. I am not a thief. I just take, and you would not dare tell me not to take. Everything in this town belongs to its people. I am a human being and I am from this town. After eight years I am back, and this time I will make some people leave. They will never see this town again. My mother was killed here. They said she was a witch who sucked the blood of children. They killed her, cut up her body into bits, and left her to be eaten by vultures and dogs. They then threw me out, calling me a thief."

Another rebel walking by his side said to him, "Show us the people and we will show them what witches and wizards can do." Our captor then drew out another can of beer from his pack. He emptied its content in one go, throwing the empty can at me.

As slaves of rebels, Kambia became our new home. Our lives were miserable. If you were caught sleeping when someone needed you, they kicked the hell out of you. When we were not helping to cook, we were either cutting wood or washing the clothes of the rebels. Our captor became our lord until his time came to go to the front. Those were not pleasant times; when he got drunk or was high with drugs he made us sing and dance for him. We received slaps and kicks as he joined the dance, but we were never allowed to say anything. When he was semi-normal, he looked for ways to punish us like spitting on our face or making us lie on the ground with him putting his feet on us and beating us with sticks. When he finished smoking, he would put out the cigarette on the back or the head of anyone who happened to be around him. We carried his weapon when he walked around the town and he introduced us as his slaves. Sometimes when he was very normal, or even sober, he was relatively nice to us, or at least not evil. Then he would tell us stories of the battles he had fought and about his past before becoming a rebel. But he was hardly ever sober so those occasions were rare.

On one occasion he returned home with three heads in a bag, and said, "These ones made me unhappy as a child, and today, they have paid. I want to see their faces every minute to remind myself that I have succeeded in avenging." He walked towards us holding what was the head of an elderly looking woman. "Never let someone walk over you. When they hit you, hit them back, and if you can't, wait, for one day your time will come." That was something he should not have said to us, for he was hitting us now and he should have remembered his words, but he was drunk. We had to be attentive so he would not lose his temper, but his words had registered in our young brains. He drank heavily that night and pissed on himself as he slept. I had to wash his clothes the next day. The stench was unbearable. I hated doing it but I had no option. Any act of defiance would surely be the signing of my death certificate.

We all had to fend for ourselves. Since food was very scarce, we spent our time helping the cooks in the preparation of the food, after which we had to wash all the pots and kitchen utensils before we were given small portions of food. We were losing weight rapidly, and I did not want such a life to continue. With the rebels, one could never be sure of what the future would bring and I was not willing to stay around long enough to find out.

•••••

The next day we tried to appear as normal as possible, doing different tasks to avoid being together. Captain Jones, who oversaw what the women did in the kitchen, called us at 10 a.m. "Do I have to remind you boys that wood is needed?" I was very happy, in my heart. He was creating our window of opportunity without knowing it. He was sending us to our freedom and it was very welcomed. I said to him, "We are going to get wood for sure. We know that is our duty. I only thought that we should wait until mid-day to do it." "What makes you think that mid-day is the best time to fetch wood? I think you boys need some inspiration. You seem to have forgotten that you are not in your parents' house. Follow me." He whacked the hell out of us despite the pleas we made. He was a horrible person who was always angry.

He was particularly unkind to us, even though we were not expecting him to be kind to us at all. "Now you will not forget what instructions are. The day you make me remind you again will be your last day in this world. Now get the hell out of here before I kick more sense into you." He used sticks to beat us. He had hit me on my head with the stick so hard that a bump formed. I was prepared to go through anything, for I was very sure it would be the last day of such treatment. The beating, I could tell, had helped to strengthen the resolve of the others too. Kofie told me, as we looked for the ropes we used to tie woods, "He can beat as much as he wants, as long as he does not kill us. Very soon, this will be a thing of the past. If he thinks we are drums he can beat, then he should be looking for new drums, for these ones are going away this time."

I was happy to hear him say that since he was the youngest of us all, he would undoubtedly have more difficulties going through what we were about to undertake. I asked Sahid if he was ready, He replied whispering, "You are asking me that? I am getting the hell out of this damn place today. I do not mind being shot out there or being eaten by a wild animal but I will not stay here to be beaten by that man any longer."

We had learnt that all of our villages had fallen into the hands of rebels. People were massacred each time the attacks took place. There were people from my village who had been captured and were now imprisoned in what used to be the old police station. They could not believe that we were used as helpers instead of being killed or turned into fighters. They were certainly treated worse than we were, but life was not easy for us either. The rebels considered us to be part of them, though we knew in our hearts that it would never be the case. "I think we do not have to wait until mid-day. That fucker will come again and if he sees us around, we will be sorry for it. Let's go now," Sahid advised. He was right.

We picked up the ropes and the machetes and started our slow march into the forest. The wind was blowing a little bit stronger that morning and it was cold. The forest was close to the town. So, after ten minutes we were out of sight. We continued in silence as we marched in a straight line towards the place where we normally cut wood, which was about 20 minutes from the entrance of the forest. When we could no longer see the town, we put the machetes and the ropes down and pretended to be cutting wood, wanting to be very sure that we were not being followed. We knew that this was not the case but out of anxiety, we were all being overly cautious. We were so close to freedom that we wanted to make sure nothing went wrong. Jack said in a whisper, "What do we do now?" Sahid replied, "We take the machetes with us until we reach a distance where we think we will be safe and we throw them away and keep on moving." Jack was not in for the idea of going with the machetes. "If anyone sees us with them, then we will be regarded as hostiles and we might be shot at. If we leave them we can argue that we missed the way to our farm and got lost in the forest."

"Forget that story. No one will buy it. If they ask you where the farm is, what will you say?" Raymond joined in. "Even a little child won't believe you. Five boys, who have all missed the road to their farms?" "I know no one takes seriously what I say, I have no brain at all. You make all the decisions, I will follow you." He moved away from us. I went to him. "This is the wrong time to start getting angry with each other. At this time, we need each other if we are to survive. Any disagreement among us will be dangerous at this point, please." He joined us again. We decided that we would take the machetes but will throw them away when we are close to Port Loko. Adrenaline kicking in, we moved hurriedly through the forest; our journey towards freedom had begun. The clothes we were wearing could not protect us from the angry wind that was furiously blowing. A storm was on the way. If it catches up with us it will affect our movement. I could see Raymond and Kofie putting their hands around their chest as they walked. I tried to be strong; we had crossed the point of no return.

•••••

Forests often have an aura of quietness and calm about them that draws strong fear when you are going through them, especially with the anticipation of coming across people you do not want to meet. At the slightest sound, the forest in its serene state becomes very noisy at the time you want quietness. You step on twigs and leaves that give your position away. The leaves rustle in the breeze as you pass. As a child I used to play hide and seek in the forest in our village a lot. But I always stepped on a twig at the wrong time and got caught. I prayed that the forest would be friendly to us today, at least for the time that we would be in it. We took routes that were not very clear and had lots of undergrowth to conceal us as we moved. Luckily, everyone had experienced the forest as kids so we moved through easily. All our villages have forests, so it was not a new territory for us. We walked for two hours, only slowing down when we needed to speak, or when someone thought he heard a noise and made a sign for us to stop. We had developed signals in order for us to minimize talking or making sounds that would attract anyone who might be close by. If we were going to come out of this alive, we would have to take every precautionary measure, the most important of which, is silence.

We had nothing to eat or drink. That had been missed out in our grand escape plan. The heat and hunger started getting the better of us all after three hours of brisk walking. I noticed Kofie slowing down and asking for a chance to rest for a while. I had been so obsessed with escaping that I had never thought of food until Kofie said to me, "I do not know how to say this, but I am very hungry. I think we should look for something to eat before moving on." Then, we heard gunshots from the direction we had come from. Even though they sounded far away, we were afraid. Sahid whose face portrayed all forms of fear said, "They know that we have escaped. They are coming after us. Let us leave here now." We were practically tearing through the forest as we ran, trying to get as far as possible before the rebels came any closer. We avoided every village in our path, going deeper into the forest whenever we saw smoke rising ahead of us, probably from people cooking or burning wood. We believed that the entire district was now in rebel hands, so any activity suggestive of inhabitation would have something to do with rebels.

After another two hours of running and fast-paced walking, going deeper and deeper into the forest, the storm caught up with us. It was a very terrible storm, with thunder rumbling and lightning flashing all over the forest. I have always been terrified of thunder and lightning because there is a belief in my village that the lightning is an axe that falls from the sky and can cut a person into two. So whenever you see it you should hide, or you will meet the same fate. Thunders are said to be God rolling his drums in heaven. Everybody was as scared as I was yet we kept on moving undeterred by the rain, thunder or lightning; our fear of the savage rebels catching up to us should we stop or slow down was at that moment far greater than our fears for the natural elements. The heavy rains however remained as persistent as we were. After an hour or more, Jack stopped us, "I cannot move anymore if I do not eat, let's find something to eat." We scouted all the nearby trees. We saw bananas that were mouth-watering. We hungrily devoured them, forgetting that the rebels may be pursuing us.

Despite being the youngest of us, Kofie had the largest appetite, and so went for a second bunch and ate it as if it were his first. Satiated from my banana meal, I attempted to drink the water that was dripping from the

156

leaves to quench my thirst, but it had a bad taste. So I stopped after the first attempt and told the others that we should look out for a stream along the way instead and not risk drinking the rainwater. Raymond protested, "What if we do not come across a stream anytime soon? I will drink this. I know it won't kill me. In the jungle, everything is good. At this moment we do not pick and choose, everything goes. I am drinking whether you like it or not." So he drank, and Kofie followed him. I could see Sahid looking at me as they drank. I was not happy with the tone of voice Raymond spoke to me in, but I knew we were all exhausted so it was easy for tempers to flare up. So I let it go and pretended to be looking for more fruits. When everyone was satisfied, we continued our journey.

No stream was in sight, but I was not prepared to drink the water from the leaves of the forest. Prior to being captured, I had fallen ill from a sickness called typhoid, which I was told by the village doctor, I had caught from drinking infected water. The memories of what I went through before getting healed were still fresh in my mind. That night we took refuge in an abandoned farmhouse where we managed to catch some sleep, though we stayed seated on the cold wet floors. The house provided little protection from the wind and the rain as most of the roof had been blown off. My sleep was regularly disturbed by the wind. At one stage, I thought I heard people moving. I went out and looked around to see if there was anyone coming. Raymond had woken up when I left as I met him peeping out of the door. The rest were sound asleep. So we tried to make as little noise as we could so they would rest well, for there would be new challenges the next day.

•••••

Around dawn, the storm subsided. We set off then, looking for food again. This time we stumbled upon an abandoned farm. I helped myself to more than a dozen bananas, guavas and mangoes. Everybody ate as if it was their last day on earth. We found a bag and filled it up with fruits that should last us for the rest of the day. Kofie attempted taking up the bag when we decided to leave, but it was too heavy. "We do not need a very big bag of fruits. We will find more as we move on. Anybody who sees us with a bag like this will be suspicious and we might get into trouble," Sahid advised. "Besides, it will slow down our movement," Jack also added. While there was sense in what they were saying I knew why Jack had made that comment. He was the laziest and would not want to take turns in carrying the bag. But he was right. At a time like this, speed was our best ally. Any deterring factor should be avoided at all cost. The day started in a promising way. I hoped it would continue that way. We reduced the contents of the bag we ate more to ensure that we would remain full for a long time. Within an hour our stomachs reacted and we all took to different directions to empty our bowels.

We continued moving as the weather improved. On approaching the edge of the forest we started seeing familiar sites, which indicated that we were getting close to Port Loko. There were plenty of rice fields. The forest became scantier and scantier due to the deforestation in the area. We started walking through rice fields, which were thick with mud. Sometimes we were knee deep in the mud, which was dangerous. But as children of farmers, we knew how to survive in swamps.

In Port Loko we found an abandoned hut in the district and decided to rest, as we were exhausted. Jack and Kofie after resting for a while began to fight over the last of the bananas. We had saved only few bananas because under the weight of the other fruits they would be easily crushed. I took a mango, and Sahid with Raymond decided to share a coconut. Kofie took the banana, but Jack claimed he was the one that put the banana in the bag, so a bitter argument ensued.

"If you do not give me that banana, I swear I will kill you," Jack said moving closer to Kofie who peeled the banana and put it in his mouth. As he did so, Jack sprang on him like a wild cat and it was all commotion. Kofie was trying to put the whole banana into his mouth and Jack was trying to prevent him from doing it. The rest of us attempted to separate them but Kofie's head was firmly tucked under Jack's arm. Jack was squeezing it with all the strength left in him. While struggling to pull them apart, we heard a familiar clicking sound. I turned immediately and saw men with guns behind us. "If you move, I will shoot" the lady closest to us said. Arms went into the air and what we had prayed against was once again our reality. There were about six rebels fully armed with leaves tied to their bodies, which I believe they had been using as camouflage. "Who sent you here? You are spies! Who sent you?" The lady asked us as we were made to sit on the ground. "No one, we were just around looking for wood so we could cook tonight," Sahid said looking a bit calm. I was very afraid, I was not sure this group would let us live as our last boss did. They seemed to be ready for action. "Which village are you from?" She asked again.

I stepped in knowing Port Loko more than all of the others. "We are from Petifu. We will return as soon as we get some wood. We do not live in this area. We only come for wood." "Come, we will show you where to find wood." I almost pissed on myself when she said that. When a rebel tells you something like that, you should be very scared as you may be killed. We were led into the forest and as we walked into it we heard sign calls. We noticed rebels on trees and some lying on the grass. A tall rebel walking behind us with the lady said, "These are spies. They have been sent to see where we are. These boys don't look ordinary to me." "They will talk." "You know me, don't worry." My fears were confirmed. We were now in hot water with no hope of surviving. I felt sad at that moment, because I was the one that had convinced the others to escape. However, I decided to forget about my deep regret in that moment. I needed to maintain a sharp focus. We were stopped when we reached a place where we met about five rebels looking at what seemed to be a map. "We saw these boys by the forest. We believe they must be spies. We should have killed them but we wanted to ask you what to do. The sound from shooting them may have betrayed our position. They said that they came from Petifu, the area close to the airport, where we expected the enemies to come from."

My heart and pulse beat increased; I had added salt to our injury. I could see four pairs of eyes piercing through my flesh. The lady called on the other rebels. "Bring them." "I am very busy here. Go ahead, try to make them talk and after that we will see what happens," the one holding the map said. He seemed to be in control. 'O.K' she made a sign to the others who led us towards the point she was heading. We were undressed and made to sit on thorny branches and leaves that were scattered on the forest floor. That was painful and it felt like my behind was on fire. I tried drawing out some of the thorns that had pierced me, but the lady thought I wanted to try something. "If your hand ever goes behind your back again, I will cut it off. Don't try being smart here. It will only make things worse for you. I know how to deal with people like you. Now, we are going to have a friendly conversation. You should tell me the truth, because if you don't you will regret it. Who wants to talk first?"

We looked at each other. Then Sahid started to talk, "We are from Petifu and we have no reason to lie. We only came to this area for wood like we said, and this will be our last time. From now on we will go somewhere else." "Do you think I am stupid? I do not want you to waste my time. If you do not start talking, I will kill you." She asked Kofie to stand up and get closer to her. Her eyes were wild. "Sit here, boy." She pointed to the ground close to her as she spoke. "I will mutilate this boy for every second you waste, and when I finish with him I will take another and another, and you will talk." We all started crying. She knelt on the ground close to Kofie and started rubbing her knife on his face. She asked her colleague, "Where do you think I should start cutting, his nose or his ears?" Everything that represents fear was in us now. I was shaking inside out. Kofie vomited on himself. It was the worst moment of my life.

"Now, talk!" she demanded, with the knife on Kofie. Sahid began again, "Please do not hurt us. We are innocent boys looking for wood. We are not spies." "You think we are joking here. We mean business. Let me show you an example of what I can do," she grabbed Kofie's head and rammed her knees into his face. She got up and kicked him as hard as she could. There was blood all over Kofie's face and I could see that one of his hands was in bad shape, since he tried to block the kick with it. I tried getting up to reach him but I was pushed down and stamped on with the boot of one of the rebels who had his gun on my hand. "One more try and you are dead." We begged the lady with all our hearts, crying to appeal to any sense of compassion, but I could see that there was none in her. She was determined to produce the result she wanted, and unfortunately there was no way we could help her, for we were not the spies she thought us to be, and to say we were would only have made matters worse. We would be killed instantly, and not freed. To continue saying we are not would only postpone the inevitable, for we would surely be killed after a long time of torture. We were now between a rock and a hard place.

"Do you want to talk or not?" We all kept silent, not knowing what to say. "I see you are hard to break. I will bend you so far that you will vomit every word you are keeping in your stomachs. I will make you talk. You will talk without knowing you are talking and if you make it easy for me, I will make it easy for you. But if you make it difficult, I will make it very difficult. I will count up to ten, and if I do not hear anything sensible, your friend suffers." "One, two, three," and when she reached eight, I spoke. "We have told you the truth, we have no business with anyone and no one has sent us here. If that were the case we would have spoken. We cannot keep quiet and die for the sake of someone else. We do not know anyone in the military and no one in the military knows us." "Shut up, you stupid liar! Boys like you have betrayed our positions and have made us fall into ambush. They all lied like you are doing. The person that trains you knows how to do his job. My business is to make you talk and I am not just repeating myself, I want to assure you." She made Kofie stand up. He could not open his eyes and I could see one was swollen. "Tell me the truth and I'll set you free. Who sent you?" she asked Kofie.

Kofie could not answer her. He could not even stand still. She then did what we never expected she would do this early. She brought Kofie very close to her, bent her head slightly to his left ear like she wanted to say something to him and then drove her knife into his heart. We could not believe what we had seen. Blood pumped out of Kofie as she drew out her knife. Kofie fell slowly holding his chest as he kicked out and came under the grip of death. It all ended as suddenly as it started. We were consumed by silence after witnessing the most horrible scene of our lives. She broke the silence by pointing at Raymond. "You, come here," she said beckoning to one of the rebels to push aside the body of Kofie. Raymond stood by her and cried, "Please, do not kill me. I have not done anything wrong, please!" "The only thing you are doing wrong is refusing to talk. You can make it easy for all of us if you talk. You know the rules. If you do not talk, I will do the same to you as I did to him," she said, pointing to Kofie. "I will begin counting again one, two, three, and four," Sahid stopped her. "Let me tell you the truth." "We escaped from Kambia. We are on our way to Freetown. We are not spies. We have never been spies," he began. "So you escaped from Kambia, where we have established peace for everyone? This fight is for Sierra Leoneans. We are sacrificing ourselves and you do not appreciate us?" With those words she shot Sahid in his stomach and chest killing him instantly.

"Now we have two stories here. What is the third one? I need the truth. You people are not taking me seriously. But I will get an answer, believe me." Then we heard rapid succession of gunshots coming from the other section of the forest. A second outburst indicated that there was an attack. The lady paused, not fully sure what was happening. By now, there was shooting all over, and the sounds were getting louder. She took a quick look at us then dashed off in the direction we had come from. The other rebels followed her, leaving us behind. I turned to Jack and Raymond. We gathered our clothes and started sprinting like springboks. I had dropped one of my slippers as I ran, but slippers I would get some day. My life, I will never get back again if I lose it. We ran for over an hour and we could hear loud explosions going off from where we had been, where our friends were lying dead. The three of us kept as close together as we could be. When we had reached a safe distance, we stopped to put our clothes back on and also to rest for a while. The shooting now sounded far away. I thought of Kofie and Sahid, who had been with us only a short time ago. But I will cry later, I said to myself.

•••••

We walked again for two more hours before reaching villages I recognised. This time we had actually taken the direction that led to the airport, the area where Petifu actually was. We kept off the main road and away from any human contact. We ate oranges that had fallen from trees and drank water from a stream that ran across a village. After another hour of walking, in silence, we saw the fence of the airport. We were very happy, for at least we had seen a sign of freedom, and we knew that the airport was under Government control. We had finally

163

made it. At that point we cried bitterly, as we remembered and mourned our fallen friends. Five of us had set out on a journey and only three were about to achieve our long awaited, much anticipated freedom.

As we got closer to the airport, we started coming across people, but we knew that they were harmless, for we had observed their activities from a safe distance and had deduced they were normal civilians. We kept on walking without talking to anyone, our only aim being to reach the airport from where we would find a way to reach Freetown. People looked at us as we walked, but we kept our focus and continued towards the airport gate. When we reached the airport gate we met ECOMOG soldiers from Ghana. We explained to them where we were from and what had happened to us. They took us to their commander who through the help of an interpreter asked us to explain, over and over again, what we had seen and what had happened. He confirmed that ECOMOG and Government troops had attacked the rebels at Port Loko, and the battle was ongoing.

"I will not keep you here. I have called the United Nations Children's Fund office and will hand you over to them soon; they will take care of you. I am sorry that you had to go through all that you have explained. I will ask our troops to look for the bodies of your friends, so they can be buried. While you wait, you can have some food." We were given yams, fish and water. Even though I had looked forward, for a very long time, to the day I would have proper food like the one in front of me, I lost every form of appetite as I thought of Kofie and Sahid. They were like brothers to me. I cried, not believing what had happened to us within such a short space of time. My tears made the others cry as well. The Ghanaian commander and his soldiers tried to calm us down. As soldiers, they understood what had happened to us, for they must have lost colleagues in the field. We were not soldiers, but victims of the harsh reality of a war we did not

164

understand, a war we did nothing to bring about. We left the food almost untouched. An hour later, the United Nations Children's Fund (UNICEF) official, a white woman by name Rose, arrived. We were handed over to her and she thanked the commander and his soldiers for reaching out to her. We joined Rose in her vehicle, as free people, but we had paid the price for that freedom in a very bitter way.

My Gun, My Life

"I hope the talks fail. I don't want the war to end. Where will we go if it ends? I can't go back to my family. They will kill me after all I did to them. If I had known that this is how it would end, I would not have joined." Kalokoh was very angry with our commanders for going to the peace talk in Lome, Togo. I understood his fears. Most of us were uncertain of what the future would bring. We had been in the bush for too long. It was now our home and we had never thought of the possibility of one day leaving it and making peace with those we had seen as enemies, those we had been commanded to kill. "You don't have to worry. Do you know how many times they have met and yet there has been no peace? Do you think Papay is foolish enough to make peace with them? If we make peace, we are all dead. Once we mix with them, they will find a way of killing us." I assured Kalokoh. I did not even want to think about the possibility of going back to my village. I knew my family would not welcome me. They would not want a rebel in their midst and I did not want to go back to them.

"Papay should know that one should never trust his enemy. Your enemy will only pretend to love you when you have the upper hand. Now the government is losing, and they know it. After the January 6th attack on Freetown, it became clear to them that they can't stop us. That's why they are asking for a peace agreement to be signed. When we were not that strong, they never asked for a ceasefire or for a peace agreement. Their helicopters were chasing us everywhere, bombing the shit out of us, and now they want peace. I don't know who is advising Papay, but he should not commit to a peace agreement." Kalokoh, who was one year older than me, had spent six years of his life as a fighter. We fought together at Waterloo while trying to enter Freetown and since then we had been good friends. We were now stationed at Mile 38 after our retreat from Freetown. Mile 38 is a beautiful town with lush green sceneries. For some time it was no man's land until we finally captured it.

"Kalokoh, let's imagine for once that the war comes to an end. Do you think they will forget about us? Papay knows there are thousands of people looking up to him and their future is in his hands. We have sacrificed a lot. I do not think he will let us down." I argued, trying to be optimistic. "Talk like a man! You are still a boy. Do you believe Papay will care about us once he is given a position in Freetown? Does he know your name or my name? We will be abandoned and left to perish in the bush. We will have to find our own way out. Haven't you been listening to the stories of the boys from Liberia? Once their Papay became president he forgot about them. They had to come here to find a way of surviving. I have never even seen Papay. I have just been hearing about him." The points he raised made me ask myself some real hard questions. What if he was right and we were abandoned? What will we do, how will we survive? "Ok, let's say we get abandoned. What are we going to do?" I asked him, perplexed. "I don't know about you, but I will kill myself. It will make things easy for me. I can't face my people after all these years. I have told you what I did before running away and joining this group."

•••••

Kalokoh was the son of a schoolteacher in Sanda Magbolontoh. He had killed his aunt and his cousin in the presence of other residents when he became a rebel and

167

had access to a gun. He said they were cruel to him, and he left the village after killing them. He knew that his people would exact cruel vengeance on him when the opportunity to do so presented itself. Any peace agreement therefore would leave him vulnerable to his past. He was a worried man. I tried to calm him down by saying "Taking Freetown is the only way to have peace. The discussions are just a show; it will go nowhere. Trust me, our commanders are very intelligent. They will not do anything that will not be in the interest of the movement. It is for them that we are fighting. Let me tell you, if anything goes wrong, we will suffer for sure, but they will suffer more than us. Let's forget about this and find something to eat."

"Moseray, all you think about is food. Is it a tank you have there, with your belly like a goat" he laughed touching my stomach and saying, "As for me, I am not in an eating mood." "Not even for fried chicken?" I teased him. I knew that was his favourite. "If it is chicken, I will take it, but nothing else." I convinced him and he followed me. I left my gun with him and climbed a mango tree that was full of inviting and very juicy mangoes. As I picked the mangoes, I threw them down to Kalokoh who caught them and put them on the ground so they would not be damaged. As I proceeded to another branch, I heard the unmistakable hissing of a snake. I turned slowly and saw a black mamba on the branch I had to use to climb up the tree. It was over six feet long and very big. I knew it was quite poisonous and that I had to avoid it at all cost. I had never been so scared in my life, especially of a snake. I had killed several them as we moved along jungle paths but with this and being in a vulnerable position, I knew I was the prey in this case. I moved up the branch gingerly. I was pointing to the snake so Kalokoh would see it and distract it away from me, but he did not notice and rather thought I was pointing to a mango.

"Yeah, it looks nice, that should be mine, throw it down so I can eat it now." I cursed him in my mind for being stupid. I avoided speaking because I did not want to create any loud or sudden noise, afraid that it would only make the snake angry. I shifted slightly, somehow stepped on a fragile branch, which snapped, and down I went. I landed heavily on my buttocks, struggled up and ran like a mad man. Kalokoh, who seemed confused by my action, took my gun and ran after me leaving the mangoes behind. I rested at a safe distance and now checked to see if I had sustained any injury or broken any bones. I was in great pain, particularly on the side where I had landed but at that point I was just thankful that I had gotten away from the six-foot long reptile.

"What happened? You scared the shit out of me. I thought we were under attack, but I heard no gun shot. What's getting into you? You almost killed yourself there." Kalokoh asked as he helped me clean the dirt from the minor bruises I had sustained. "I saw a poisonous snake on the tree; a black mamba can you imagine." I managed to say. "A snake? You can't be serious. Is that why you ran as if the devil himself was chasing you? Ah, just because of a snake! If you had seen a lion, then you would have collapsed immediately." He said, laughing tirelessly. "If bullets have not killed me, I will not let myself be killed by a snake. It's better I run from it and remain alive than face it and get bitten and die." I was angry at him for making light of my close call; and what a senseless death it would have been – to have survived all those fights and bullets only to die at the hands of some stupid snake. But after a while, I started laughing as well when I thought of the way I got up and ran thinking that the snake would fall on me. Kalokoh refused to return to our base without mangoes so he went back for them and we ate them as we walked back to the base.

Four days later, a meeting was scheduled at the base for 5:00 p.m. that afternoon. Kalokoh woke me up to inform me. I yelled at him, "You should have waited till I got up. I was on guard last night and now you have ruined my sleep." But Kalokoh was insistent, "My friend, you better get up. You were not like this. Now you sleep every minute." He was right. I had become lazy since we entered Mile 38. We had not had a military operation since. I wanted to catch up on sleep as I had a backlog I needed to clear. I covered my ears as he continued to talk, "I heard that the peace agreement has been signed. That is what they want to talk to us about this afternoon."

Adrenaline instantly pumped through me; the lethargy shook off. "That cannot be true. What do you mean?" I said, fully awake. Kalokoh answered sarcastically, "I do not know. Ask them when you see them. I told you these guys only care about themselves, not us. You never take what I say seriously, but now you will believe me." "Where did you get this information?" I asked him, as I sat up completely surprised that our leaders could agree to peace at a moment when we had the upper hand. "The commander asked me to fetch him some water and when I returned he was speaking on the radio with someone. I overheard the person instructing him to tell everyone about what was happening. He did not seem happy. He was swearing when I left him." "If all the commanders do not agree on this, I do not believe it will work. First we have to hear what they have to say at the meeting" I said, struggling to be hopeful. "What do you think they will say that's different from what they have been instructed to tell us?" Kalokoh was killing every ounce of optimism in me and it was very painful; I knew he was right. However, I refused to believe that our commanders would abandon us. These were people we relied on for our security. If they let us down, we were doomed. As I sat in silence, I started thinking of my past and my future, what my life outside the movement would look like, and what my chances of survival were.

•••••

At the age of twelve, I became a rebel after being forced to kill my mother and brothers. Under the influence of drugs I shot them without even flinching. Though I had a thin frame, I was quite tall and strong. The height was from my mother's side. I was told my father was a short man. The Madingo people, the tribe from which my mother was from, are tall, elegant, dark skinned, and have sparkling white teeth. Because of my towering height and ruthlessness, I became famous as I joined other boys of my age and went into challenging battles. This made our commanders proud of us. I went to my village several times; killing people who had not treat me right when I was a child. With time I became known as 'The Terrible', a name I adored. Despite meeting children of my age and fighting with them, I seldom spoke to them. Kalokoh was the first person I could call my friend. As my thoughts alternated between my past and present, my fears grew stronger as I agitated over what the future held for me. Patiently, I waited for 5 p.m., which felt like light years away.

•••••

The commander came to the field where the meeting was to be held. I saw him with two white men and a man that looked to be Sierra Leonean standing by a white Toyota jeep. They were dressed in brown jackets, with sunglasses and hats on. Four chairs had been set up for the commander, the black man, and the two white men. The rest of us sat on the grass. I observed the facial expressions of the others; everybody was eager to hear what was going to be said. The commander began by introducing the two men, Hans Kroeger and James Forde from the United Nations (UN) Headquarters in New York. Desmond, the black guy, was their interpreter. Hans who seemed to be older than James was smiling as if he had discovered some hidden treasure. "Comrades, I called you here today because something very important is going on and I want you all to know as early as possible. You have

171

been the foot soldiers. You are the movement and the movement is you." We all applauded. The commander was a brilliant speaker and could easily move people. He continued as the clapping waned, "Papay and the government have been in Togo dialoguing and they have signed an agreement to bring the war to an end." No one clapped. I could see some people talking in groups.

The murmuring got loud and the commander demanded order, "Order! Listen to what we have to say and you will have time to ask questions," he continued, "The international community has told us that they will ensure that each and every one of you is assisted to become normal civilians when the peace agreement is implemented. Besides, you will all have a role to play in the process that is beginning now. In the coming weeks, we will be told what to do which I will communicate to you. But from now it is an order. We have a ceasefire and no one should use his or her gun. I repeat, No use of any weapon! If any combatant is caught violating this order, that person will be severely dealt with." I loathed the commander as he uttered those stabbing words. "I will now call on our visitors who will tell us what happened in Togo and what will happen in the coming days as the peace process begins."

Hans started speaking, as Desmond interpreted. It was good that they brought Desmond because no one could understand what he was saying, "One week ago, the world watched as the Government of Sierra Leone and the Revolutionary United Front (RUF) met in Lomé, Togo to find a peaceful solution to the war that has lasted for close to a decade. The war has caught the attention of the world. People are suffering in this beautiful country and we want to help solve the problems that led to the war. Big people, like my boss, the Secretary General of the United Nations, and presidents from different counties here in West Africa, were able to reach the leadership of the Revolutionary United Front and the Government of this country.

Yesterday, they were finally able to commit themselves to begin a peace process that will allow everyone to live in peace."

"Your place is not in the bush. You deserve to live a good life. That is what we intend to assist you achieve. Now I want to tell you what will happen in the coming days. What I am telling you is what we have all agreed to. Very soon, we'll have peacekeepers from all over the world coming to Sierra Leone. These peacekeepers will be responsible for the security of the country and will ensure that the fighting does not continue. They'll then begin a programme called Disarmament, Demobilisation and Reintegration of Ex-Combatants. I will break it down for you so you can understand. During the disarmament period, you will give up your arms and ammunitions. These arms and ammunitions will be collected by the United Nations peacekeepers who will store them in a safe place until we decide what to do with them. You will be given some money for every gun, or ammunition that you turn in. The experts will determine how much you will get. After the disarmament process, you will move on to the demobilisation phase. In this phase, you will be helped to change the way you think at the moment and prepare you to enter normal communities. You will no longer be part of the RUF but citizens that are returning to their communities. Children do not go through demobilisation as they are not recognised as fighters. They would be handed over to specialised agencies such as the United Nations Children's Fund (UNICEF). UNICEF and other similar agencies will facilitate their reintegration process."

I almost died inside when first he spoke of taking our guns from us, then also of returning us to our communities. I looked at Kalokoh whose eyes and expression clearly said, 'I told you so.' I continued listening. "However, we do not want you to go back to your communities with nothing to do, sitting idly at home. So we are now designing programmes that the United

Nations and other agencies will fund. Everybody will be trained in the work they want to do. For example, if you want to be a carpenter, we'll train you and we'll give you materials to begin your work. If you want to operate a computer, we'll train you to operate it. If you want to go back to school, we'll send you to school and support you for a specific period of time. This will be part of your reintegration programme. After the demobilisation programme, we'll get you back into your communities of origin, for those who would want to go back there. For those who do not want to go back to those communities, we'll help you resettle in an area you would like to live in." I turned to Kalokoh who seemed somewhat relieved by this alternative. He made a thumbs-up sign to me to which I reciprocated.

"In the coming days, when we are sure that all parties are committed to the peace process, we'll begin negotiating with communities and together with them, and the leadership of all the parties involved, we'll work out a reintegration plan which will make everyone happy at the end of the day. The reason we are here is to ask all of you to help us make everything I have said here work. Now if you have questions, I'll happily take them". The commander got up and said, "He will take five questions and your hand should be up if you want to ask a question." Several hands went up and 'Crazy lady', a woman any man will have to think twice before confronting asked the first question, "Thank you for coming here to tell us this." I was shocked, that was the first time I heard the words 'thank you', from her. "You spoke well, and at least I know I will have something to do when I leave here, but what will happen to the movement, Papay and our commanders?"

Hans smiled before answering the question, "That is a very good question, thanks for asking it. The peace agreement that was signed in Lomé made possible the establishment of a government of national unity in which the RUF will be playing a crucial part. There will be ministers in the government that will come from the RUF. In fact, the head of the RUF will have the status of vice president. The RUF will now become a political party instead of a fighting force and if anyone here wants to be a politician, he or she can. Your commanders will be helping us in the Disarmament, Demobilisation and Reintegration programme I spoke to you about, as they are all very important people in the peace process."

The second question was asked by Sergeant 'Ta Faikor' which is the Temne word for let's kill him, "If any one refuses to give up his or her gun, what will happen to that person?" "We sincerely hope that everyone will see the benefit of wanting to give up his or her weapon and help move the peace process forward. I strongly believe that you have been fighting because you thought something was going wrong in your country and you wanted to fix it in one way or another. You succeeded in catching the attention of the world. Now you are not alone in the struggle. There are people coming to help, but we want to do it in a peaceful way so no one gets hurt and you can all live to see the changes you dreamed of, changes you were prepared to sacrifice your lives for. I see no reason why anyone would want to hold back his or her weapon. We are fully committed to helping each and every one of you to do what you want to do in life and help move this nation forward. Give this some thought. Think about it and you will see where we are heading."

Kalokoh got the third question slot, "You spoke as if returning to our communities is an easy thing. Do you know what they will do to us if we go back? Some of us might get killed. Taking our guns will make us become vulnerable and our lives will always be in danger." That to me was the most brilliant and important question by far. I patted Kalokoh on the back as he sat down. Several others sitting next to me also patted him and shook his hands. That question was asked for all of us who shared this fear and had spent sleepless nights trying to find a solution but to no avail. We were very attentive as Hans answered the question, "We are very much aware that there are several challenges lying ahead. We know for sure that difficulties are bound to come and some communities will find it difficult to re-accept former combatants. That is why we want to involve them in the designing of the reintegration programme, so they will understand and support the process. Responses may differ depending on the community, but we are sure that by now every community is fed up with the war and wants peace, so no community will want to be seen as the spoilers of peace. If you do not want to return to your community of origin as I said we'll find a place for you in another community that will be willing to accept you. We'll not take you anywhere we think your life will be at risk."

"What if the government is not sincere and they break the peace agreement; will we be free to fight again?" asked Ann-Marie with a coarse voice that had succumbed to marijuana. Hans responded in his usual soft tone, "We have a team of peace monitors that are already in Sierra Leone as we speak, and they will soon be deployed. The United Nations will attentively monitor the peace and will report any breach of the agreement. There will be consequences for any party that breaches it. There are several of my colleagues in every one of your bases doing what I am doing here, so everyone will get the message and will support the process."

The last question was from Colonel Snow, a Liberian, "What about us who are foreigners? What would you do for us especially as my country is not stable?" Hans scratched his head before answering. It seemed like the question was a complex one to answer. "We are aware that there are people from other countries fighting in Sierra Leone. Once the experts who will be handling these programmes come, they'll tell us what is going to be done. You do not have to worry. We'll figure something out.

Thank you all for paying attention to me. You'll be seeing more of me in the coming weeks and we will come to know each other better." We dispersed as the visitors walked with the commander to his house. As I walked back with Kalokoh, I knew he was eager to talk but wanted to avoid talking in front of the others. When we were away from everyone he asked me, "What do you think?" I answered him, "Honestly, I do not know. Let's wait and see."

•••••

Hans and his colleagues continued to visit and with time we felt comfortable with them. One month later we were informed that the disarmament programme would begin. We were told that for weapons and ammunitions we could get some money. There were people in our command unit who served as load carriers, and so did not have guns, meaning that they started looking for some to steal. Everyone started taking good care of his or her gun. I tied mine to my body one day as I slept, so I would know if someone tried to steal it. Everyone was making fun of guns. They became important to us, this time in a different way; not to kill, but to sell. We were going to sell the thing that had empowered us. I thought about this for a long time. I tried talking to some of the other rebels to make them understand that giving away our guns would bring us no good, but only few listened.

Later in the year, United Nations Peacekeepers came to Mile 38 and took over the security of the town. The ceremony was colourful but I felt hopeless watching it go on. It was that day that the movement died, at least to me. I believed that nothing beneficial would come out of the peace process for us. I told Kalokoh, "We are no longer of any importance. They will start maltreating us soon. We have to go back to our villages." I was completely depressed. I spent most of the days sleeping, eating, and smoking marijuana.

The peacekeepers were friendly and they asked us to play football with them one day. The match was very funny, as most of us could not play soccer very well. While we played aggressively against them as if we were fighting a war, they were relaxed and composed. We tried picking up a fight with them when their defender brought one of our men down. The captain of their team intervened, "We are friends, and friends don't fight. We play peaceful games. Now we play again." I made a mental note to kick the hell out of him and see how he would react as a friend. We were down 2-0. We were not even optimistic that we were going to score any goals at all. Our goalkeeper had spent the night smoking marijuana and taking cocaine.

I enquired what was wrong with him and asked him to pull himself together only for him to tell me in a sluggish voice, "it's not my fault. I'm seeing four balls instead of one, and the one I try catching is never the real one. I will try to catch the real one." He was completely stoned and I wondered why they had put him in the goalpost. He kept running out of the post trying to chase the ball. We continuously had to remind him that he was our goalkeeper and not our attacker. When I saw the ball passed to the captain of the peacekeeping team, I ran to him and kicked his shin pretending I was trying to tackle the ball. He fell to the ground screaming. I gave him my hand to raise him up saying, "Friend, peaceful match, no fight, just football." He gave me a mean look. I knew that the friendly thing was a lie, at least at that moment. I laughed to myself as I saw him rubbing his shin. We were defeated 4-0 and in fact our goal-keeper had fallen asleep at the post when the fourth goal was scored.

•••••

The DDR registration programme started few weeks after the game. We were all given identification and ration cards. We had people talking to us about peace and reconciliation, subjects I never cared to talk about and had no knowledge of. The sessions were very boring and I was asleep by the time we were half way through. Kalokoh and I were among the last people to give up our guns. We received some money for the guns, ammunition, and bayonet we turned in. By the evening, we had spent the money at a local bar that had been opened in Mile 38. We were no longer getting girls for free so we had to pay. There were so many prostitutes in the town from nearby villages. Money was flowing in their direction not only from us, but also from the peacekeepers who like us, also had manly needs to be met. The girls were ready to render the service, as long as the peacekeepers were prepared to pay. Some girls were maltreated, getting nothing but food as payment. I was surprised by how easily we interacted with civilians who used to run whenever they heard that we were coming.

Our demobilisation camp was not the most comfortable of places. One day the officials at the camp asked us to tell them what we wanted to do in life. People were suggesting all sorts of things, from carpenter to truck driver. I told the officers that I wanted to be a pilot. They were shocked. One even asked me, "Why do you want to be a pilot?" I answered him, "You asked me what I want to be and I said I want to be a pilot. What is wrong with that?"

That sparked up a whole discussion as he explained, "We are asking these questions because we would like to get you into training programmes that will help you find something to do with your life. We cannot train you to be a pilot because we do not have the money, training or facility. What we can do if you want to pursue your dream, is to help you go to school. If you do, you might be able to become a pilot at some point in the future. If you become an excellent student you will get a scholarship, and then you could study to be a pilot." The thought of going to school had never crossed my mind. I told them I wanted to think about it for a while, and that I

179

would return the next day. Kalokoh registered to be trained as a welder, which was what his father was doing before the war. "What did you register to do?" He asked me looking excited for the first time since the DDR programme began. "I have not registered for anything yet, I am still thinking about it. I want to be a pilot and they say that will only be possible if I go back to school," I replied. "You and your big dreams! You never stop dreaming. My man, come down to earth for once. You will never be a pilot and you know it." "Kalokoh, you were with me in the bush and you saw the jets and helicopters that were coming to bomb us. They were so powerful. We ran like animals when we heard them coming. Do you think they were flying by themselves? There were people piloting them. They are human beings with blood in their veins like me. If they can do it, why can't I do it? You want to be a welder, fine! Be a welder! I will be a pilot one day."

•••••

Since the first day I saw a helicopter, I always wanted to be a pilot. Jets amazed me beyond my comprehension. During our days in the bush, whenever I heard them coming after us, I forgot that they were sent to kill us and always tried to get a glimpse of them as they flew over us. I was determined to be a pilot one day and fly jets, and have people admire me. Nothing was going to kill that dream, not even Kalokoh. The next day I registered to go to school. Kalokoh did not seem happy about it, as he had wanted me to be a welder like him. He told me that we could even set up a workshop together. After a while he left me alone knowing he could not change my mind, "They say make money now, and you say school. You have no sense in that coconut you call head!" He slammed the door heavily as he moved out. After the demobilisation, I was told that the programme would support my education for two years and I would continue paying after that. Though that brought several doubts into my mind, I was determined not to give up. I made Kalokoh go with me to Hans who was witnessing our demobilisation that afternoon. He knew something was wrong when he saw us, "What's wrong, my friends? Come let's talk."

He was a very approachable person. I explained to him our problem, "My people will not want to see me at the village. I fear that they will kill me." "Why should they want to kill you?" He asked and we explained to him the atrocities we had committed in the village before running away. He told us that he would go to our villages with a reintegration specialist and talk with our families, to see what could be done. He wrote down the details, and explained our situation to the head of the centre, Dr. Conteh, who said he would see us the following week. I felt better inside having explained to someone else other than Kalokoh about my past. I took relief in knowing that Hans was taking interest and was willing to help. The period of waiting was quite challenging as I imagined every possible reaction from my family members at the news of my return. Kalokoh was faced with similar thoughts.

One day I asked him and he said to me, "My people believe in revenge. I only hope they do not harm Hans." I stood up shocked, "I was thinking of the same thing, how come?" Kalokoh laughed, "You always forget that we have the same problem. The only thing that will save Hans is that he is a white man. Let me tell you a story that has to do with revenge in my village. One day a man went to his house and met his wife with another man. He went to the house of the man, raped his wife and daughters and killed them before returning home to kill his wife, who stupidly was still there. There was another man whose cow got killed by his neighbour. He went to the house of the neighbour and killed the child of the neighbour, which led to family confrontations that disrupted the village for two weeks. When I say I am afraid to go back, I know what I'm talking about." That week we played another match with the peacekeepers. By then we were referred to as ex-combatants and not rebels. The peacekeepers were not as friendly as they were during the first match. They were kicking the hell out of us. The captain I had kicked during the last match made several attempts to kick me, but I skilfully dodged every time. During the last few minutes of the game however, I was not very lucky. We both jumped for a header and he went for my head instead of the ball.

•••••

The following week Hans sent for us. I was filled with anxiety as I sprinted alongside Kalokoh to where he was. "What do you think he will tell us?" Kalokoh asked me. "If I knew I would have told you." Hans was happy to see us. "Guys, your families were hard to persuade; but we succeeded in the end to get them to agree to have you back in your communities. We also met with the community leaders in the two villages and some young people who know you. They are happy that the war is over and are willing to forgive and forget." Kalokoh was not convinced, "They can easily say so. Probably they want to get us to return so they can kill us. I know those people. What they say is different from what they do." Hans stopped him, "Young man, I won't put you in harm's way. We had the leaders in your villages commit themselves to peace as well as pledge to re-accept all former combatants and make peace with them. They were happy to do so. In your village, Kalokoh, we have fifty young boys and girls like you that will be returning. You are not alone. In Moseray's village, there are about seventy-three young boys and girls like him returning. We'll have social workers that will help you become members of those communities once again. You'll not be left alone. We have arranged for you to be transported to your communities and provided with the necessary support that you need. I have work to do and will be talking to you in the coming days about the details of your reintegration process."

"He is the best human being in the world." Kalokoh could not hide his excitement, "Without him I would have perished. I only hope those people mean what they say. If not then I will only be able to complain after meeting God." I packed the few clothes I had in a plastic bag and started counting the days. Three days before I left, Dr. Conteh told me about the school I would be attending in the village next to mine, and gave me books and school materials. He made me sign for them. He also gave me the name of my contact person in the school and some money, which I was to use for lunch. Three days later, I said good-bye to Kalokoh who was also leaving later that day for his village. We were going to face our past. We had created them separately, and now we going to face them separately. We cried as we bade our farewells knowing that we won't see each other in a long time, possibly ever again. There were other people with me in the truck. Five of them were going to my village and the rest were going to villages close to mine. The scenery was green and beautiful. I loved it, but as I started seeing familiar places and knowing that we were reaching my village my heart throbbed with fear. "Are you scared?" I asked one of the boys. "I am very scared but they won't do anything to us" he remarked optimistically.

•••••

As we entered the village, we saw people gathered all over with women singing and dancing. The song was a welcoming song; its words allaying my fears:
Our children have come home again,
Yes they have come home,
Our children are our children,
No matter what, they are our children.

I could not believe my ears. The song was a traditional song of forgiveness and love. It is for prodigal children. As we came down the truck, I looked for my

183

relatives not knowing what I would do if I saw anyone. Dr. Conteh had sent two of his workers with us who led us into the community. Families were celebrating the return of their children. I saw my aunt and uncle, the ones I would be living with. They were from my father's side and were not as annoyed as those from my mother's side. They welcomed me and took my plastic and school bags. We were taken to the chief who, together with elders of the village, performed a traditional cleansing ceremony for us at the riverside. We were washed with water and native soap to remove the perceived evil spirits in us. After washing us a very smelly ointment with suffocating scent was rubbed all over our body, they said, to protect us against evil spirits. My mother's elder brother who was present at the ceremony laid his hand on my head as a sign of forgiveness. He cried as he touched me and I cried with him. We were made to confess and apologise for all the things we did during the war. We did our best to look remorseful, but most, if not all of us, were genuinely remorseful. We were children when we became rebels, but we were now young men prepared to live a different life. Our mouths were washed with salt water and wiped as a sign of the last contact with the devil. I thought of what Kalokoh would be going through at that moment.

After the ceremony, I followed my uncle who escorted me to my new home and new life. I resolved within me to completely divorce from my past life as a rebel. I turned a new page, and began another chapter of life

The City of Change

"Welcome to the City of Change. Here we have people with different challenges, ranging from drug addiction, torments by evil spirits, mental disorders and post-traumatic stress disorder (PTSD). We have been operating in this centre for twenty-five years and there are none better than ours. After the war, we treated over 500 ex-combatants and over 800 victims of the war. Treating post-traumatic stress disorder is our strength and we treat our patients with the highest level of professionalism, which could be hardly seen even in Europe or America. As you may be aware, this country has only one psychiatrist who himself is said to be in need of psycho-social assistance. So we are the only people anyone in the right or even the wrong state of mind should turn to." In spite of the seriousness of the situation at hand, my mom could not suppress her giggles. The comical figure talking to us could indeed help to ease stress and bring laughter. Looking like someone harassed for over a decade by tuberculosis mixed with an unusual case of typhoid, the lanky fellow parroted away while wearing the serious look of a Nazi concentration camp officer lining up his victims for the gas chamber.

He continued without the slightest hint of noticing that my mom was laughing, "We now have one hundred people in residence and the facility itself can accommodate 120 people at any point in time. Our catering service is one of the best in Freetown, even the restaurants cannot compete with us. We have ten women, all born-again Christians, who have dedicated their lives to serving people in need. Three of them were healed in this very centre when the devil made it its business to disturb them. Pastor Alfred Jones is the head of the Centre and he is a true man of God." My mother continued examining the centre, trying to reassure herself that it was the right place for me to be. My recent outbursts at home had reached a new height where I started attacking people. I was going crazy. I wanted access to drugs but my mom was determined to stop me from taking it. For me, life was not worth living if I had no access to drugs. It was the only source of comfort I had. It was the only thing that made me see life as an interesting thing, something liveable. My mother stopped giving me money when she realised this. When I could not get the money from her, I started stealing and selling stuff so I could pay for the drugs. Cocaine, heroin and marijuana were like food to me. Lack of it heightened an internal tension that led me to cross paths I never thought I would cross. It had all began six years ago.

•••••

1996 was a year of hope for Sierra Leoneans. Democracy was in transition and the military had committed itself to conducting multi-party elections and handing over power to a civilian government. The people were sick and tired of the regime, which they had openly welcomed on the 29th of April 1992. Unfortunately, the military disappointed the people who were also quick to understand that the regime was not that different from the government that it overthrew. Promises made were not kept and the regime started experiencing the wrath of the people. By then, the war was getting worse and the rebels were spreading their terror like California Wildfires across the country. In the midst of these frustrating times, there was a palace coup in January 1996, which ushered in a second version of the military regime (National

186

Provisional Ruling Council II). The people decided that enough was enough. There were several protest marches across the country, the most memorable of them being the march by some women who stripped themselves naked in the centre of Freetown. The military, realising that the people of the country were desperate, called a National Consultative Conference at the Bintumani Hotel (the conference was titled Bintumani 11 as Bintumani 1 had been held in 1995), asking the people to be given time to end the war before going to elections. The people of the country, unified in their resolve to have the military leave the political stage, out rightly stated, 'No'. Thus, elections were held in June 1996.

It was during one of those days in 1996 that I followed my friend Joseph to Sackville Street, a street known for dubious activities. Joseph had a strong influence over me and I had a blind sense of loyalty to him. He was older and street smarter than I was, though he was no match for me in school. We were always together as we lived in the same neighbourhood. Of course this had implications for my food and money which I equally shared with him whenever available. We entered a three-storey building with stairs that left one breathless, not because they were long and winding but because navigating the stairs always proved challenging as it was crammed with people smoking marijuana. Some were fearfully and tightly clinging onto their lovers as if when they let go of them they would automatically disappear. The terrain was unfamiliar and eerie to me; it was like entering a world you know is very much unlike yours. I was caught in the dilemma of wanting to return home and of staying with Joseph as I had promised to accompany him. I put up a brave front and traced the steps of Joseph who confidently ascended the stairs, patting the backs and shoulders of those who showered him with titles like 'commander', 'manager', 'chairman' and 'investor'. He reciprocated having a different title for all those who had one for him.

Surprise and fear gripped me. The two are a deadly combination that could send one over the cliff in a matter of seconds. I had known Joseph for a quite some time now but had never suspected that he was friends with people like those I was meeting. Horrible thoughts of the police raiding the premises and arresting me or me being killed or wounded should the police raid the place or a bloody fight erupting raced through my mind. Even the cool evening breeze could not save me from sweating. Joseph was not a mere acquaintance, he was in fact romancing with the bloody law breakers who had faces that would scare even the most hardened criminal in Alcatraz. Joseph my good friend had fooled me. He told me he was going to collect a book, which was why I followed him.

We entered a large room on the second floor. "Josie the man, big boy, you nar better person, come sit. Who be this, nar your friend?" With the funnelled shaped mouth that ran like a tap, a light skinned man with the height and ears of an elf simultaneously rained greetings and questions on Joseph. He introduced himself to me as Femi. "My guy, you came right on time. We just had a supply of the best grass in the country. It will turn your head like crazy." I was looking at Joseph for an explanation but he was not even looking in my direction. He said to Femi, "You know I am a strong man. So nothing can shake me. The last time I had three jumbos and you could not take more than two. I walked out of here strong leaving you snoring." The alarm in my head went off. I was shaking like a jellyfish and even a blind man could have seen the sweat streaming down my face. I had followed Joseph to hell. I said to Joseph, "My mom will be waiting for me. I think I should go now."

Femi looked at Joseph, wearing a frown. "You came with a mommy's pet? Has he been baptised?" Joseph said no and Femi moved towards me. "Your mom will wait today. We are going to baptise you. Trust me you will like it. If you saw the way Joseph was crying when he first tasted grass, ha! You would have believed he was going to die." "I am a Christian, and my mom says Christians do not smoke grass or drink alcohol. I can't try it." "You think we are not Christians? I know the Bible better than your pastor. Even in heaven they smoke weed. Do you think Bob Marley survives there without weed? Tell me bro, who made the weed?" "I don't know. I have never seen it". I was being truthful; I had never seen the weed before. "Don't be silly, boy. God himself, who is the greatest of all Rastafarians, made it. He planted it on Solomon's grave so the intelligence of Solomon will not die with his body. He wanted mankind to smoke it, drink it as tea so that part of Solomon would be inside us. This opens the eyes of people whose eyes are closed, like you. You become creative and you do things you never knew you could do."

I thought for a second, that probably this was what was making Joseph more street wise than me. If I tried it, maybe, just maybe, it would make me become brilliant too. I asked him, "They say people who smoke grass get mad after a while. Is it true?" "Those are statements by stupid people who do not know anything. People say bad things about something they do not know. All of the ministers and professors you see in this country smoke weed. Without it you cannot think properly, you will remain forever in the dark. Most of those who oppose it later come to try it, smoking it until the day they die. Don't you see the ministers as they pass with their dark glasses? Behind the glasses are red eyes. They can even read the minds of people. The grass has a power that no human being can explain. It is a medicinal herb. It cures asthma, and other illnesses we do not even know about. Have you seen Joseph falling ill in recent times?" I was in a total state of confusion. I knew in my heart that I did not want to smoke, but slowly, slowly, I was coming to believe there might be some truth in what they were saying.

"Bro, let's try a jumbo," Femi said to Joseph who started wrapping one. They took two long draws each before passing it to me. "We have not died, have we? Try it. If you do not like it, you stop." Joseph told me. I took the grass and drew on it; I coughed like I had never coughed before. The taste in my mouth was very strong and it was unlike anything I had tasted before. My chest tightened. "You see, it is clearing your chest and your lungs. It is killing every sickness in you. You must be happy for this. Now you will be a strong boy," Femi said as I passed the grass back to him. I pretended to have taken it like a man. I smoked more as they passed it to me. The sensation became more and more overwhelming. I remember at one stage telling Joseph, "This is good." He smiled. Femi continued preaching to me about the greatness of the grass. "Our parents are not people who want to try things. They are comfortable with the things they know. Their fear of the unknown is strong. With our generation it is different. We see something and we want to try it. That is why the world is improving. You can only know if something is good or bad if you try it. You will see from today your life will improve. You will stop thinking like a boy. You will be thinking more clearly than your parents."

Joseph said to him, "Man, this grass is hot! Where did you get it? I need some for tonight. I need to be stoned tonight. This is beautiful." He answered, "I went to Waterloo yesterday and I bought it from my friend, the one I told you about who has a farm there. He is a wonderful man. He waits for me to buy his grass, if even he has someone willing to pay more. I will take you there one day so we can smoke fresh grass and drink tea. Maybe we can go with your friend here." "We should have tea there this week. I believe Umar will like it. What do you think, Umar?" By then, I was completely stoned, so I just stood, smiling and nodding my head. I don't remember when we left. I felt like I was being dragged by Joseph, who seemed very normal, a veteran of smoker I guess, and I was just a novice. I jumped into bed the moment I reached home. I slept till midday the next day. I remembered opening my eyes and seeing my mom checking my temperature. She was worried that I was sick.

•••••

I started frequenting Sackville Street with Joseph in the coming weeks and I sometimes even went alone when Joseph was not around, because I had also become Femi's good friend. When I did not want to go far, I would go to Horton Street, where there was a former military officer selling grass by Devere Street. It was a new discovery for me. I started doing it excessively. Most of the money I was getting for lunch went to buying grass. I made friends in this way. I even came to realise that most of my peers were also taking weed. I was once taken by surprise when Mr. Sandy, my agriculture teacher, met me smoking marijuana at Sackville Street. I got up to leave but he said, "My friend, in here, there is no teacher. I am John and you are Umar. We are equals. I smoke, you smoke, but if I hear this from anybody I will know you told them. We never met here, do you understand me?" I said, "Yes sir, I understand," and we continued smoking. The next day I sat at the back of the class to avoid him. He went about his class as he usually did, never once looking in my direction.

My mom started noticing changes in me and demanded to have a talk with me. "What is wrong with you, my son? You seem to be sleeping a lot these days, and your eyes are always very red. You had measles and chicken pox when you were a baby so I am not sure they are related to what is happening to you. Tell me what is wrong with you?" She asked. "I am okay, I only have slight headaches in the evening, but that is mostly because I play football after school. It is fatigue." I could not look straight into her eyes. She was determined to continue the discussion, "You have been playing football after school since you were ten but you have always been fine. I told your dad when he called yesterday that you don't look alright. He said I should take you to the hospital so we get to know what is wrong." "I am fine mom, you should not worry. I will stop playing football after school and I believe everything will be fine." "You are just 15 years old. I should worry. I have suffered a lot with you since your father left to study in the United States. Or is there something wrong that you do not want me to know? I see you are avoiding me these days. When you come home all you do is eat and sleep, you no longer sit and chat with me or kiss me good night. Talk to me, son, something is definitely wrong. You have always been so very close to me."

"Mom, all is fine, believe me. It is the football I play after school." Realising how much she loved me, I felt a tiny pang of guilt, but I just wanted the questions to stop. They irritated and grated on my nerves. "Or have you found a girlfriend that is taking all your time and attention and now your mom is no longer important?" In the end, I talked her out of the discussion but I grew very worried. My mom was not someone who easily forgot things. She noticed everything and everyone around her. I could see from that moment that she kept a close eye on me. So I tried to be very careful and pretended to be playing when around her. Two days later, I went with Joseph to Towerhill, which was one of our hideouts. Towerhill has beautiful sceneries and from there you can see the eastern part of the city, particularly the quay, with all the beautiful ships and boats docking there. Late in the evening you would find lovers using it as a love nest. Once, we caught a couple having sex behind a large tree. We seized their clothes and made them pay us before we returned their clothes. We tried that once on a giant of a man whose partner we heard screaming in climaxed excitement. We were given the beating of our lives. After that we stopped looking for trouble.

•••••

"Joseph, my mom has noticed that something is wrong with me. She confronted me recently and I lied that all is well." "What do you mean by you lied? It was the truth that you told her. Is anything wrong with you? What did you tell her?" Joseph seemed annoyed with me. "I told her that I get weak when I return home because I play football after school. But once I stop I will be fine. She does not seem to believe me. She spends most of her time at home with me, and tries talking to me all the time. She thinks I have something on my mind. She is a very smart person and I am very worried." "You are smarter than her and you have to prove that. You have to keep our secret! If you betray us we will not be happy with you. She will know I have something to do with it and she will not let me into your house again." "What should I do? What should I say if she suspects?" I asked Joseph. "One, you should always have a chewing gum or pepper mint in your pocket. As soon as you finish smoking you should chew the gum and suck the peppermint. That kills the scent immediately and she will not catch it from your breath. Then, you should learn to brush your teeth when you go home, and if you are completely stoned, don't sit near her, go and lie down."

"I will try, but then maybe I should just stop," I wondered out loud. Joseph exploded "Well, go ahead. That is your choice. I know I can't stop and I don't want to stop. This is my God and everything in the world. I cannot afford a pint of beer, but grass I can afford at times. When I can't, there is always a brother willing to share. You see, the problem is that you do not know what is happening in this world. When you go home, there is food, your mom gives you lunch, when you are sick you go to the doctor, and your dad is in the United States sending you beautiful stuffs. For me, life is shit. I have none of those things. I am completely empty. I sleep in an unfinished building. I pay my own school fees and no one cares. Some of my relatives are rich but they do not want to hear about me. When I was staying with my uncle, I was sleeping in the garage with his dog. Even the dog was treated better than I was. I was the first to get up, clean the house, and light the fire to warm water so his kids of my age could take their bath. I was the last to go to school and the last to sleep. I would only eat after everyone else had eaten, and it was the crust that I had. Even the dog was given meat but I could not have any.

I was always beaten and once my hand was broken because he hit me with a chair. I was a slave in my uncle's house. He never let my mother stay at his house when she came from the village, forgetting that it was my mother who had to sell her farms to help him go to the University. Now he behaves like a white man and we are nothing to him. Life has never been nice to me. It was then that I discovered the grass from Solomon's grave. It became my solace and since then I have not been as bitter as I was before. It gave me the courage to move out of my uncle's house and to stand up for myself. It opened my eyes. Now I am a grown up man. I have seen different worlds and I have survived them all."

I felt sorry for him as I was touched by his story. It was the first time that he had told me about himself and his past in such an expressive manner. I only knew he was a caretaker in the unfinished house he was living in. He lit a jumbo and smoked it without sharing with me. After he had taken four draws, I took it from him and smoked, damning the consequences. On my way home, I bought Hollywood chewing gums and peppermints. I thought I was going to beat my mom on this, but behold, she would come to know sooner than I expected.

•••••

One day I returned home and found my mom fuming with rage and crying the hell out of her life. Even a first class idiot would have realised that something terrible had happened - my mom is not someone who easily shed tears. I sat by her side asking what had happened.

She screamed at me, "You have killed me, Umar, you have completely killed me. Congratulations! You succeeded in fooling me, but not anymore. I should have thought of this long ago." As she spoke my heart navigated through rough waters trying to nail what she was driving at. Finally, I settled on the possibility that she had known that she has a drug addict for a son. That could be the only reason she could be so mad at me. I was petrified, I thought of vanishing into thin air. I looked around her to see if she had a cane or stick, but on second thought wiped out the thought of her beating me. She stopped beating me when I turned 15.

She wailed "Umar, what have I done to deserve this? Have I not been a good mom to you? What is there that I have not done to make you happy? What have you ever asked for that I have not given you? Tell me, Umar, tell me!" "I don't know what you are talking about mom, tell me what's going on," I said to her, meekly. My voice quivered, I knew. She went to her room and brought out a sling of marijuana. I went limp, almost consumed by a catatonic fit. My worst fears had come true. My secret was out, now she knew. I had never been so ashamed of myself all my life. Clutching at straws, I decided to deny with all my heart and soul. If I conceded, then she would lose faith in me. I knew she trusted me and would believe me if I denied firmly enough. After all, all this while she had not seen through my lies, even though she suspected something was amiss. Now she had evidence in her hands but I still believed that my words would be greater than the evidence she had. To achieve this, I realised I need to put on an act so convincing that even the best director in Hollywood would give a standing ovation to.

"Now tell me where this comes from?" she asked. At which point I instantly put on a pained expression, and spoke in a voice tinged with disappointment and hurt that she would think so low of me, "Mom, is this the reason you were crying? You should have asked me. I found this on my way to school one day and I do not know the reason why I kept it. I guess I should have thrown it away. If I were a smoker, I would have smoked it, but I left it there. You should know I couldn't do something like that, mom. I am disappointed that you would think of me in a way like that." The look on her face instantly changed and I knew my words had hit her hard. "Are you trying to tell me that I am wrong after seeing this in your pocket?" Of course I was lying but what did she expect me to say. I landed the second decisive blow with confidence and grit "Mom you are wrong, in fact you owe me an apology. If I were a smoker you would have known, wouldn't you? I have never involved myself in anything like that, and you know I never will." She kept quiet for a while, and then with a deep, unstable voice, she said, "I pray to God that I am wrong. If what I am thinking is true, then I will never forgive you. Never, in fact I will disown you, I swear to God I will. You will not bring shame and disgrace to my family. If you want to behave like the other boys, then go out and join them, but you won't do that in my house." I was slightly surprised that she stood her ground for a moment; this was unlike her but I suspected that despite my sterling convincing performance, she had drawn a link between the marijuana and my recent behaviour and looks.

I got up and walked to my room, pretending to be angry with her. I locked the door and stayed in the room for the rest of the day. She tried opening the door several times, calling on me but when she realised I did not want to talk to her she gave up.

•••••

My behaviour changed the following week. I went home the minute school closed and I stopped smoking. I even refused seeing Joseph, who was always knocking on my window, late at night. I did not want to hurt my mom.

I knew she had tightened her watch on me. Any simple mistake would land me in hot water. But the desire to smoke grew stronger and stronger. I was now jumpy and irritable. I snapped at anyone who talked to me. Finally, the craving became irresistible. They were right. It seemed everything was clearer and made more sense when I smoked. On Sunday night, I opened the window when Joseph knocked and jumped out to join him. I explained to him what happened. He was shocked but congratulated me on the way I handled the situation. "You see this is what I told you about being smart. You cannot be outsmarted by anyone who does not take the grass. Now you are a clever boy. Where is the grass she found? Did she throw it away?" "How would I know? Whatever she does with it is her problem. I do not want to have anything to do with it. Do you have some on you?" I was desperate for some. "No, but since everyone in your house is asleep we should check with Femi. He has fresh grass."

We strolled to Femi's place. It was full of people that night and there was loud music playing, to which everyone was dancing. An organisation called 'Friends' was running an advertisement for their show that was coming up the next day at the Paddy's Night Club in Aberdeen. We danced as we moved through the crowd making our way to Femi's. Business was good for Femi that day. People were moving in and out of his house buying grass. He asked us to wait for him since he had something new he wanted to show us. When the place became quiet, he led us to his room where he showed us a powder I had never seen or heard of. He called it heroine. It was crazy but incredible. We were completely knocked out by this new discovery, harsher than grass by a thousand times.

It was that discovery that completely threatened my life and got me kicked out of my house. That night I found my way to my room after five in the morning. I started doing badly at school and my grades went down even further as I continued taking weed and heroine. My teachers complained to my mom. My body was negatively reacting to this new drug. I had scabies all over my body. Besides that, I was always weak and hungry. My mom noticed the changes and when she tried to force me to tell her what I was taking, I fought her, taking a knife and threatening to stab her. I left the house and moved to Joseph's unfinished building. I was safe from my mom because by then she did not know where Joseph lived.

I helped Femi to sell his grass and I could smoke for free and have heroine when business was good. I became addicted. I did not know what I had got myself into. Life became very tough and the things that I took for granted when I was staying with my mom, I now had to struggle to get. Sometimes I could go for days with nothing to eat. Getting food never worried me like getting grass or heroine. It was then that the May 25 1997 Armed Forces Revolutionary Council (AFRC) military coup took place. It opened a new chapter in my life.

"Fellow citizens, our national integrity has been mortgaged to foreigners, and we Sierra Leoneans continue to suffer. We have little access to education and poverty is killing us. The government came and they disbanded the national army, an army that was made up of patriots who would sacrifice themselves for this land. The Kamajors were given more powers and the army was badly treated."

The announcer of the coup sounded angry as he spoke. In five years we have had five heads of states, four of them military. With the election, I thought that we had seen the last of the military, but it clearly appeared that I was wrong. The country turned upside down and the President fled and sought refuge in Guinea. The next day, a military vehicle parked outside Femi's house and four soldiers came up to where we were sitting. I wanted to run but Femi held me still. "Where are you going, boy? These are friends, don't be a fool."

The soldiers greeted us. They seemed very friendly, shared their grass with us and asked us to join them in a mission. I hesitated but they convinced me to go with them. I had little else to do and they pushed me hard "Look, man, this is our time, don't joke with it. Join us if you want to avoid poverty forever." So I went with them. I carted goods to the vehicle from the stores they broke into along Siaka Stevens Street, and Krootown Road. We had everything from televisions and mobile phones to cameras and radios. By every indication, I was becoming rich as long as I stayed with these guys. Joseph and Femi seemed to be on top of the situation. They were even helping with the door breaking process. We carted all the commodities we looted to the soldiers' apartment at Wilberforce Barracks. They asked us to stay so we could continue our business over night. We ate, smoked more grass and had heroine. A whole packet brought by Femi quickly disappeared in record time. Femi had seen and taken a huge bunch of U.S dollars in one of the supermarkets we broke into, and had put it in the small bag he had with him. We ate and slept for a few hours. That night the three of us who were not soldiers were made to dress in black. We also wore masks. We were in addition given machetes since we could not shoot a gun. The soldiers brought a bigger truck this time and we were joined by four of their colleagues who appeared to be as desperate as we had been when we joined the soldiers.

During our ventures, we could see that there were other soldiers looting. We pretended not to notice their activities. Some of the goods looted were stored at Femi's place, but most were taken to a garage in Kissy, owned by one of the soldiers as they decided against using Wilberforce Barracks. During this mission I was prepared to look for cash and by the time we finished I had no reason to worry about cash for a long time. I was a rich man by every standard. The next day, we were taken to the beach where we were trained to shoot. It was very easy. I mastered it better than Joseph, but Femi was by far a better shooter.

We were provided with uniforms and the soldiers told us that we were part of the People's Army that would liberate the fatherland from the hands of Nigerian soldiers who were bent on taking it from us. Our comrades gave us a hero's welcome whenever we went to Sackville Street. I wondered what my mom would say if she saw me in a military fatigue. I had not thought of her in a very long time. I always avoided passing by our house to avoid contact with my relatives.

•••••

As the revolution progressed, I became deeply entrenched in the people's army. More boys of our age and some who were older than us joined. We were losing most of our boys as the Nigerian army had superior firepower and whenever we made attempts to kick them out of the airport, or from their base in Jui, we suffered severe casualties. In one of such battle I was shot in the arm but fortunately was treated at the 34 Military Hospital at Wilberforce. I was a fighter by then even though I was only 16, and not of the age to be a soldier. Who cared? The regime wanted recruits and I was ready to fight. Boys as young as 10 who wanted to fight, were given guns especially by the RUF, which was now in Freetown following an invitation of the AFRC.

We were however having difficulties with the rebels as they refused to take orders from our commanders. They only listened to their own rebel commanders who came with them to Freetown. The soldiers told us that it was a major blunder to invite the RUF to join the revolution, but they were only pretending to be at peace so the Nigerians would not suspect that the marriage was not going on well.

We became part of the convoy of Colonel Turay who had the reputation of being a brilliant soldier and a hard-core fighter. He was in charge of protecting the eastern part of the city from falling into the hands of the Nigerians. So we accompanied him as he did regular monitoring of the area, assessing the situation. The heaviest battle we fought was in December when we suspected that the Nigerians were flying troops into the Hastings airfield. We launched what was supposed to be a surprise attack but the response of the Nigerians sparked the fear that someone very senior in the regime was spying for the Nigerians. The battle lasted for six hours but it was very bloody and brutal. We lost over one hundred soldiers. I saw soldiers and rebels running as the Nigerians bombed the hell out of us. They had the advantage of air support and effectively used it. We only had one military helicopter, which could not face the military jets the Nigerians had.

In February 1998 we were kicked out of the city and we used the peninsula to retreat into the interior of the country. The Nigerians would have caught most of us if they had closed that route. They left it as an escape route since they thought that closing it would only intensify the fighting in the capital, which could have actually led to more casualties among the civilian populace.

•••••

We ran all the way to Makeni, though most of our colleagues set up their base at Okra Hill, which is closer to Freetown. I stayed at the rebel command post where Colonel Turay continued to work with the rebels. The rebels captured all the soldiers and volunteers, like Femi, Joseph and I. We learnt that there had been a fall out with the head of the revolution, who had been taken captive in Kailahun by the ground commander of the rebels. We were tortured every single day. Every day brought more suffering and pain. What kept me going were my friends, Femi and Joseph. We tried to survive together. Sometimes I hated them, for without them my life would have being a happy one. My happiness ended when I came to know them, but I was always quick to kick that aside for it would only make things worse for us. After eighteen long months, we were released and asked to be part of the disarmament, demobilization and reintegration programme. We would be demobilised and sent back into the communities destroyed by the fighting forces. I opposed the idea of going back but by then I was very sick and was having memory problems and found it difficult to keep up with conversations. The constant intake of drugs was taking its toll on me. One time, I told Femi and Joseph that I wanted to go home to my mom, but they said they would join the DDR programme since it had some benefits for them. The reintegration phase of the programme will take them to their communities. I did not want to be part of the DDR programme, so early the next morning I asked for a lift on a truck that had supplied camp materials and I was taken to Freetown.

When I reached my mother's house I weakly knocked on the door. She screamed when she saw me and quickly reached out to catch me as I collapsed into her arms. She gave me a good scrub, dressed me like a baby and fed me. She asked me over and over, what had happened to me. Each time she asked I turned my face away, not knowing where to start and not wanting to talk at all. I knew my face looked different to her now. I was sick and I needed medical help. Even in my state, I could tell my brain was not functioning properly. That afternoon she took me to the Connaught hospital where the doctor told her that I was suffering from serious post-traumatic stress disorder and gave her a long prescription of drugs to buy and what should be done to help me. The thought of more drugs exhausted me.

As relatives streamed in to see me, the next day I felt ashamed of myself, and my depression heightened. I was constantly bombarded with a barrage of questions, which I never answered. It made me look stupid and hopeless. I asked my mom to stop people from coming to see me. My dad called one time but I told my mom that I just wanted to rest and not talk so I did not talk to him. I took the medicine for three weeks but it was not helping. It was then that one of my mother's friends told her about the City of Change. She decided to take me there. I was happy about that and hopeful that it would bring me back to my senses, because it would save me from the embarrassment of having to sit at home to face people who wanted to ask me questions I did not want to answer.

Everything appeared suspicious and fearful to me as they led to flashbacks. If I saw a bag in the middle of the road, I would think it was a dead body, if I saw a knife, I thought that the holder would try to stab me. I had to wear glasses as I was becoming visually challenged. I cried to myself without noticing that I was crying. I easily forgot things and was totally depressed. I had the desire to take drugs but tried very hard to stop myself. My mind was a troubled one. I really needed help. As we were taken through the City of Change, we came across the head of the institution who immediately walked towards me, held my hands and asked me to look into his eyes. I was taken aback by this unexpected command, but I looked into his eyes, and he said to me, "Your worries are over, God will heal you." He had a powerful presence. I knew that it was the beginning of the end of my long journey. After making all arrangements, my mom kissed me good-bye and told me she would see me the next day. She didn't want to leave, but she couldn't help me any other way.

That afternoon Pastor Alfred Jones took me to the garden where he prayed for me. After praying he said, "My son, only God can heal, no human being can. I called on him because I want him to intercede and take possession of your life. Before you begin talking to me, talk to God and ask him for forgiveness. Pray in your heart, and then tell me your story." I knelt down not knowing where to begin. Tears streamed down my face as I closed my eyes to talk to my God. I told him my story and after a very long time, I asked him for his mercy.

Healing Wounds

The room was full. There were people from all corners of our town witnessing the proceedings of the Truth and Reconciliation Commission. I was wearing a white T-shirt and shorts, bought by my elder brother who I was staying with. He told me that wearing the symbol of peace would help with my testimony and with asking for forgiveness from the Koroma family. I was nervous. I tried several times to take a deep breath to calm myself down but it was not working. This was a moment when I had to be very composed and talk from the bottom of my heart. I had done things someone of my age should not do. Actually, I had done things no human being is supposed to. I had hurt a family and I could never bring back or replace their loved ones I had killed. I saw Mrs. Koroma sitting very far from me with sad eyes following the events in the courtyard. Her eyes met mine and she turned her face away. I wondered what was going through her mind, and what she would do to me if she had her way. My sins were unforgivable and I will understand if she cannot forgive me. It would take more than a Christian heart garnished with Christian resignation to forgive what I had done.

•••••

My reintegration process into the village was not going well. Instead of mixing with other people my age, I withdrew from them, afraid that someone might attack me. My nights became troubled, with horrible and disturbing nightmares. The ghosts of yesterday had come to haunt me. Restless and wandering spirits, ghosts of lives taken, were tormenting the tormentor. My elder brother, Suma, worried that an evil spirit had possessed me. He took me to the chief and village priest who performed numerous ceremonies to rid me off the spirit, but my condition only worsened. The high priest said to me one day, "There are dead spirits haunting you. They are very powerful and they cry for revenge. They want your blood, so you must confess your wrongdoings and ask for forgiveness. That is the only way through which you can attain peace." I thought of the things I had done but there were so many that I could not say anything that would help the high priest and me. I told him of how I had killed people, raped women, and burned houses. He looked at me and said, "I have heard all what you have said but go home and think. There are many people you have hurt, so search the dark rivers of your heart. You might remember a clear case where you should not have killed someone or a family, yet you went on and did it. See me again in two days."

He spat on his hands, poured some black powder on the spit, mixed it and rubbed it on my face, "Leave this on you till tomorrow, and wash it very early in the morning." The wide mouth of the high priest was walled at the front by only two stained teeth, which produced a disgusting spit that now coloured my face. The fact that the unwholesome effluvium from his mouth had been deposited on my face only added to my trauma. However, I had to endure, and endure I did. My brother was worried about what was happening to me so much so that he offered sacrifices every day, asking the gods to forgive me of my sins. That night after seeing the high priest I thought of the things I had done. After several hours of soul searching, I remembered a family I had attacked in our neighbouring village. I had killed the father and the two children, and raped the wife. The children begged to be spared but I made them watch as I raped their mother and then killed them, with the mother watching as I slowly but expertly denied them their right to life. I went to my brother's room, woke him up and told him of this.

"Do you still remember this woman?" he asked me. I said I did. "I want to go to the village, look for the woman and ask her to forgive you," he said. But I was afraid they might hurt him. "The woman will be very angry and might hurt you when she learns we are brothers," I said. "That is true; maybe we can find an elderly person who will want to help us. Go to bed, I will talk with the chief and the high priest in the morning. I will handle this. Go and rest." That morning when we had breakfast, my brother made me retell my encounter with the woman and her family. I was bleeding inside as I spoke. My brother sensed that I did not like repeating the story and he said to me, "The more you explain the easier it becomes on you. You have been keeping all these things to yourself and now they are hurting you inside. They want to be let out; you should not suppress them anymore. Talking makes things easier for you and it makes you feel better. I am your brother and the only family you have left, you have to talk to me. I do not want to see you like this; Let's help each other on this, please."

I felt encouraged to continue. I narrated all that had happened with the woman's family and my role in it. I also told him several stories of the things I did while I was a combatant. I felt ashamed of myself. I knew that my parents would not have been proud of me if they were around to hear my stories. I wondered if my brother hated me for what I had done. However, he did not show any emotion. After explaining, he asked me, "Do you remember any family member of the other victims?" I could not remember, "Most of them were killed as we moved from one place to another. The boys under our command brought some of them to us. Some we captured along the way. I remember the woman's family because it is close to here and I personally went to their house." I was very honest and open for the first time in my life. My brother took me to the chief. He explained to him and the high priest what I had told him. My head was bowed the whole time he spoke. I was ashamed of myself. The chief asked the high priest, "You've heard him. What do you have to say?"

The high priest asked me to raise my head. He looked into my eyes, "Only the truth will set one free. As our people say, there is no bad forest to throw an evil child. I will go to the village and find this woman. Where did you say the house was and what does it look like?" Trying to remember every detail, I described and directed the place to him as best as I could. The chief then asked me, "Have you heard about the Truth and Reconciliation Commission (TRC)?" "What is the TRC?" I asked him, not having a clue about what he was driving at. He continued, "We had some people who came to the village and told us that they were trying to solve some of the problems of the war by getting people to come out and publicly say what had been done to them. Those who did something wrong to them during the war will confess and ask for forgiveness." I had never heard about it and neither had my brother. "Would you like to go through it? If we see this woman, would you like to publicly ask for her forgiveness, so you can put this behind you and begin living a normal life?" the chief asked, but the high priest did not like the idea so he said, "You believe in the ways of the white people. We can handle this our way. He does not need to go public. What if someone from that village comes to know of his whereabouts and tries to harm him later? What will we do then? Let's meet this woman and after she agrees to forgive him we can find a way of appeasing the gods."

The chief laughed, "Oh! Foday, I was just suggesting it to him. Okay, let's start first by looking for this woman." "Suma, you do not need to worry, Foday will go there. Just leave some transport for him." My brother left Le 5000. As poor as he was, I felt sad making him go through all this for my sake.

•••••

On Friday evening, the chief sent for my brother and I. My brother was out of the house. I went to his workshop where I found him making a chair. We were almost running instead of walking to the chief's compound. I tried not to think of anything as we went. The chief, high priest and two elderly men with full grey hairs were in the chief's veranda with two stools already placed for us. We greeted them and were asked to sit. The chief led the discussion, "Two days ago I told you that Foday will go to the village of the woman you told us about and will try to find her. Fortunately for us, he found her. So today we have two people from her village who came with Foday to meet with me on the sensitive issue. Suma, the people are here. What do we say to them?" the chief asked my elder brother who knelt on the floor before him and the people. I knelt down with him.

My brother then said, "Chief, I want to say that we are very grateful that you sent our high priest and today we know the woman is still in the village. Now that we have her people here, Chief, all we are asking for, is for you to find a way of helping us ask for forgiveness for what my brother has done. We know that the lost souls will never be brought back to life. If there were anything that could have been done to bring them back to life we would do it. My brother was not in his right state of mind when he did the things he did. He was drugged and we all know what happened in this country within the last ten years. Please help ask for forgiveness. We are on our knees. You are our father," My brother was crying as he spoke. "Sit up and stop crying. We have heard you. Foday, what do you have to say to our strangers?" The high priest cleared his throat before speaking, "Chief, when we received the former fighters that are living with us now, we did the traditional cleansing ceremony for them

208

together. Since then I have been monitoring the activities of each and every one of them, as we made a promise that we would help them live like one of us. While the others are happy going up and down doing work with some attending school, Alex stayed indoors and never mixed with his age group in this village. I became worried and started asking his brother what was happening to him. He was brought to us. I then realised that there was something disturbing him. A few days later Suma brought him here to tell us what he explained to him at home."

The chief interrupted him, "Foday we know that part. What do you have to tell our strangers?" The high priest had the reputation of stretching discussions by beating around the bush before coming to what he actually wanted to say. "Chief, I want our strangers to get the full story, with no doubt in their minds. Where was I again?" My brother reminded him. "Good, when they explained to us, the chief asked me to go and find your daughter in the village and talk to her about what our son had said. We would then find a way of bringing the two together so our child could ask for her forgiveness."

He turned to the chief, "Where is Fatu? I want her to bring more water and kola nuts for our strangers. They have come from afar." "Fatu, Fatu!" the chief shouted. The young wife of the chief answered, "Yes, Chief." "Bring more water and kola nuts for our strangers. Also bring some fresh palm wine." I saw the faces of the two men brighten. They seemed to appreciate the chief asking for the palm wine. The strangers gulped down full cups of palm wine and refilled their cups before the high priest could speak, "After I reached the village, I went to the area our son described to me and I was taken to the woman who is called Rachel Koroma. She is quite young and beautiful. She spoke respectfully to me and I carefully explained to her why I was at her place. She asked me to wait while she went to call her elders so they would also listen to what I had to say. I explained to them my mission. My brothers here decided to come and meet with you the paramount chief, and to see the boy with their own eyes."

"Now we are here. This is the boy," he said, pointing at me as he continued with his intercession, "I want to tell you that he is very sorry for all that he did. Violence is not part of our culture. His family had a good reputation in this village before the war. His father and mother died in a car accident as they were escaping to Guinea. He lives with his older brother and he has not caused any trouble since he returned to this village few months ago). My brothers, on behalf of the people of the village, I want to ask that you help us beg our sister to forgive our child. Even teeth and tongue sometimes quarrel, but they always find a way of settling their scores. Our child has hurt your child and we want you, the wise people of her family, to come between them and help solve this problem. For now, that is all I have to say." When the high priest had finished speaking, the chief accidentally spilled some palm wine on himself as he tried to put his calabash down to speak. "I think the gods are angry that we have not poured palm wine for them," he remarked. He proceeded then to pour some on the ground saying, "May our gods and our ancestors lead us in the right direction, and may they protect us from our enemies. Now our friends and brothers, we have spoken our hearts to you. You have heard what Foday and Suma have said. What do you have to say? We know your hearts are heavy but we are men and we should talk to each other as men. Our ears are yours."

The elder of the two men placed his empty calabash on the stool in front of him as he started speaking, "Our brothers, we are happy to meet with you today even though the issue that made us meet is not a happy one. It is a tragedy that will be remembered in our village for a very long time. Even the young children will remember it as they grow up. Our villages have lived in peace and happiness until the war started. Our people are your people and your people are our people. We are one and the same. So we are not strangers here. We came today because we want to help solve this problem too. Our child has suffered for too long. We believe that if she could forgive the one that caused her sorrow it will help her let go of the past. No one ever wished for war in this country, so we are happy that it has ended. The boy here is young and was a small boy when he did what he did. Only God knows what got into him. I do not want to go into that again. We will help you talk to our child. Satan really used all of us during this war. We will not give up in fighting against him. We will talk to her and we will let you know when we should meet again. She is the only one who can say for sure whether she will forgive him or not. Since night is coming and we have a long way to go, I believe we should suspend all discussions for now. We shall explain to our chief what we discussed here, and we will talk with our daughter." The two men poured full calabashes of palm wine again, gulped them down, wiped their mouths, and were ready to go.

"We appreciate your wisdom and your desire to help us with this matter. Let us help you with transport". The chief thanked them for coming and then called my brother into his house. They came out shortly after. The chief gave some money to the older man, and while he said that the chief should not have bothered since we were all of the same family, he nonetheless hurriedly pushed the envelope into the back of his pocket lest the chief changed his mind. The high priest and my brother went out to see them off. After they had left the chief asked me to stand before him and he held my hand, "I have children, some of them your age. Two of my sons got killed in the war and my other son joined the rebels and I have never heard about him since the war ended. He was my favourite son. We became very close after his mother ran away from the village because she no longer wanted to be my wife. He was abandoned. I think of him always. Whenever I see you I think of him. You know him right?" I answered, "Yes, he was my play-mate before the war. However, I never saw him during the war. Our force was big, people were stationed in so many different areas that you would never be able to meet or know everyone."

The chief continued, "Your parents were good people. They were loyal to me and very helpful in the village. Your brother is liked by the elders, because he is respectful. When he has a problem he comes to me. I advise him like I will advise my son. We won't let anything bad happen to you. We will talk to the woman and help you find peace. Try not to create any problems while you're here. Try to go back to school. You should be going to school, not staying at home. No one will harm you here. We are a one people, and you must know that you are part of us." The high priest and my brother walked in as he was talking to me. "Are they gone?" he asked them. "Yes, they are on their way now," the high priest responded. "Suma, let's talk a little before you leave. I was telling your brother that he should go to school and stop staying at home. I believe that the more he mixes with other children, the more relaxed he will be. He is part of our family and should behave like it. For now, continue talking to him while we wait to hear from the woman." "Chief, tell him. I talk to him every day. If I were here this boy would not have left this village in the first place. I will do all I can to help him. Chief and Pa Foday, I am grateful for the support you are giving us. Without you it would have been difficult for us," my brother said.

"Why do you think I am chief? I am the head of this village and I am responsible for the welfare of everyone. Whatever problem you have is also my problem. Without people there would be no need to have a chief. You do not have to thank me for doing my duty. Take the boy home. We will call you again when we have news." The high priest gave me some ointments to rub on my body before sleeping saying that I should use it for ten days and that it would protect me from evil spirits. When I reached home I smelled its contents and it was more horrible than the spit. My mind settled the entire night on the piece of encouragement and advice the chief gave me.

•••••

Three days later, outreach officers from the TRC visited the village again to meet with the chief. The chief remembered them and he was happy to see them, "You are welcome my brothers, I hope your work is going on well." "Chief, we will be holding the first TRC session in Bo. We are in charge of this village and we would like to begin our work as soon as possible, just as we told you the last time."

"Okay. Let me get the elders so that you can talk to all of us. Fatu! Fatu!" "Yes Chief," his young wife answered. "Please call Mohamed for me." Mohamed came in running, tripping over a bench as he entered the room. "Take care my brother, you will hurt yourself," one of the visitors told him as they helped him up. "He is always like that. Don't worry about him. Mohamed, go and call all the elders for me. Tell them they should be here as soon as they can. We have people that want to talk to us, do you hear?" "Chief, I will do that now," Mohamed said, leaving the room. "Let's wait till they come. I do not want you to talk to me and have to repeat everything later. Let's wait". "No problem chief. We will wait for them," the leader of the group said. Twenty minutes later, Mohamed returned with the high priest, Pa Kallay, Pa Barrie and Pa Santigie, the elders of our community. "Ha! They are here. Welcome! I am sorry that I had to send for you at such short notice. Pa Foday, I told you the last time about our visitors from the Truth and Reconciliation Commission. They want to talk to us and I want all of you to be here so we understand what they want us to do. My brothers, since everyone is here you can now talk."

The leader of the group cleared his throat before beginning an endless verbal marathon, "Thank you very much Chief. I want to introduce the group before I begin explaining what we are here to do. I am Abdul Karim Koroma, the leader of the outreach group for the South. My two colleagues are Brima Samura, and Munde M'bayo. They are also outreach officers. The war in this country came to an end recently when all the factions fighting in the war signed a peace agreement in Lomé, Togo. During the course of developing the peace agreement, all those present agreed that a Truth and Reconciliation Commission should be set up to help us bring together victims of the war and those who hurt them and their families, so as to promote peace and reconciliation". The heads of the chief and the elders bobbed in unison, like an Agama lizard. "The war has brought forward several questions that we want to answer as a nation. For instance, we are faced with the questions of what made people take up arms? What happened during the course of the war, and how do we face the current challenges to save the country from relapsing into another violent conflict? These questions are not easy to answer; they actually lead to more questions. The only way we can know what went wrong and how we can fix the challenges faced is to bring together the victims and perpetrators of the violence, and get them reconcile. The perpetrators will ask for forgiveness from the victims. If this is not done we will have continuous deep-seated grudges that will erupt in years to come. This is why the TRC was formed."

The chief asked him, "Who are those that are leading the TRC? I don't trust Sierra Leoneans. They will only use it as a money making machine." Abdul Karim laughed, "I understand your fears. So many things have gone wrong in this country that we no longer trust ourselves." The chief interrupted him, "No, I am not talking about you; I am talking about those in Freetown. They will make you work whilst they will be eating the money, using big words but not doing anything." "I understand your concerns. The head of the TRC is a Sierra Leonean, a Bishop who is of good moral standing. We have some commissioners who are Sierra Leoneans and some who are foreigners. The TRC will bring forward many problems in our country, like the ones you talk about, which are matters of corruption. We believe that if there is trust among Sierra Leoneans we will be able to solve our problems in a positive way instead of taking up arms. People have lost faith in the system, so we hope we will be able to help restore trust and patriotism in this country. Most of the work will be done by Sierra Leoneans; since the problems were created by us, we are the ones who will fix them. We will get help from foreigners, but we have to make this work to help transform our country."

The high priest asked him, "You talk about justice, but do you believe that anyone will come up and testify if they know that they may be arrested and jailed? Only a fool will do that." "When we talk about justice, we are not saying that anyone will be arrested and jailed after testifying. Justice in this case means that the victims will feel satisfied by hearing the people who have wronged them come forward publicly to acknowledge their crimes and ask for forgiveness. There are people who cut off the hands and feet of other people, or killed other peoples loved ones, and even members of their own families. Those people will be humbled when they stand to testify. Note that it is also not easy for them. It will be difficult, for they will be reconciling with their past and trying to enter a new phase wherein they would want those that they have hurt to forgive them. No one will be arrested, I want to assure you." Pa Kallay asked him, "If ex-combatants testify, don't you think that they will be endangering their lives? People may have been looking for some of them for years. By revealing their identity they will be open to attacks. If I can think about this then others will too. People who have meaningful contributions to make will not come forward, out of fear."

"You are right. We have discussed this continuously, and we are fully aware of the challenges that the perpetrators of violence face. We do not believe that anyone would want to harm someone who has publicly admitted to a wrongdoing, and who has asked for forgiveness. In all our programmes, we call on every Sierra Leonean to help us make our work easy by supporting the country in moving from a violent past to a future in which the rule of law and human rights are respected. In answering a question like the one you have just asked, I will say that the community and you, the leaders, have a crucial role to play in helping us protect those who have been reintegrated into local communities. You can help us by sensitising your people about the need to live peacefully. The TRC is not saying that we should forget our past. It is important for us to remember it so that we will never go back to it. It was violent and brutal, and a repeat of it would not be good at all. I believe we have all learned our lessons." Pa Barrie asked, "Can children testify too?"

Munde, the other member of the team, stepped in to answer that question, "We believe that children, like some older people, played a crucial role in this war. A significant percentage of every fighting force was made up of children. Children were both victims and perpetrators of violence. They too have their stories to share and we are encouraging them to come forward and tell their stories. Some people are against this, and are saying that they are too young to go through this process, as it will only add to their trauma. We believe that it is a vital part of the healing process, and helps them to openly reveal the challenges they face and ask for the support of their communities. The psychological burdens of their acts are weighing heavily on them, and they need to let go. We believe that speaking out helps to heal. We do not compel but rather encourage people who feel that they have something to say." "How do you identify these people and reach out to them?" the chief asked.

Munde again answered, "We have travelled through every village, every town and every city of this country since our work began. We have crossed every river and have travelled through every mountain in this country to look out for those who want to testify. We do not care about whether it is the rainy season or the dry season, or whether it is a good or a bad road we are going through. We owe this to our country and we will do it. We will reach every community, meet the elders, as we are doing here, and then we talk to the entire community. We get volunteers and there are some people identified by the elders or members of the community. We talk to these people, hear their stories, and encourage them to come forward. Our work will never succeed without the help of the communities. That is why we count on your support." The discussion was like a roller–coaster, endlessly turning. It was decided that the next day Abdul Karim and his team would talk to the entire village.

•••••

I was awakened from my slumber by the sound of the town crier beating his drum. It was done in such a solemn way that it sends chills down one's spine. He would hit the drum and talk, hit the drum again, sing a song and hit the drum again. I had never gotten used to it and really hated it. I took my pillow to cover my ears but I stopped myself on second thought, curious to hear what he was saying. I wondered why the chief was calling an urgent meeting for the entire village. So I decided to go and hear what it was all about.

By noon, the community centre was full. Whilst good at many things, punctuality was not the chief's forte. He always arrived thirty or forty minutes after the appointed time. On this day he was thirty minutes late, and even then he moved at the annoying pace of a tortoise. He

217

arrived in his best three-piece batik gown, which had survived several stormy years. Taking care of that gown was one of the full time assignments of his wife Fatu. She could be seen starching and ironing it after every occasion to ensure that it was ready for the next. Nonetheless, the chief was liked and respected by all so even though he had kept everyone waiting, we were all cheering as he climbed the stage with his visitors. After introducing the visitors, he asked them to tell the people what their mission was. Abdul Karim spoke on behalf of the team. He spoke very well and was interrupted several times with long applauses. I saw my brother in the crowd and I walked up to him. He was surprised to see me. "So you came?"

"Yes, I did not want to be in the house alone," I answered, As Abdul Karim continued speaking, I realised how much I wanted to go and testify, and I made up my mind that I was going to do it. I told my brother and he was happy to hear that. After all the questions were asked and answered people began dispersing. My brother walked up to the team and asked Abdul Karim for his contact details.

•••••

At home that day we discussed the pros and cons of me testifying but my mind was made up. We decided to see the chief and tell him of my decision. When we entered the chief's house, he was having a huge bowl of foofoo and okra sauce. Looking at his thin frame one could not help but wonder where all the food he ate ended up. He invited us to join him, "Come and eat with your father, I have a better appetite when people eat with me." Three quarters of the food was already gone, leaving me wondering what he meant by "better appetite". Even though he was almost through with it, we washed our hands and joined him as it was considered impolite to reject an invitation to partake in a meal, more so when it was coming from the chief of all people. Though tempted to eat some of the meat on the tray, I politely pushed them to the chief and my brother as it is disrespectful for a child to be meat-grabbing when eating with adults.

After eating, we went outside where the chief listened to what my brother had to say to him, "My brother has told me that he wants to testify at the TRC, and we would like to tell the people that came today about Mrs Koroma and get her to go to the session so my brother can testify and apologise to her there." "That thought also thought crossed my mind today. The TRC is a golden opportunity to make peace. You remember I initially mentioned it to Foday that we use the TRC but he thought that I was becoming completely influenced by the ideas of white people. Now we all know that it could work. The team will be coming again on Wednesday to register all those who would like to testify. They will be at the community centre at 11 a.m. so your brother can go and be registered. I will also speak with the people, but they know what they are doing. Alex, when you go to them, explain properly what happened, leave no detail out. Also tell them the steps we have already taken. They will tell you how they will help. Don't worry. God will help you in this." We thanked him and said good night.

•••••

Fortified with prayers, I set off to give my testimony at the TRC hearing. The meeting hall had the ambiance of a night party with endless loud pockets of discussions flowing over the collective noise in the hall. Women and men brilliantly dressed, some to show off their new clothes and others to reasonably step up to the occasion, moved across the room showering greetings and blessings on all.

After days of dialogue, Mrs Koroma consented to hear me testify. It took constant dialogues with our chief and the TRC people for her to finally consent to forgiving me and letting go of her past. I was transported to the session with my brother, some elders from the village, the high priest, and the chief. While the people from my village interacted with the woman and her family, I did not. I never knew where to begin, so I decided to wait patiently for the session to begin. Abdul Karim told me that there was one testimony before mine. At 10:00 a.m. four people, among them a white man, entered the room and took the high table. I knew that some of them were working for the Truth and Reconciliation Commission I was not surprised, as Abdul Karim had told me there would be commissioners among those who would be leading the session. The session was called to order and there was an interpreter who was translating between Mende, our language, and English. The white man was chairman of the programme. I could not even remember his name, which sounded very funny. He exploded like an old vehicle, with a leaking exhaust pipe. Even the least attentive people stopped their pocket meetings and turned to him. His voice was unlike his frame. He was of medium height and slight built with a strangely shaped head with the looks of a relative of the buffalo family. "Friends, today I am happy that we are in Bo, and we are beginning the series of testimonies and reconciliation processes in an area of the country that suffered from the war, an area that was the subject of occupation, attacks and counter-attacks. The people of the south, like the people of the other regions of the country, suffered immensely during the course of the war. Today we want to turn to a new page in the history of this beautiful country. So we are asking everyone to speak up and let us know what is on their minds. We want Sierra Leoneans to come together and strengthen the fragile peace that exists in this country now. We want an end to suffering, and grudges, in this country". He stopped and gulped a glass of water before continuing.

"Today you will hear six people testifying. Three will tell us what was done to them by people who were in fighting forces. After each of them, the persons who hurt them will tell us what they did to them and they together with their families will ask for forgiveness from the injured party. This process will show us that peace and love should be the dominant forces in our lives. If we learn to forgive we will always be in peace." The other panellists introduced themselves. Then the first two people were called. I recognised the first as a man I had been in the RUF with who had ripped open the stomach of a pregnant woman to see whether the baby was a boy or a girl. The husband of the woman, by name John Yambasu, explained how he was forced to watch this happen. He said that over time he had submitted his life to God and had come to understand the power of forgiveness and was forgiving the man we had called "Commander Take No Shit." As I listened, I felt repulsed by the horrible things we had done. Then I silently prayed in my heart for God to forgive me. Commander Take No Shit in his usual dramatic style, though more composed and looking remorseful and responsible, knelt down while talking and said, "I have wronged this man and his family. There is nothing that I can explain that will make sense here. I am asking all of you to please join me in asking for forgiveness." The husband rose, touched the back of Commander Take No Shit and in tears proclaimed, "I forgive you. I will no longer hold any grudge against you." They embraced amidst thunderous applauses, took photos and spoke like old friends. I knew it was difficult for the husband who had lost a wife and baby in such a nasty way, but he had chosen to put the past behind him and to move on.

The case of Rachel Koroma and Alex Momoh was then called. My brother squeezed my hand, and asked me to breathe in and out four times before beginning to speak, so as to calm myself down. The woman began testifying after being made to introduce herself, "It was on a Monday morning that the rebels attacked our village. We were preparing our daughter, the last one, for her first day to school. She was very excited and we had waited

221

anxiously for that day since she was always crying that she wanted to go to school.

We heard sporadic gunshots, which took us by surprise because after the first rebel attack we were told that the rebels had been driven completely out of our area. We closed the doors and the windows, and knelt down to pray as the fighting raged on. One hour later our door was broken down. Two rebels entered our house pointing their guns at us. One of them is the boy standing here today. The other boy said to him, "You deal with them; I am going to the next house." He was so young that I thought he would not harm us. We begged him and gave him money but he shot my husband in the stomach and then in the head. Seeing no escape route and sensing the rage in him, I grabbed my two children and started pleading for him to spare our lives. He asked me to lie on the ground in my husband's blood and raped me in front of my children who were seven and four years old. After raping me, he shot my children and laughed as he went out of the house. I shouted out after him and asked that he should kill me as he had taken all I ever had in life. My world stopped rotating on that day, and I have been living my life like a zombie ever since. The only people that truly mattered to me died on the same day, killed by a stranger whom we had done nothing to hurt."

Though I was the perpetrator, her story touched me to the core and it was like a tragedy written by Shakespeare. It made me lose all the composure I had earlier gained, and as I was asked to stand up and testify I could feel the fiery darts of several pair of eyes pinned on me (I know some would have loved to lynch me at that point). Instead of three or four as advised by my brother, I must have taken over a hundred deep breaths to try to regain my composure so that it appeared as if was gasping for air, so I stopped. I started by introducing myself and stating how I came to be a part of the RUF. I recounted how I was abducted and made to do things that I never thought I would do in life. "I was a very young boy who did not understand the difference between good and evil. People who only wanted to see blood, and achieve their political aims manipulated me. We were the foot soldiers who won battles and made them famous. Several of my friends, most of whom I was older than, were killed as we moved on to make our commanders happy. We were children who lost our innocence in fields soiled with blood, deceit, and criminality. We were the slaves of people we came to trust, people whom we were told were fighting a just cause. Our happiness depended on their happiness. We were given drugs and other very harmful substances that children of our age should not take, to suppress any compassion in us so we could act without questioning what we were doing. I was in one of those moods when we entered the village of Mrs Koroma. All that she has said is true. I killed her husband, I killed her children, and I raped her. I was a rabid dog to whom everything smelt of death and destruction. I was killing without knowing why I was killing. To me it was like a game. Everything in front of me looked useless and in this frame of mind, it was always a case of kill or be killed."

There was complete silence in the room as I spoke. One could have heard a pin drop. I had succeeded in catching the attention of everyone and even my brother and our chief were looking as if they were hearing me speak for the first time. I had found strength deep within that was propelling me to speak up. My system was sick and tired of harbouring the filth in me and it was desperately spitting it out. I continued. "Mrs Koroma is not the only person I offended. She is not the only woman whose family members I killed. Several victims fell as I shot or used my knife on them. The relatives of these people are not here today; they may never see me or may never know what I did to their people. I am not proud of the things I did and if there was a way to go back into the past and erase all of it, I would do so. To Mrs Koroma and all those whose family members I hurt, I want to say I am very sorry. I have been having serious challenges since I returned to the village. I cannot sleep at night; I am restless and dying inside, and I know that unless I am forgiven by the relatives of those I hurt, I will never have peace in my life. I am very sorry and I would be very happy if you forgive me." I knelt before Mrs. Koroma to beg her. She started crying and I burst into tears. Several people in the room were crying as I knelt down holding her feet. One of the Sierra Leonean commissioners came forward and sat close to Mrs Koroma and said to her, "Please forgive him. He was just an innocent child who did things he never understood, please." Mrs Koroma touched my head as a sign of forgiveness. Our two families came together and she embraced me and told me that she had forgiven me. Before we departed the chief called her aside and prayed for her. After they had spoken I went up to her and said good bye. She said to me, "I have forgiven you. Always try to be good. Bye." As the car drove us back to the village I looked at the open fields and the beauty of nature and thought of how beautiful my life would be if I tried to live in peace with myself. I felt easy and free. For the first time in a very long time I felt normal, relaxed, and very light inside. The burden of yesterday had gone away. I was glad that I had testified and I knew it was the right thing to do. I held the hand of my brother and as he turned to look at me, I said to him, "Thank you."